MAGIC REMEMBERED

CORALIE MOSS

Published internationally by Pink Moon Books, British Columbia, Canada

ISBN: 978-1-7752646-8-2

Created with Vellum

❦ Created with Vellum

For my husband, Martin.
Thank you for manning the cappuccino machine.
Thank you for making the hot chocolate *my* way.
Thank you for picking up my slack.
Thank you for asking, "But what happens next?" and thereby volunteering to do it all again.
And thank you most of all for being my rock.

For the witches.

MAGIC REMEMBERED

CHAPTER 1

I rued the day I downloaded ShiftR, the dating app designed for witches and the like. My first experience with swiping found me grimacing at my ex-husband's smug face and wondering why the avowed magic-hater was trolling for non-humans. Swiping in the other direction—over and over—eventually netted two possible matches, both of them werecougars living across the channel on Vancouver Island.

After a cluster of dating disasters, I wanted a no-strings-attached romp. Choosing one shifter over the other because of a shared interest in vintage Airstream campers, a romp inside a restored, aluminum-sided Clipper was exactly what I got. But even in his fully human form, the werecougar's combined size and enthusiasm may have led to a busted condom.

And now, my period was almost two months late, and I couldn't make myself pull open the glass door of the medical building, step over the threshold, and show up to my appointment at the women's health clinic.

Calliope Jones, you can do this.

Not emphatic enough. I needed a middle name. I hadn't been given one and before I could tumble onto the map of dead ends that comprised the missing pieces of my ancestry, the glass door banged open. A very pregnant woman lumbered out. I gripped the door handle and watched as she waddled to her nearby car.

That could be me in seven months.

Nursery décor themes danced in my head as I entered, registered and accepted a plastic cup. I dutifully peed and followed a nurse's Medicinal Pink-clad backside down the hallway and into Dr. Renard's office, where I used the wait to review my options as a possibly pregnant forty-one-year-old divorced mother of two teenaged sons.

I helped myself to the water cooler, swallowing against a rise of nausea. Another wave from the center of my agitated belly to the base of my throat sent my eyelids slamming shut. Nausea had been an issue nineteen years ago, when I was in my first trimester with Harper. It was going to be an issue again.

Shit.

I finished the water, crumpled the cup, and opened my eyes to Dr. Renard's concerned gaze. "What brings you here today?"

"My period's really late." Goddess, those words stung when uttered aloud.

"How late?"

"Six, seven weeks." *Eight. Maybe, nine.* I hadn't been keeping track of my cycle.

Dr. Renard scanned the medical records displayed on her laptop and glanced over thick green eyeglass frames to the nurse hovering in the doorway. "Did we get Ms. Jones's urine?"

The nurse nodded. "Three more minutes and we'll have the first results."

The door snicked closed, and my belly clenched again. Dr. Renard leaned in, placed freckled hands firmly on my khaki-clad knees, and looked at me head on. "Calliope, we haven't known each other very long, but you *are* under my care and you can tell me what's going on."

"The guy I was with suffered a condom malfunction," I blurted.

The kindly doctor arched both eyebrows over her big, cornflower-blue eyes and *hmm*ed. I fidgeted with the snap on the flap of my pants' thigh pocket as my feet broke out in a sweat.

"My sex life since my divorce was finalized has been the stuff of legend. You know, the kind of legend that's fodder for someone else's comedy routine." The calendar tucked in my underwear drawer—a place I knew my sons would never explore —recorded one dating disaster after another from the moment I decided to dip a toe in the proverbial pool.

Hands tapped the outsides of my knees, and another comforting *hmm* reached my ears. Dr. Renard pushed her rolling stool away from the upholstered chair as a soft knock sounded at the door.

"Come in."

The same nurse handed over a piece of paper and slipped out of the room. Dr. Renard read the results, glanced at me, and smiled, folding the paper in half and half again, before tucking it into a pocket of her lab coat.

"Calliope, I have some good news." She leaned back and crossed her legs. "You're not pregnant. The more likely scenario is you're starting menopause."

I exhaled in relief and quickly inhaled confusion. Menopause meant the end of…of rapturous sex and luxurious hair, and I was in no way prepared to give up on either, especially since I had yet to experience the kind of sex I was currently on a mission to find. "But I'm only forty-one!"

"Have you been experiencing any sleep disturbances?" she asked, folding her arms across her chest. "Night sweats, unexplained weight gain, vaginal dryness?"

"Every couple of weeks I sleep the night through, but mostly I wake up at least two or three times." And here I thought it was the stuffy air from July's heat and seasonal forest fires. "And my vagina is fine. I'm…" I sighed and smirked. "I'm more the opposite. I can't stop thinking about sex." Hence my personal mission and current predicament.

"So, heightened libido, sleep patterns are off, and you're sweating. Anything else?"

My sons, Goddess love them, were simultaneously charging toward manhood and clinging to their childhoods with tenacious fingers. "Does an increasingly *laissez faire* attitude about parenting count?"

That elicited a chuckle. "Actually, yes. It's not uncommon to care less about clean toilets and getting dinner on the table and more about pursuing whatever makes you happy." She returned to reading through my records. I distracted myself by longing for her saffron curls instead of my dull brown waves. I'd run out of argan oil, and my hair was suffering. "Let's do a PAP test while you're here and a full work-up for STDs."

"Ready for the sexy robe." I undressed and waited, wobbly on the inside from the whiplash-quick switch from picking baby names to cursing my hormones, and scratched at the tattoo inked directly over my left ovary. Doug, my vexatious ex, had talked me into getting matching designs after our second son was born. Once the divorce was finalized, I had considered getting the tattoo done over so the original design was unrecognizable. Now, I just wanted it off. The ink might have faded, but its presence was a sore reminder of someone I no longer loved.

Or even liked.

Dr. Renard returned, warmed her hands at the sink, dried them on paper towels, and settled herself at the side of the table. "Are you doing regular self-exams?" she asked, lifting the gown and palpating the area around my breasts. When she moved the modesty sheet covering the lower half of my body, she sucked in a quick breath. "Anything you want to tell me?"

The flush blooming across my chest was hidden by a yard of hospital-blue polyester blend.

"You mean about the bruises?" The werecougar and I had tried the dating thing again, but it was clear the only thing we had going was mutual horniness. As much as I liked sex and wanted a steady lover, I wanted more than a well-endowed fuck buddy.

Dr. Renard leaned her hip against the side of the table and removed her glasses, tucking the sheet snug against my outer leg. "Those are more than bruises on your thighs, Calliope." She tapped the eyepiece against her chin before sitting the glasses back on her nose. "Did your date have…"

"Claws?" I dove in. I trusted Dr. Renard—plus, the pentacle she was wearing had started to glow green—and the day couldn't get any weirder than admitting your date had a hard time controlling his ability to shift while in the throes of arousal.

"Yes, for starters," she said.

"Those marks are a physical record of my dalliance with an enthusiastic…" I faltered.

The look in her eyes was still kind and very direct. "Shifter?"

The tension along my spine released into the Naugahyde cushion. Shifter sounded so very normal when spoken aloud in a clinical setting. I nodded.

"I only pry if I suspect there's been any kind of abuse, Calliope." She made a point of continuing to stare at me.

"No abuse," I assured her. "Just an abundance of arms and legs maneuvering in a very tight space. Electric cars weren't designed for making out."

She chuckled, patted the unblemished section of my leg, and moved to the foot of the table, opening and closing drawers and snapping on a pair of exam gloves. "Tell me, what rituals does your coven use to welcome their members into menopause?"

"What do you mean?" Her question startled me out of my pre-exam disassociation. Two of my fingers were firmly wedged in a knot of fabric, and now I had to consciously relax the muscles in my hands and unstick my knees.

"You know, rituals that mark the milestones in your life? First menstrual period, being accepted into a coven, giving birth? You've had all of those, right? And you're going to feel the speculum, there...can you tilt your pelvis slightly? Yes, good, okay."

I clung to my breathe-in, breathe-out mantra during the rest of the exam. Coven? I'd been without a formal education in the magical arts since my mother's death left me in her sister's care. My aunt was a good ten years older than my mom, and apart from the loss, my childhood had been rather unremarkable. The trauma of losing my only known parent had given way to a bland and predictable routine. Passable for a young girl in a family with low expectations and less than optimal for a budding witch.

"Now that I think of it," I started, "I can't recall a single ceremony aside from birthday parties. And I've never belonged to a coven."

Dr. Renard stood and removed the disposable gloves. "Scoot back and then you can sit up."

I used the small sheet to wipe the excess gel from between my upper thighs before pivoting my legs to the side. I offered up both inner elbows for Dr. Renard's inspection and looked away as she drew three vials of blood. When she finished, she opened the door and called for her assistant.

"Rachel, can you please send Calliope's samples to the Grand St. Kitts lab in Vancouver? Thanks." She closed the door, hooked her foot around the rolling stool, and pulled up close. "If you're truly at the start of menopause, there are specific ceremonies you must participate in to advance your magical abilities before your moon blood stops for good."

The hot fingers poking through my belly slid to the back of my neck, dropping fiery bits of slag along my hairline. "What do you mean? And how do you know?"

"Has no one talked to you about this?"

I shook my head, choking down the bubble of loss threatening to rise and burst. "My mother died when I was six. Her older sister raised me. I'm a witch, like my mom, but my magic is..." I turned my hands and studied both palms, as though I was a fortune teller and all the answers lay somewhere between my thumb mounds and a lifetime's accumulation of forked lines. "My magic isn't very strong." Shrugging, I rubbed my now-sweaty palms on the examination smock, unable to fully breathe out. "I've tried to use my mother's old books and notes to teach myself basic spells and counter-spells, but there's nothing in them about what to do for…for menopause."

"Calli, would you like me to put you in touch with my local contacts?"

"I would," I said, feeling hopeful for the first time in days. Months. "Are you in a coven?"

She nodded. "I am. And I'm trained in Western medicine too. Obviously. What about your ex-husband? And your sons?"

"I suspect Doug's mother had some magic. And I think my boys do too, but…Goddess, this is hard to admit, Dr. Renard…"

"Rowan. Please, call me Rowan."

"Rowan. Okay." I sucked in a big breath. "I've never actively sought the company of other witches. I mean, I haven't *avoided* them, but my husband—my *ex*-husband—insisted I not use my magic and it was just easier to not practice, to not even talk about magic."

"Tell me about your sons."

Relief. "Harper's eighteen. He'll be a senior in high school this coming year, and Thatch is sixteen and a half."

"And their magic?" Rowan asked, speaking over her shoulder as her assistant knocked on the door and entered.

"Doctor Renard, the hospital called. Lolly Brooks has gone into labor, so…"

"I'll be right out." She turned to me. "Let's talk later. I want to hear more about your sons. And you. I'll call with the results of your tests within the week. And here." She scribbled on the back of a pamphlet. "My coven is based in Vancouver. We're all healers and followers of Airmid, but Belle and Airlie live here on the island. Their addresses and phone numbers should be listed in the local directory. The other woman, Rose, can be challenging, especially if she doesn't get a good first impression, but give her a chance."

"Thanks, Rowan. For everything." I extended my arm and accepted the hug she offered instead.

I took my time changing into my clothes. Zipping my pants, I stared at the wall without seeing. My entire body deflated when I sighed. I wasn't pregnant, a state of being I had some familiarity with. I was entering my menopausal years, completely unknown territory. I wasn't about to watch a life grow inside me, I was about to...I had no idea. Doug had slowly isolated me to the point I had few female acquaintances and no real friends. Post-divorce, I'd been trying to connect with other women. But shy of wearing a sandwich board advertising my loneliness, I hadn't figured out how to find a bestie.

Folding Rowan's note, I slipped it into the back of my cell phone case and half wondered if there were apps for updating one's magical abilities and for gathering friends.

At least I was on top of things at work.

Next up was a visit to the Pearmain orchards. A manila envelope with no return address had arrived at my office via Canada Post. Inside, a handwritten message—accompanied by a few out-of-focus photographs—accused Clifford and Abigail Pearmain of using banned herbicides on their certified organic apple orchard.

As an acquaintance of the soon-to-be-retired growers, I doubted they dabbled in forbidden chemistry. As a Provincial Agent for the GIAC—Gulf Islands Agriculture Commission—it was my responsibility to investigate. What troubled me was the accuser's apparent desire for anonymity.

I arrived at the turn off to the orchard without remembering a thing about the drive out of town. The untrimmed grass growing in the center of the single lane dirt road brushed the undercarriage of my car. I parked on the verge next to a dented pickup truck, grabbed my cross-body bag, and pocketed my phone. Making sure my wand—more ceremonial than useful—was in the bag too, I peeked into the truck's cab. There was nothing unusual about the portable coffee cup in the built-in holder or the soft leather briefcase on the passenger's seat. I flipped the door handles; both were locked.

The winding driveway to the farmhouse and outbuildings was pitted and unkempt, which *was* unusual for a thriving apple farm. Grasses going to seed lined the former sheep path, and berry canes, heavy with blue-black fruit, grew more dense and entwined the closer I got to the main gate. I'd been working for the GIAC long enough to be wary but not overly alarmed at the lack of activity. Farmers were busy people and far more likely to be out in their fields and greenhouses, monitoring their crops.

"Clifford! Abigail! It's Calliope," I hollered, banging on the combination split wood and wire enclosure. Trinkets hanging from bits of string and knotted straw rattled every time the side of my fist hit the frame of the homemade gate. One last forceful smack of the heel of my palm and the rusted latch acquiesced to the pull of entropy and dropped from loosened screws. As the gate creaked open, its bottom edge scuffed a break in the curving line of salt placed across the surface of the dull brown dirt.

"Cliff! Abi...?"

A filmy silence settled over my shoulders, flowed down my body, and pooled over the ground. No insects, bird calls, or rustling leaves interrupted the leaden quiet. I sucked in a breath and peered into the shadows between the trees to my right and to my left. Nothing moved, even the breeze held its breath.

Anchoring my boot-clad feet, I raised my hands, fingers spread and palms facing out, and tested the strength of the salt circle's magical charge. If it was active—like an electrical wire—I'd feel a resounding zap if I got too close.

Nothing.

No vibration, no sensation of skin meeting invisible membrane, no static, no...nothing. Stepping further onto the Pearmain's property, I crouched, brushing my fingertips over the salt's pearly-white crystals before bringing a few to the tip of my tongue.

A pungent darkness rolled over my taste buds and coated my nostrils, a sensation akin to swallowing a surprise mouthful of seawater. For a moment, my shoulder-length hair flowed away from my body like kelp from an underwater rock, and the light that penetrated my eyelids filtered a murky emerald green.

Mama.

I swayed in place, spitting the dirt and undissolved crystals off my tongue. I knew this salt; it was produced locally, from seawater pulled out of the deep trench off the coast of British Columbia. But why it called forth memories of my mother and the Atlantic...

I left that for another time.

Straightening, I brushed my fingers over my pants and headed away from the circle and the gate. When I last walked this property earlier in the spring, the grass was newly trimmed and the fruit trees were covered in delicate, pale pink blossoms. But in the heat and sharp yellow sunlight of high noon, the place appeared deserted. I pulled out my cell phone, brought up the Pearmain's phone number, and waited for theirs to ring.

In the distance, long, insistent peals from a landline pierced the stillness. Rounding the final curve in the road, I stopped and gaped, the cell phone forgotten in my hand.

Clifford Pearmain sat upright in a once-red rocking chair on the farmhouse's wrap-around porch. Abigail sat in another, her hands resting on a faded, flower-print apron. Both stared forward, rocking slowly in time with an invisible force. Abigail's feet left the porch every time the front of her chair lifted and settled softly on the boards when she pitched forward.

Competing telephone rings snapped my attention off the

zombie-like couple. I thumbed the red circle on my phone and ended the call, stopping the other phone in the middle of a trill. The rockers continued their syncopated rhythm. Beside me, grasshoppers clung to chest-high stalks of Sea Holly thistle and kept their silence.

I pocketed my phone and crouched again. Knees and palms to the ground, I spread my fingers and waited. The soil was dense underneath its warm, powdery surface. I took a slow breath, exhaled in a stream through pursed lips, and pressed down, reaching toward the house and the gate, the woods and the orchard.

Earthworms slumbered. Tree roots remained mute to my probing.

The quiet underneath my waiting palms connected with a dull pang feeling its way blindly from the vicinity of my heart. Once again, I would be forced to admit my magical skills were functioning below par, call it a day, and count on local law enforcement to solve whatever mystery I'd stumbled onto.

CHAPTER 2

I stood, made a fuss of brushing off my hands to give my urge to mourn a moment to ease, and palmed my wand before heading toward the porch. Scanning Clifford's face and chest for signs of life, I stopped beside his rocking chair and placed a hand on his shoulder. A short-sleeved, tattersall plaid shirt draped over the protruding bones.

Closing my eyes again, I sensed my way through the threadbare cloth to the ropey muscles of his bare upper arms. I could do this; Cliff was connected to his land through his years of stewardship and the dirt clinging to his boots, and at the very least, I was adept at reading dirt.

I waited. The grasshoppers remained silent.

A pulse rose—a heavy, viscous bubble—and bounced against my fingertips before it turned and made its way back toward the innermost chambers of the older man's bones. I squeezed Cliff's arm. Not a flinch or a quiver. Whatever held him mute was heavily cloaked.

I gave Abigail a quick glance and stroked the old woman's gnarled fingers and wrist. More of the same lethargic slumber. A momentary breeze lifted wavy strands of silver hair off her cheek and settled them on yellowed skin sagging with the weight of her seventy-plus years.

Catatonia.

Once, I could read my aunt's basic spell books, and before I understood that waving a wand around had very real consequences, I practiced magic on our barn cats. As soon as my aunt de-spelled the catatonic felines, the book disappeared. And I never saw that wand again.

Shaking off the memory, I rechecked Cliff and Abi's pulses. Satisfied they were alive and hopeful they would remain so, I opened the screen door and stepped into the farmhouse's dark interior. In the sitting room—preserved like a museum display from the early twentieth century—dust motes twinkled in lazy spirals. As my eyes adjusted to the dim light, my gaze was drawn to a carved couch littered with needlepoint pillows, all of them variations of dainty pink and white blossoms on black backgrounds. A grouping of photographs was displayed on the wall behind the couch's curved back.

Horsehair stuffing crackled as I kneeled gingerly on the cushions and lifted the first frame off its nail. The glass front needed cleaning; the back was dusty but unremarkable. Tiny brass tacks around the edges looked undisturbed, probably since the frame's initial assembly. Plucking a tissue from a box covered in more needlepoint roses, I wiped the glass.

The image underneath revealed younger versions of Clifford and Abigail seated stiffly on the elegant settee with three young men arrayed behind them and everyone dressed in finer clothes than farming required. I found nothing unusual in their semi-blurred features before returning my attention to the frame.

Like others arrayed across the wall, this one was hand-carved. And old. Probably a family heirloom.

I squinted, holding it farther from my face. A repeated decorative element of curving lines turned into roots and branches, with tiny, carved apples and pears dotting the branches. On closer look, four faces emerged, one near each corner, each graced with an elongated nose, slightly pointed ears, and hair that intertwined with the tree.

I scanned the wall. All the frames in the grouping over the couch were carved in a similar fashion. Rehanging the one in my hands, I stepped into the middle of the room and listened.

High-noon cloaked the house with a blanket of heat and kept the grasshoppers on mute. The creak of a floorboard as I made my way back to the hall startled me into joining the ambient stillness.

It's an old house, Calliope.

Blowing out a short breath, I squeezed the duct-taped handle of my wand, wished it was a knife—and that I knew how to use it in self-defense—and entered the kitchen. This room had a much more lived-in air, with dishes in the rack by the sink and a table set for two, complete with a vase of drooping flowers. I hesitated in front of the refrigerator; I really should have put on gloves before touching the picture frames.

I pocketed my wand, extracted a pair of gloves from my bag, and tugged on the old appliance's dented aluminum handle.

The interior was neat and organized. I poked at the assortment of deli meats and cheeses, checked the purchase dates, and sniffed the bottle of cereal cream. Nothing was close to spoiling. Closing the refrigerator, I shifted my attention to the small pantry. Decorative dishware took up most of the shelves behind glass-fronted doors, and the usual dry goods were stacked behind the others. A chest freezer occupied the back wall. Its heavy lid fought against being opened until the suction finally gave way with a *whoosh.*

A blast of cold air offered a welcome respite from the stale heat. Inside, two squarish wire baskets were half filled with paper-wrapped packages stamped with the local abattoir's logo and labelled in black marker. Below the baskets, bagged in plastic, were larger packages containing pork and beef roasts. I went to close the lid.

Light coming over my shoulder highlighted a peculiar shadow in one of the clear bags. I separated the wire baskets, reached for the plastic, and gave a quick tug. I had to stifle a scream.

A *nose*.

I had grabbed a frozen nose, and it wasn't a pig's nose. Those were wrapped and clearly labeled in the basket at my elbow. I pressed the back of my free hand to my mouth and frantically scanned the shelf to my left for something to count. A full blown panic attack would not help me or the Pearmains.

Twelve. Twelve neatly stacked dessert plates.

When I was done counting and gagging, I reached forward, pinched the plastic, and turned the bag. A severed head, its pasty gray skin covered in a fine layer of frost, stared out, eyes unseeing.

"What the...?" I jiggled the wire baskets farther apart, took out my phone, and snapped a few photos. Needing better light, I removed the bagged head and placed the frozen bundle on the floor. Carefully.

Shit. I dropped the freezer lid and stepped into the kitchen, searching the countertops for something to cut the plastic. Poultry shears. Grabbing them by the handles, I kneeled on the faded black-and-white squares of linoleum and cut open the thick plastic bag. Flakes of ice tumbled over my knees. I brushed them away and pulled the crinkling material from the face.

The long nose and pointed ears mimicked the features carved on the picture frames in the sitting room. I was able to take another photograph before the bile rose again.

Stepping to the window at the far end of the narrow room, I opened the bottom sash and sucked in gulps of apple-scented air. Catatonic orchardists and a severed head were a couple steps above my pay grade. I was trained to investigate environmentally-based complaints and spats between organic and traditional farmers, not death.

Not *murder*.

I gripped the windowsill, sank into a crouch, and leaned my head against one arm. I ignored the buzzing from my phone. I'd *have* to get the Provincial authorities involved now, but—

"I see you found the heads," a man's voice said.

My heart damn near punched a hole in my chest. I pivoted on my knees and grabbed the shears I'd left on the floor. Angling my gaze upward, the sunshine slanting through the back door effectively blocked out the man's facial features and endowed him with a temporary halo.

"I'm Tanner Marechal," the voice continued. "Ministry of Forests, Lands and Natural Resources. And who are you?"

I palmed the shears and took a deep breath, standing quickly and pivoting so the sun wasn't in my eyes. The better angle revealed a man clad in regulation-green pants and a light khaki shirt.

"Calliope Jones," I answered. "I work for the island's Agricultural Commission."

Birds landing on the feeder outside the kitchen window made a sudden racket, pecking for seeds and dominance.

I shifted my grip on my weapon as my heart beat twice for every second. "Could we exchange IDs or something? This is a crime scene and—"

"The uniform and hat aren't obvious enough?" One sable eyebrow raised, slow and deliberate.

I held my ground. The man with the shoulder-length hair might be dressed as an employee of a province-wide government agency, but this was *my* island and *my* investigation and death was in a bag on the floor behind me.

Plus, he was wearing flip-flops.

"I don't think we've ever met," I said, straightening my spine and mimicking his wide, confident stance. "And in my official capacity as steward of the island's orchards, I'd rather err on the side of offending you than ruffling local feathers."

Note to self: Make sure someone adds 'She was brave' to my tombstone.

He didn't shift his gaze off my face while he unbuttoned the breast pocket of his shirt and removed an embossed identification badge. I tried to make a mental sketch of his features, in case I had to describe him to the RCMP, but I didn't get farther than topaz eyes and minty aftertaste.

After placing the shears on the countertop and peeling off the gloves, I extended my hand, palm up. Tingles darting across my skin alerted me to the presence of magic.

Ooh. My gaze went back and forth, from the man's face and the crystalline clarity of his eyes to the shiny badge. I confirmed his name, memorized his employee number, and when I stroked the pad of my middle finger across the back of the metal, one of those tingles pulsed rapidly before piercing my skin.

Ouch. I flipped the badge. A pentacle glowed green then started to fade. Today was my day for meeting other Magicals.

"So. Natural Resources is hiring witches?" I asked.

The agent's eyes widened. He shook his head. "No, not intentionally. The pentacle tells me *you're* a witch."

Oh. I had no idea government-issued IDs could be customized to detect magic.

"And what are you?" I asked, ready to go tit-for-tat.

"Druid."

Agent Marechal may have been the first druid I'd ever met, and I didn't know what to say or if there was a specific protocol I was supposed to follow. I went with my most over-used icebreaker. "What brings you to Salt Spring Island?"

He tucked the badge in his pocket and buttoned the flap. "Over the past three months we've received multiple reports of disturbances in orchards all across the Gulf Islands and into the San Juans, as well as coastal areas of British Columbia and Washington State." He pivoted and pointed at the Pearmains, still slowly rocking. "This is the third incidence I've come across of orchardists placed under the Catatonia spell."

"How are the others?" And why hadn't I gotten even a whiff of information about problems with magic in the agricultural sector?

"All were released successfully and have recovered without side effects. We're working on tracing the spells' origins, but not a single one of the victims remembers who put them under."

"And why did you come here?"

"Because the Pearmains were accused in the same manner as the others of using non-organic farming practices."

"Were those accusations filed in person or anonymously?"

"Anonymously."

Bingo. "Same here," I said. "So why didn't you contact my office?"

"Because..." Tanner hesitated, brought his hands to his hips, and scuffed the floor with the toe of his flip flop. The birds continued to squawk and toss seed. "Because there's nothing in my files about the GIAC having a witch on staff. And something was left at the second site."

"What kind of something?"

He pointed to the bag at my feet. "A severed head. Like the two here."

I swallowed. I wasn't aware a second head waited in the freezer. "I'd like to put this one back and get the RCMP's Forensics team in here."

The agent tensed, looked out the window, and rubbed his jaw. "I'd like to propose a different tack. I have other druids and witches who work with me. I'd like to bring them on board and keep this—" he circled his shoulders to indicate the kitchen and beyond—"between us."

"Are you saying you'd like to lend your expertise to *my* investigation?"

"I'm saying…" he huffed out. "Yes, Ms. Jones, I can put my resources at your disposal. In return, I would ask for quid pro quo. And that you not inform local, human authorities."

"Agreed." I extended my arm, starting when he took my right hand in both of his. I half-expected a return of the tingling I'd felt when I swiped the back of his badge. Instead, my feet warmed in my boots, heat rising up my legs like bathwater. I jerked my hand away and rubbed my palm on my pants, my legs rubbery but solidly my own. "What did you just do?"

Tanner had the grace to blush. "I'm overly curious that you've managed to fly under my radar, and I apologize."

"Next time you want to know something about me, ask." I turned and went to one knee.

The frost coating the head was melting in the warmth of the enclosed space. I pulled on another pair of disposable gloves and folded the halves of the cut plastic over the nose, whispering an abbreviated prayer. Now that I wasn't hovering around panic mode, I could see the head was more child-sized, though the features were clearly adult.

"This shouldn't stay out any longer," I said. "Can you please open the freezer?"

Tanner jumped to help. His phone went off as he lowered the lid. "I'll take this outside."

I washed the poultry shears in the sink, left them in the drainer, and took my time checking the kitchen thoroughly, even opening the tiny freezer inside the refrigerator. The compartment was barely big enough for two aluminum ice trays, let alone body parts, but I was aiming for professional thoroughness.

The sitting room, located on the north side of the house, was still dim. Taking out my phone, I compared the image of the severed head with the faces carved into the picture frames. I swept my flashlight over the rest of the photographs, getting close enough to sneeze from the dust and ascertain there was more than a passing resemblance to at least two of the younger men. It wasn't a perfect match, but it was close enough to call: the heads in the bags weren't one-hundred percent human. And neither were some of the Pearmains.

W hen I peeked out the kitchen window, the Provincial agent was standing in a patch of sun, slapping his hat against the side of his thigh, the other hand holding his phone to his ear. I lingered on the details of his physique, highlighted by the cut of his pants. There was no way those were off-the-rack Carhartts.

He noticed me when he finished the call and beckoned me to join him. I noticed his shoulder-to-hip ratio and declared it perfect.

"You ready to walk the orchard?" he asked.

"I don't remember much about the specific layout of this property."

"The photographs you received. Can you pinpoint where they might have been taken?"

I should have been making that suggestion, instead of gawking at the man's backside. Pulling out my phone to compare the images, I shook my head. "Let's start with the oldest section of the orchard." I showed the pictures to Tanner. "The trunk of this tree is too gnarled to be less than fifty, sixty years old."

"Lead on." He dipped forward in a mock bow and swept a half-circle with his hat.

"Let me check on Cliff and Abi first." I followed the wrap-around porch to the front of the house, my boots' wide heels echoing dully on the weathered boards, and squeezed Abi's hands and then Cliff's. I quietly promised I would figure out whatever was happening on their land then completed a circuit of the porch, satisfied nothing was obviously amiss. "They're the same. Any idea when your contacts will get here?"

"Within the hour."

"Do you think we should stay here and wait, in case…?" I slid my hands into my back pockets and shrugged. The air around the house and grounds remained unnaturally quiet for a summer day.

"I'll know if anyone steps onto the property."

I started to ask how, wavered my foot over the bottom step, and closed my mouth before giving in to the crush of curiosity. "How?"

"How will I know if we have visitors?"

"Mm-hm."

"You're an Earth witch, right?"

"And you know that because…?"

"Because the pentacle glowed green," he said, "and there's dirt ground into your knees and the palms of your hands."

I looked down. Okay, he paid attention, and some of the clues were pretty obvious. "So your powers of observation are good. What else?"

"Druids are connected to the earth as witches like yourself are, but…differently. I knew when your car crossed the property line. As long as my feet are on the ground—this ground—I'll know if others do too."

Later, I'd ask him why he waited to show himself to me. For now, I would keep him within eyesight. "You ready to go look for damaged trees?"

At his nod, I turned my back to the farmhouse and contemplated the two paths. I chose the one bordered with reddish-purple fireweed and trailing curlicues of vetch and indicated Tanner could go first.

CHAPTER 3

The trail soon sloped toward a trio of ponds, each edged with plump, brown cattails. Past those, the ground rose into a shoulder-like ridge that eventually connected the property to one of the island's tallest mountains.

Pausing at the crest of the valley, I shielded my eyes and scanned the area. "There."

The south-facing slope, where winter frosts nudged boulders at random and generations of deer carved narrow trails through the meadows. The older trees had long since ignored the directives of annual pruning and instead twisted and turned with the pull of the sun and the push of the wind.

I paused at the first wild rebel, caressing its patchy, lichen-splotched bark. The lowest limbs were suspended in a cathartic dance, the upper ones covered with ripening fruit.

"We'll start here," I said. "We're looking for trees with wide trunks that may have split."

"Ashmead's Kernel."

"What?"

"It says this tree is an Ashmead's Kernel." Tanner reached over our heads and pointed to an apricot-sized apple with a blemished, dull green skin. "Not very pretty on the outside, but one of the oldest varieties grown on the island. And one of the tastiest," he continued. "This trunk's in good condition, and I don't see evidence of pesticide use or other topical residue on the leaves. Let's keep moving."

I swept my gaze across the uncut grass. "Look at the ground too," I reminded him. "In the photographs, it looks like someone —or something—was digging near the bases of the trees."

Tanner kept his lead along the path. I lagged behind, running my hands over the roughened bark of every tree we passed, gathering tidbits of their lives through my fingertips. I smiled to myself, giggled softly, wished I could take off my boots and meander, eyes closed and senses open. The orchard's occupants had triggered my witchy curiosity, making it difficult to stick to the plan.

"What's so funny?" he asked.

I shook my head. "These trees have stories to tell, and if we weren't here on such gruesome business, I'd still be hugging old Ashley back there and listening to what she had to say."

"Ashmead," Tanner corrected me with one eyebrow up, and the side of his mouth quirked in a half smile.

"Ashmead," I echoed. "Got it." The sudden trill running along the bones in my chest had nothing to do with tasty apples and everything to do with the timbre of Tanner Marechal's voice.

Focus, Calliope. Focus.

My inner compass didn't warn me soon enough. Fingers trailing lightly over low-hanging fruit, sun-warmed apples releasing their scent and inciting thoughts of desserts—apple crumble, apple pie, Marechal a la mode—I stumbled on a rock and fell to my knees.

"Ouch!" I went to press myself to standing, only to be diverted by a swath of flattened grass. Rocks the size of my head and larger, loosened from some prior event, rolled away easily when pushed. "Tanner. Get down here."

I clambered forward on hands and knees to where roots, bent like the knuckles of a giant hand, plunged into the dense, dry soil. The center of the tree's trunk was split and slightly hollowed, its interior darkly shadowed.

"Whoa." I used my flashlight to illuminate the grotto-like opening. Fresh gouges on the outer bark, close to the ground, confirmed a match with one of the photographs. Gouges meant claws—or thick nails—and perhaps a struggle, and it wasn't clear to me on first look whether the struggle had been to get in or not get pulled out.

Leaning forward, the cool air hovering inside the trunk cast a wave of goosebumps over my neck and down my back. I hadn't come to the orchard prepared to find severed heads, and I wasn't prepared to come across the bodies formerly attached to the heads. If there had been a fight here...

Strands of hair and bits of faded fabric snagged on the interior surface confirmed that possibility. Tanner kneeled, his thigh pressed against mine, and added his light. Two-by-fours, roughly cut and splintered by use, framed a hole in the ground. Below that, a ladder made from thick branches disappeared into the inky darkness. I inched closer until my head and shoulders were inside the trunk. Shining the light over the ladder, I counted the horizontal pieces of wood. The top two were lightly gouged and the rest descended to a depth of at least ten or twelve feet.

"I think we should see where this goes," I said, claustrophobia and childhood trauma be damned. I had a lead to follow, and Tanner was much too broad-shouldered and tall to maneuver through the opening. "Whatever was here—*is* here—feels benign, like their work is done."

"How can you tell?" he asked.

I wiggled backward until I was fully out of the tree and could sit. A clump of sticky spider web, stretching from inside the trunk to the back of my head, set my skin to crawling. Tanner reached for my ponytail, removed the stringy mess, and wiped his fingers on the grass.

Pressing both hands to the ground, I closed my eyes and surfed for input. Every point of body-to-earth contact buzzed softly. "Bees. Happy humming. Like they're getting ready for sleep at the end of a long work day."

I lifted my palms, blinking at the transition and the oddness of not actually *seeing* any bees.

"Happy humming?" Tanner stared, his voice echoing the skepticism telegraphed by his posture.

"Yes." I nodded hard, once, certain of what I'd felt, though uncertain of the why. "When I explored the area near the salt circle," I continued, eager now to share because honestly, when was the last time I'd talked about my magic with anybody, "I felt nothing, like the ground had been...vacated. Here, it's like the tree and the ground are happy, content. The feedback I get is these trees, this entire section of the orchard, is being cared for. Nourished."

I was practically bouncing in place.

"So we have a section of the property that feels dead and a section that feels alive."

"Very alive," I agreed. "But I wouldn't say dead, more like asleep."

"Which could be a side effect of the catatonia spell." He'd put it together before I did, but I was seconds away from the same conclusion. He continued, "I'm betting you'll fight me on going into that hole, but would you agree to wait until the other agents are here? Please?"

I could give him that much, but joy, and one small success, made me ambitious. "In the meantime, I'd like to look more carefully at every other tree in the area."

Tanner stood and offered his hand. "Agreed."

He snapped a photo and noted the tree's approximate location. I put my hands on the trunks of others nearby. We found two more with hollowed cores, both with wood-framed entrances to tunnels of similar depths. And both trees matched the photographs sent anonymously.

"Tanner, are you seeing what I'm seeing?"

We had meandered far out of sight and sound of the farmhouse and outbuildings. The apple trees in this section were gnarled to the point of appearing exhausted, unable to bear the weight of fruit-laden branches. None were completely dead, and most had at least a few branches—shiny green and optimistic—reaching straight to the sky from limbs propped by rotting crutches or stacks of large stones.

"These don't look so healthy," he offered.

"Or maybe they're just very old. And tired."

The terrain was rockier, and the angle of the afternoon sun created more shadows and shade. The bee-like humming I heard at the first tree had morphed into a steady drone of sound.

"A heartbeat," I whispered. "A very slow heartbeat." A very slow, melancholic heartbeat.

Tanner slid his thumb down my forearm and took hold of my wrist. "Calliope, stop. What did you just say?"

I didn't turn to look at him, but I did stop, softening my knees and spreading my fingers, palms down. He released his grip. I blurred my gaze, loosened my joints until my body was a more fluid conduit of information and followed the beat. The ground gave a series of slow, rolling undulations and settled. I held my breath.

This was it; this was what I had been waiting for. The earth was talking to me again, and the beat was faint but present.

"Did you feel that?" I turned to face Tanner.

Gold sparks flickered at the tips of his hair, along the exposed skin of his arms, and around his eyes. "Yes."

"It's like this part of the orchard is alive, not just the trees and the bees but...everything." Scanning my memories, I could find nothing that mirrored this moment. At least nothing I could verbalize. But I'd felt this before, and that achy, uninhabited place in my heart leapt. Whether in hope or recognition, I wasn't sure.

More faint reverberations made their way from the ground into my legs. My joints loosened in anticipation of another undulation, another clue, another connection. Instead, the beats thundered closer to where we stood.

"Those're my agents," Tanner said. "Be right back."

I floundered then sank to the ground. When I'd seen the salt circle and pressed my hands to the nearby dirt, I was certain the lack of sensation meant my magic was weaker than ever. Now, I was ready to reverse that opinion. Something was alive under this very ground, and its life-beat had reached up and made a connection to mine. I stroked the crushed grass, ran my hands over desiccated clumps of moss, murmuring to myself and to whatever might be listening.

"I'll protect you," I whispered, giving the ground another pat before standing, wobbly-kneed and covered in hitchhiking grass seeds, at the sound of approaching footfalls.

Tanner squeezed my elbow and let go. "Calli, this is Wessel Foxwhelp and Kazimir Wickson. Wes, Kaz—Calliope Jones. She's with the island's ag commission."

The men had firm grips and clear eyes. Wes's brilliant red hair flopped in tight curls around his ears and across his forehead. Kaz stood shorter than his two coworkers, with a wrestler's build and an unstoppable grin.

"How're Clifford and Abigail?" I asked.

"Resting," said Wes. "We got them into their beds. River and Rose are here too."

Both Tanner's eyebrows lifted. "Rose tagged along?"

Kaz crossed his bared his forearms over his broad chest and shrugged. "River wanted her for medical support. We agreed it was best to encase the Pearmains in a slow-release sleeping spell, given their age. Those two'll stay with them until they're awake and settled. River's promised to let us know if they say anything."

"Thanks," Tanner said, before turning to me. "Ready to show these two what we found?"

At my nod, we retraced our steps to the first tree.

"Kaz, how are you with tight spaces?" I asked, comparing his height and girth to mine.

He grinned, coppery flashes igniting his irises. "Live to get myself stuck, Calliope. Extracting me gives that fellow something to do." He winked at Wes. "Where would you like to begin?"

"Right here. It's the tree closest to the house and the road."

Kaz was on his knees in a moment, pocket flashlight in his teeth, peering into the trunk and down the shaft. His head circumscribed most of a circle as he scanned whatever lay underground. "Tunnel," he proclaimed, once he'd crawled backward and gotten off his knees. "Looks like we might have a waystation."

"Waystation?" I asked.

"Think of it as a stop on a rail or subway line."

I pivoted to scan the orchard and note the locations of the other trees in question. I pointed toward the first one we stumbled on. "Any chance the tunnel heads in that direction?"

Kaz nodded. "Sure does. And then it heads over that-a-way."

He gestured toward the third tree, out of sight behind a slope in the land.

"You up for exploring?" I was so, so ready.

"Aye, but we'll need to come back tomorrow. With equipment. Which means we need to stay the night."

The tiniest bit deflated and with another complaint to review, I left Tanner and his cohorts to work out amongst themselves who would do what, given the twists in the orchard investigation. I didn't get to meet River and Rose. They were occupied inside the farmhouse with working healing spells on Cliff and Abi and made it clear they could not be interrupted.

On my final stop before home, I parked near the outdoor farmer's market in the center of town. I was reaching for my stash of cloth shopping bags when Tanner knocked on the passenger's door and planted his elbows on the window opening. He'd ditched his hat, pulled his hair into a low ponytail, and donned a pair of sunglasses, sending a quiver straight to my knees. The man was achingly handsome.

And my addled hormones were responding. Strongly. "Hey."

"Do you have time to talk?" The obsidian glass shielding his eyes couldn't mask the concern drawing tight lines across his forehead and to the sides of his mouth.

"I do," I said. "But I missed lunch, and I really need to pick up some things for dinner."

"I'll help. Then we can go eat."

"We?"

The lower half of the serious face cracked into a smile, and he lifted his glasses. "Agent Jones, would you care to have dinner with me this evening so that we may review the events of this day and discuss how our offices might proceed to work together on this investigation?"

I thought about his offer for all of one-point-five seconds. "Sure."

Summer's crush of tourists meant I had to lock my car. I divvied up the bags and let Tanner follow me to the stall selling apple cider mini-donuts. Munching on a couple of treats would stave off my hunger and give me time to think about dinner. I paid for a half-dozen cinnamon-and-sugar covered confections, nabbed the one on top, and offered the greasy paper bag to Tanner.

"Dessert first?" He peered at me over the top edge of his sunglasses. The glow I'd seen at the Pearmains' was present in the golden sparks glinting in his faceted eyes.

I'd had my feet in exam room stirrups first thing that morn-ing, silently swearing off intimate encounters with magically-enhanced men, and here I was, losing my resolve at the earliest opportunity. And what was it with the sparkles? Was it a druid thing?

I'd ask another time. Instead, I answered, "Always."

Belly growling, I ate another donut while I collected and paid for a bag of basil and paper produce boxes of wild, sweet strawberries and yellow raspberries. I never tired of the bounty of the island, and to touch, taste, and smell all the life around me was a welcome respite after my encounter with a chest freezer loaded with death. I shuddered and pinched off another sugary bite.

"May I?" Tanner held a cloth bag open. I deposited my purchases, and he followed my methodical pace, asking. "Do you feel obligated to buy something from each merchant?"

"Am I that obvious?" I moved to the next stall and was about to bury my nose in the cleft of a plump heirloom tomato when my phone vibrated.

"MOM," read the first text, followed quickly by "PIZZA" and "Dad says he needs our help this weekend."

Funny how my sons always had time to communicate when the topic was their hunger. Tanner moved ahead to a tent displaying desserts while I texted Thatch and Harper.

"CHORES"

"DO THEM"

"HOME SOON"

I looked up in time to see a smiling young woman with chin-length hair and a spiked collar place a lattice-topped pie into a box. Her profile was familiar and her name was on the tip of my tongue, though I couldn't retrieve it. Tanner handed over a credit card while I searched my brain.

"This okay?" he mouthed, pointing at the box being wrapped with string.

I nodded and waved my arm in the direction of the bank of shops and restaurants flanking the side of the temporary market. I ordered two pizzas to go at the Italian place and found an empty table where I could sit and wait. My unexpected dinner companion cast a long glance over the milling crowd before heading in my direction.

"Calli," Tanner said, his voice low, "put down your phone and look at me like we're flirting or something." He slid the red-lettered pie box onto an empty chair. "Don't look out the window. Look at me."

Working against the urge to turn my head and do precisely what he'd asked me not to, I placed an elbow on the table and rested my chin in my hand. With poured concrete under my leather-shod feet and glass and metal to my right, I couldn't get a read on what might be happening outside the restaurant.

"We're being monitored," he said.

"Since we left the orchard?"

Tanner shook his head and reached across the table to touch his fingertips to my elbow. "No, since we entered the market."

"How do you know?"

"They're probing. It's subtle, but I can feel it."

"Can you sense what they're looking for? Or who?" Magicals got hungry too, and I'd noticed a couple of familiar signatures as soon as I exited my car.

The young man behind the counter hit the order bell. "Two Margherita pizzas."

"That's ours," I said.

Off-balance at Tanner's mild alarm—and the sensation of his fingertips on my bare skin—I stood a little too suddenly. My chair teetered and quickly righted, Tanner's foot looped around the closest leg. While I paid, he retrieved the boxes and stacked the pie container on top.

"Can we take your car?" he asked.

I nodded. "But where's yours?"

"I let Wes and Kaz use my truck. I'll have them pick me up when they're done." He held the door open with his back. When I passed in front of him, he tensed. "Calliope, take the food."

"Why?" My left arm brushed his chest, meeting a solid wall of warm, tensed muscle.

"Because I'm not sure what it is we might be walking into and I can't defend us if I'm also trying to save our dinner." Tanner hitched the straps of my bags higher on my shoulders before handing over the stack of fragrant boxes. The bottom one was hot. He bent forward, brushed his lips against my cheek and whispered into my ear, "Go to your car. Put the food on the floor, start the engine, and wait for me."

My urge to gawk at his backside cooled even as my cheeks burned. I hightailed it to where I'd parked, keeping my eyes forward and daring any driver to get in my way.

Damned if I was going to play the damsel in distress.

And damn Tanner for making it so easy to pretend there was something between us.

I stashed the pizzas and the pie behind the driver's seat, readjusted my cross-body bag, and leaned against the car door, slowly scanning the street and sidewalks. If he could feel the presence of another magical, then so could I.

Maybe. Probably.

It was worth a try, especially with the boost to my confidence earlier in the day. Slipping off my boots and wincing at the gravel underfoot, I kept my eyes open—always a challenge when I was sensing—and fed my awareness out in concentric circles.

CHAPTER 4

I couldn't recall the last time I tapped into the energy of downtown Ganges with the purpose of tracking Magicals. The energy was always thicker in the summer and especially on market days, when the collective magic resembled a tangled mass of root balls. Familiar signatures—ones I could attach to specific shops and offices—burst here and there, like tiny buds and flowers.

I gloated when I located Tanner's citrine-colored signal in the park. The druid was likely surrounded by toddlers and hula-hoopers and...

Oh! A peculiar, solitary point tugged on a section of entangled energies at the near side of the marina. The knot was close to where prop planes took on and dropped off passengers, which could mean whoever was giving off the signal had just arrived, or was preparing to leave. Wiping the soles of my feet on the inside of my pant legs, I wiggled back into my boots and headed in the direction of the harbor. I had to cross a main thoroughfare and jostle my way through clusters of bodies. Holding firm to the unknown entity, I kept to as straight a line as possible.

Once across the busy street, I released one foot from its boot and wiggled my toes into the soil underneath the shrubbery lining the sidewalk.

Maybe Tanner was on to something with his quick on, quick off footwear.

The ominous presence pulsed oily and cold among the boats bobbing in the crowded harbor. My toes recoiled. Following the line of energy to its source had just gotten exponentially harder. There was no way I was going swimming in that water.

Moving forward, I tried to be unobtrusive. I mean, I lived here. I knew almost all the shop owners and the staff at the marina, and on a normal day it could take me twenty minutes to get from where I was to where I needed to be. I retied my pony-tail, threw up a deflective mirror shield with four flicks of my right wrist, and hoped everyone was too busy with the time-honored practice of separating tourists from their dollars to pay attention to the witch on a mission.

I honed in on the handful of yachts at the first dock, in partic-ular, the sharkskin gray, custom-painted exhibit of excess floating close to the pulse of darkness. My ex's family ran a realty firm. Along with a roster of exclusive listings, they owned a fleet of gas-guzzling vehicles and a yacht.

In fact, they owned *that* yacht, *The Merry Widow*, Doug's mother's nod to her marital state, not the famous opera.

I had no way to reach Tanner through non-magical means, but I could blend in better without a six-foot-tall druid by my side. I made it to the booth at the head of the boarding ramp the same time a float plane took off. The slippery connection flew from my grasp, whip-like and slick as the plane headed toward open waters.

Dammit.

Shielding my eyes, I could see heads behind the plane's tiny windows. I flagged the navy blue-clad baggage handler rolling his cart up the ramp.

"Where're they headed?" I pointed to the plane and made sure he acknowledged the badge affixed to my waistband.

"Vancouver. Private charter."

Nothing else I could do. My hope sank as the plane disappeared. I turned to walk back to my car, discouraged but still alert to other signals, when the baggage guy added, "If it's any help, they were staying on *The Merry Widow*."

S ix o'clock had come and gone. Market stall workers were breaking down their tents and mismatched trestle tables and loading their vehicles. I made it to my car, only to find Tanner pacing bumper to bumper.

"Where were you?" he demanded.

Fingers tapping on the roof of my car wasn't the signal I was looking for. Even if those fingers were long and elegant and could play a tune across any surface. Metal. Tree bark. Skin.

I pinched the bridge of my nose, unlocked the doors, and slid into my seat. This shared investigation was *not* going to work if I had to report every move to him or wait for him to approve my decisions.

Or deal with a crush.

I blamed my fluctuating hormones.

Tanner slid in beside me and buckled his seat belt. "Stay to the speed limit," he ordered. "And take a different way home. I don't think anyone will follow us, but do it anyway."

I fiddled with my keychain and pondered a shortcut. "What happened back there?"

He propped one hand against the dashboard and kept his gaze out the back window. "I smelled dirt. Really old dirt, combined with...engine oil, maybe?" He pressed into the seat and threaded his fingers through his hair. "I'm sorry for yelling at you. And for making assumptions."

"We don't know each other, and we don't yet know how to

work together," I offered. "And thank you for the apology." I put
the car into reverse, ready to be home, ready for some breathing
room. "By the way, I felt it too, and I traced it to the marina. And
a boat belonging to my ex-husband's family business." His look
went from irritated to possibly impressed. "But the connection
disappeared when a prop plane took off."

O nce we were at my house, Tanner insisted I park the car
so it faced down the driveway. "In case you need to get
out of here in a hurry" was his offered explanation. I went with it,
scooping up the pizza boxes so I could be the one bearing dinner
and thereby have my sons' complete attention.

"Guys," I yelled, tapping my toe against the bottom of the
screen door. "Food's here." Footsteps thundered down the inside
stairs, followed by gangly limbs and smiling faces. "You two get
your chores done?"

"What chores?" Harper lifted the pizza boxes out of my arms
and held both high above his head as he twirled.

"Harper Flechette-Jones, put those back and go set the table.
For four." My eldest sent the boxes sliding the length of the
kitchen's narrow island. Thatcher—taller, skinnier, and, eight
times out of ten, hungrier—stopped the boxes from toppling over
the edge.

"Mo-om, I *love* you," he said, flipping the lid and inhaling.
"And you got one of Sallie's pies!"

That was why the young woman's face was familiar. She was
related somehow to Harper and Thatch on Doug's side of the
family, which probably made them cousins. And solved one of
the day's mysteries.

"I'd love you more if you two would do your chores without
me having to remind you all the time," I said.

Harper coughed and adopted a serious tone. "Mother. Did
you happen to look in the wood box? And did you observe the

empty dish rack?" He swept his arm toward the staircase. "And I didn't notice you inspecting our rooms in the three minutes you've been home, so I think—"

I swatted his shoulder. "Did you two *really* do all that, or are you just desperate for food?"

"Both," they answered in unison as Tanner knocked at the kitchen door and let himself inside.

"This is Tanner Marechal," I said. "He's an agent with the Ministry of Forests, Lands and Natural Resources, and he's working on a case with me."

A round of manly handshakes and deliberate eye contact followed, behavior I hadn't noticed my sons exhibiting before. All movement toward getting food to the table paused as they assessed one another.

"Guys? Food?" I waved utensils and cloth napkins in the air. "Thatcher, can you please make a pitcher of lemonade?"

Once settled at the table, the teens inhaled their first slices of pizza and settled into a more sedate pace with their second. As usual, they were more interested in eating than in making conversation.

"What does your dad need your help with this weekend?" I asked.

"Is it okay if we go?" Points to Harper for swallowing first.

"Yes. But you still need to answer my question."

"Dad bought a condo in Vancouver, near Granville Island, and he wants our help packing up his apartment in Victoria and assembling a bunch of furniture from Ikea for his new place. You know Dad. He wishes he had a magic wand so he wouldn't have to get his hands dirty with menial shit."

The bite of pizza got all cardboard-y in my mouth. How could Doug be one of the few people able to afford to move *into* Vancouver? Lack of money was his chronic lament. I wanted to spit out my mouthful of half-chewed dough, pick up my phone, and harangue my ex, but that had never worked in the past.

"You have someone to cover your shifts at the farm and the market?" I asked. The brothers nodded in tandem. "Then make sure your father pays for the ferry and see if he'll cover your lost wages."

Tanner focused on eating. Harper and Thatch discussed the logistics of getting to a concert they wanted to attend later in the summer, while the sounds of rhythmic chewing and swallowing filled my ears. Splaying my bare feet against the cool maple floor boards, I connected with my house and, below that connection, with my land.

A quiet burp, followed by an, "Excuse me" and chairs being pushed away signaled the teens were finished. They cleared the table, rinsed the dishes, and disappeared upstairs, plates of pie in hand. Following their movements, my heart clenched, wanting to hold on to the little boys inside the young men they were becoming.

Tanner shifted his left knee and made contact with my leg. "Good kids," he whispered.

"Mm-hm," I agreed.

He tapped the side of my knee again. "We should talk."

"Let's sit outside."

A heavy three-seater swing took up one-third of the narrow deck off the back of the house. I placed my glass of lemonade on the low table and nestled into weather-hardened cushions. My house abutted a heavily wooded area, and when the sun dropped behind the hill that shouldered the long side of the property, the temperature shifted rapidly. I unfolded a shawl and wrapped it around my shoulders.

Fir trees were shrouded in summer-weight capes of light and dark greens, their edges decorated with ripening cones. Faint whisperings within the overlapping branches pricked my awareness, while an argument raged between the resident raven couple and a flock of interloping crows.

"Do you encounter a lot of witches in your work?" I asked

Tanner once he settled in the opposite corner. "Or shifters and other Magicals?"

"Here and there. I've collected a core group I trust, including the two you met at the Pearmains' and the two you didn't, River and Rose."

"Are they druids as well?"

"The three men are. Rose is River's sister, and she's a witch."

"I know almost no one," I confessed. "And today has been very unusual compared to most Tuesdays or any other day."

A handful of persistent crows now had the full attention of the raven pair, and a storm of dark wings and sharp calls shattered the cozying twilight.

Tanner's gaze went right to the section of woods off the deck, honing in on something I couldn't yet see.

"What is it?" I asked.

He curved his left palm over my thigh, stilling my urge to stand and move closer to the railing. The birds flew off, taking their argument elsewhere and leaving behind falling feathers and a large splat of guano near the corner of the deck.

I picked up a low growl.

No, not a growl, a chant or incantation, and the sound was coming from Tanner. This day was getting more unsettling by the second. Darting my gaze from his face to the edge of the woods, I found the upside-down, bat-like creature that riveted his attention. Like a flag unfurling in a slow breeze, the animal unfolded one wing, smoky black and opaque, from where it wrapped a fir tree.

Behind us, the house shook with the pounding of teenage feet and bodies hurling themselves down stairs.

"Mom, something weird is..." Harper hurried the sliding screen door open and stopped, his brother plastered to his back.

Tanner kept chanting while the creature separated its other wing fully from the tree. Only the hold of its claws kept it from plummeting to the ground.

"What *is* that?" I whispered.

The boys froze. Tanner rose from our shared seat and vaulted over the railing. I bumped my shins against the table, toppling my glass in my rush to see if he'd injured himself on the eighteen-foot drop to the ground. He strode to the tree without limping or trailing a broken leg, his right hand aimed at the creature's head with its pointy ears and elongated snout. The bat's scrawny body wobbled as it climbed backward down the tree.

Thatch bent down closer my ear. "Mom, what is going on?" he asked, his voice quiet but harsh.

His natural curiosity fought against the palm I pressed to the center of his chest. "I'm not sure. Give Tanner a chance to deal with whatever it is he's got there. Then we'll talk."

"You bet we're gonna talk, Mom, because this is seriously weird shit."

"It's been a Seriously Weird Shit kind of a day."

With his left hand, Tanner pulled a section of binding rope or vine out of the air and looped it over the creature's neck. Harper backed out of the doorway and took the more traditional route to the yard. He slowed his approach to a stop when Tanner extended his arm behind him. Harper then crept forward when beckoned.

I was on the verge of hollering at him to stay away.

Low, masculine voices rose from below, their steady timbre punctuated by high-pitched keening. Harper knelt and touched the bat. The whimpering stopped, and the tension in its body released. Tanner raised both hands, palms up. Harper paused then straightened from his crouch. The creature used its claws to climb up his leg, and once it was high enough off the ground to extend its wings, it wrapped them around my son's ribs and chest, blending the two into one in the gloaming light.

I covered my mouth with a shaking hand, one breath away from cursing Tanner into the middle of next week. Thatch grabbed my wrist and hauled me into the living room. He opened the screen door for Harper and his new companion, making soothing sounds as they entered.

"Calli." Tanner slid around the trio and took my other hand, keeping his voice conversational as he spoke. "I think Harper has a natural empathy toward winged creatures. This looks like a fruit bat, but it's nowhere near its natural habitat." He continued, as though encountering giant fruit bats in coastal British Columbia was so common as to be passé. "I've seen a few, but I've never seen anything in the chiroptera family take to a human as fast as this one bonded with your son."

Harper's eyes registered shock and disbelief, coupled with a possessiveness I was not at all used to seeing. "Mom, what have you not been telling us?"

I darted my gaze back and forth between my sons. My weird day was getting weirder. I turned to Tanner. "Will that thing hurt Harper?"

"I don't think so."

"Then can you please give us a minute?" Time was marching on, and I had a major, unplanned confession to make.

The giant bat rustled its wings, soft clicking noises coming from its mouth. I had to force myself not to insinuate my fingers between its claws and Harper's chest or at least shove an oven mitt in there.

Tanner took his cue. "I'll go outside and see if it's brought companions. They're shy, and they can't echolocate. Maybe it's... lost." He shrugged and ducked out the door.

My youngest still had hold of my wrist. "Mom?"

"Do you believe in magic?" I asked.

Two sets of eyes stared at me, three if I counted the bat.

"That creature is not like other bats," I started with the obvious. "And I'm not like other moms." I touched both sons simultaneously, focused on my love for them, and channelled a bright pink ribbon of light from my heart through my arms to my hands and outwards.

"Mom? What are you doing?" Harper twisted his arm to disconnect from me.

Thatcher looked down, eyes wide.

"I'm kind of a witch," I admitted, "and what I just did with my hands was transmit love."

My youngest snorted and tugged his hand away.

Harper increased his glare. "*Kind of* a witch? How can you be *kind of* a witch? And what does that make me and Thatch?"

"Sons of a witch?" My attempt at humor fell flat; this was not going well.

The bat shifted slightly. Harper looked down the front of his body and stroked the bony claws threatening to make lace out of his tee shirt. "Shh," he soothed. "Shhhh…"

Thatcher took hold of my hand again, twisting it one way then the other, as if he wanted to unscrew it from my wrist and have a closer look inside. "Mom. You mean to tell us *now* that you could have…" He shrugged. "I don't know, done our homework for us? Cleared up my pimples?"

I had no strategy for this moment. I went with the truth. "My mother was a witch, the aunt who raised me was a witch, and you two might carry the potential for magic. You might not. Your father's side of the family does—or *did*—but he made it clear he thought our lives would be less complicated if we kept quiet about our abilities. We did such a good job of keeping quiet, I almost forgot I had any." I pointed to my oldest and the creature girdling his torso. "But I think it's safe to say you've inherited some magical skills. Or 'affinities,' like Tanner said."

Harper shifted his gaze to his brother and bored two new holes in his head.

"What?" Thatch threw his arms out to the sides.

"You know what. Show Mom."

"She'll never let me keep her."

Harper hugged the wings folded over his ribs. "I'm keeping this one."

I squirmed. My head zinged back and forth between my sons as I tried to translate their shorthand. "One of you want to tell me what's going on?"

"Wait here, Mom." Thatcher took the stairs two at a time and reappeared with a raccoon perched on his shoulder. One of its paws clutched a clump of my son's hair; the other held a chunk of pie crust. The animal's bushy tail, ringed with stripes of black and gray-ish brown, fluffed when it spied Harper and the bat. The raccoon dropped the crust, steadied itself with both paws scrabbling for purchase, and delivered a severe and pointed lecture. The creature continued its tirade of chitters and hisses, calming only when Thatcher picked up the piece of crust and handed it back.

"Shall we sit?" I asked.

Thatch extricated nimble-fingered paws from his hair, opened the front door, and led the raccoon outside.

Harper tried to sit, but the bat wouldn't ease its grip. "I'll stand."

I swallowed, took a brief moment to stabilize by reaching into the ground below our house. "Guys, I met Tanner today on an inspection at an orchard. He figured out I was a witch, let me know he was a druid, and our day progressed from there."

"A druid. Go on."

Boys.

And men. Tanner appeared outside the screen door, the raccoon attached to his pant leg.

I waved him in and continued. "After dinner, we went to the back deck to talk. The ravens gave their alert, and you two saw what happened next."

On his way to the couch, Tanner appraised my offspring. "I run a mentoring program for magic-blessed youth. Would either or both of you like to check out what we do?"

Thatch's face lit up. He straightened his spine and scooted to the edge of the seat, turning his body to face Tanner. "You mean like learning how to communicate with animals and cast spells?"

"That's a part of it. Mostly, we teach you how to identify and work with your particular magic, how to keep it healthy, help it grow."

"How to keep us from joining the dark side," Harper joked.

Tanner considered Harper's comment and shifted his body to include both boys in his comments. "There's a dark side to everyone's magic. We encourage you to acknowledge all aspects of your gifts *and* understand what it means when we say actions have consequences."

Both sons nodded, enthralled with Tanner's offer, Thatcher perhaps more than Harp. I was irritated. I was the parent in the room, and whether my boys entered a magic-mentoring program was at least partially within my purview to yea or nay.

Or perhaps I shouldn't impose my feelings about my own lack of nurturance onto my sons. I could teach them and would do so gladly, but they had to want it. And maybe a mother wasn't the best, or shouldn't be the only, teacher for boys approaching adulthood.

"Does a parent get any say on this?" I asked.

"Would you rather your sons not understand their gifts?"

I pressed my lips together and glowered at Tanner. "I barely understand my own."

"Which is why I'm making this offer."

I tried to muster a fresh batch of righteous indignation, and I couldn't. "If you two are interested, you have my conditional blessing."

They both turned their attention to Tanner.

"When do we start?" asked Thatcher.

CHAPTER 5

Harper and Thatch accepted a last-minute invitation from a group of friends to camp on the southern part of the island. Once the bat was settled in the shed below the deck, they left with promises to exercise caution, show up for their day jobs, and return home by dinner the following night. I stood in the driveway, staring into the darkness long after their Jeep's tail lights disappeared.

Tanner suddenly standing at my back didn't startle me. I was getting used to the druid's stealth-mode way of moving from one spot to another. I asked, "Wasn't I wondering hours ago if this day could get any weirder?"

"Yes, I believe you were," he answered.

"It got weirder." I turned toward the house. "I hope that giant bat thing was the last of it."

"I think I should spend the night," Tanner announced, resting his hands at his hips and relaxing his posture. A relaxed Tanner Marechal, Provincial agent and druid, thrummed with a kind of take-charge sensuality I found completely disconcerting. "Who-ever—or whatever—sent those photos is either trying to point the finger at wrongdoing or manipulate an outcome. And frankly, I'm leaning toward the latter."

"I agree. I have a very hard time believing Cliff and Abi are deliberately undermining the health of their trees." I snugged my shawl closer around my upper arms and mounted the stairs. My relationships with most of the farming community on the island were solid, and if any one of them was in trouble, the others were far more likely to rally around than take advantage, let alone commit murder. "What else can you share?"

Tanner followed and held the screen door open for me to pass first. "The other orchardists were close in age to the Pearmains, and both had family members waiting to take over day-to-day operations once they retired."

Interesting. "Back in May, Cliff and Abi threw a party to celebrate their fiftieth wedding anniversary. They mentioned two of their grandsons were planning to move to the island come September."

I yawned. The long, strange day was catching up with me. If Tanner was spending the night, I had sheets to change and should probably put a load of towels into the washing machine.

"I want you to be safe," Tanner said.

The statement startled me. "I've never felt unsafe here or anywhere else on the island. I don't feel unsafe now."

He emphasized his skepticism by crossing his arms over his chest and flexing his forearms. "Let me at least place wards around your house. You're an untrained witch and—"

"Rub it in, Tanner." I glared at him in the dark and shared my most pressing concern. "Do you think my sons are safe?"

"No one's ever one-hundred percent immune to the unpredictable; you know that, Calliope, but in general I'd say yes, they should be fine."

"In general?" I asked. His nod triggered my maternal worry reflex. "Should I have made them stay home tonight?"

"Magic will seek them out once their power has been awakened. They're still dormant."

"Dormant? Did you see how that bat climbed Harper and would not let go?"

"All right, mostly dormant."

"But that creature—"

"That creature saw kinship, recognized Harper's compassion and his lack of fear."

I shook out my arms and rolled my shoulders. Truth be told, I would rest better knowing the house was protected, even temporarily. "You can have one of the boys' rooms upstairs. And you might want to check the closet and look under the bed before you go to sleep."

Unable to settle, I dumped the wicker basket of clean laundry onto my bed. I had started the day stressed about the possibility of raising another child. I was ending it stressed about raising the power of my magic enough to protect the two children I had. There was nothing like pairing up socks and folding underwear to settle me in reality.

Yet, how could there be a deadline to improving this ability I was born with?

I stared at my hands, nails trimmed and unpolished, fingers free of rings. They performed so many mundane tasks without a hitch. They were also gifted with sensors that, as I learned during my visit with Rowan, came with expiration dates. I snorted. Yet another cruel joke played on my womanhood by my advancing age.

I couldn't remember my aunt ever mentioning the necessity of regular rituals. When her dementia became unmanageable and my cousins moved her to an eldercare complex, they'd offered her house—*this* house—to me. And because I'd grown up under the steep roof lines of this A-framed structure, coming back to its embrace after divorcing Doug was more than a homecoming. Every tangible belonging of my mother's had been stored, waiting for me, in the attic.

I slid my underwear into the drawer, refolded a jumble of bras, and cast a scathing look at the calendar I used to track my dating life. Outside my bedroom, Tanner's footfalls reverberated through the floor and the solid wood door, adding to the stack of reasons why I couldn't settle my mind. If the man was aiming for stealth while he went about warding, he wasn't succeeding.

I pulled on a pair of drawstring pants and opened the door to the hall. "Tanner!"

No answer. I ducked into my closet, pulled my arms out of my long-sleeved T-shirt, and wrangled myself into a shelf bra.

"What?" His sudden appearance in the outer doorway startled me.

I brought one hand to my throat, knocking my elbow against the corner of the bureau. "Ow! You're making a lot of noise."

He backed away and gave me space to enter the hall.

"And I can't sleep," I added.

"I'm sorry if I kept you awake. I was just about to set wards around the perimeter."

"Can I come with you?"

"They're just simple words, nothing terribly interesting or complicated."

"But I've never watched someone set up protections around a house." I held his gaze—or maybe he held mine—and my house held its breath. And when was the last time I watched anyone practice magic? I mentally rifled through my years under this roof, one with my mother, so many more without. The few displays of magic I could recall were tied to mundane things, like giving dropped plates a soft landing or knowing who was on the phone in the days before answering machines had caller ID.

Even as a little girl, I knew magic existed around me and in me. I knew not everyone was gifted with magical abilities, I knew to keep quiet about mine, and I knew it was safe to play openly within the confines of the property.

Tanner pulled out one of the oak kitchen chairs and sat. The topmost buttons of his shirt were undone, and a cord of intricately knotted threads looped his neck. Whatever hung from the cord was hidden underneath his shirt. He'd rolled up the bottoms of his pant legs, and left his flip flops by the front door.

I went from stirring the mists of memory to a minor revelation—Tanner Marechal had gorgeous feet. One heel rested on a chair rung, the other leg stretched forward. That I might have a foot fetish was news to me, but I wasn't complaining. Nope. No complaints at all.

"Calli."

My gaze flew to his, and my cheeks warmed.

"I have an idea," he said, "a way for you to participate in the actual warding. I'll do a simple three-part, basic protection: Warn. Protect. Defend. *Prévenir. Protéger. Défendre.*"

"Is that French?"

He nodded. "French was my first language. We'll lay the perimeter ward first then come inside and apply wards to the windows and doors."

"How can I help?"

Tanner slouched deeper into the chair and brought one heel to rest on the edge of the seat. He rubbed his bent knee, his gaze on the fingers playing a random rhythm against the bare wood of the dining table. "We're going to brew a concoction using plants from your land. And some of your blood."

"My blood? Isn't blood used for...for *bad* magic?"

"The addition of blood creates stronger wards, and using your blood will tie the protective spells to you and your kin. There are wards in place already. They're weak, but they're blood-bound too."

That was news to me. "Can you tell whose blood was used to create the wards?"

"I might be able to with time but not tonight." He stared at me a moment and continued, "Do you get many visitors?"

"I don't," I said, shaking my head. "But the boys do. Lots of their friends come in and out, sleep over, that kind of thing."

"I'll set the wards to admit anyone directly connected to the three of you."

"Can you keep out my ex?" I was joking. Kind of.

"Seriously?"

"No, I'm just a bit upset with him right now." I busied myself with rolling the waistband of my at-home pants, which were a little long for traipsing through the woods.

"Has he been bothering you?" The golden glow I'd first seen earlier in the day flickered around Tanner's eyes and lashes. The faintest crackle split the air around his agitated fingertips.

"Physically, not at all. It's..." No, I wasn't going to spill the details of my failed relationship to this man, not yet. Not until he put shoes on and stopped *glowing*. "It's not important." I started for the front door. "Is there a particular plant I should gather?"

"Anything with thorns."

Basket handle over one arm, clippers in the other hand, I gathered leaves and a couple of hard, unripe fruit from the crabapple tree in the center of my backyard. I wasn't sure if Tanner wanted me to collect the actual thorns; I snapped a few off the tree just in case. The patches of wild blackberries and cultivated raspberries yielded stems, leaves, and juicy fruit. Closer to the woods, low-growing salal whispered its presence and offered up sharp-tipped leaves and ripening purple berries.

I stopped in the middle of cutting a sprig. Bears loved salal, though the island didn't have much of an ursine population. An inner urge said to add the plant, but actively seeking and trusting my intuition was an atrophied muscle so I paused. Fur brushed the side of my thigh, and a wave of protective energy surrounded me from the ground up and over my head.

"Thank you," I whispered, dropping three clusters of waxy leaves and dark purple berries into my basket.

Was Tanner expecting me to drink the tea? An image of the two of us walking the ambit of my property, peeing at strategic points, offered a giggly respite to the stress still playing through my body. I wasn't sure what else to add to my collection of thorny things, so I sat on the ground and asked my land what more it had to offer, not expecting an answer but eager to see if I was on a roll.

Mullein.

The opposite of thorny and a purported apotropaic, mullein harbored the ability to ward off evil spirits. More esoterically, its flowering stalk was used by men to designate their romantic intentions. A cluster grew outside my garden's fence, year after year.

I cut one tall stem bursting with small yellow flowers, collected a few oversized, velvety leaves, and headed to the house.

Tanner had a pot of water simmering on the stove.

"Lots of thorny things and some mullein," I said, tilting my haul for his perusal.

"Mullein?" He tried unsuccessfully to hide his grin before instructing me to chop everything I'd collected and add it to the water. "I'll need a paintbrush. Preferably one you haven't used."

"Anything else?"

"Your blood."

I shivered. I'd already had blood drawn today, stored in vials on their way to a Vancouver lab which, I assumed, handled the testing of biological material taken from Magicals, not humans. "How do you plan to get it?"

"I'll prick your fingertip. This tea doesn't require much."

Tanner positioned another cutting board next to the one I was using and set about chopping and mashing handfuls of plant matter before dumping them into the cook pot. Once we were done and had scrubbed most of the stains off our hands, he took his laptop to the living room while I tackled the laundry.

Towels washing, and dryer emptied, I sat at the dining table and watched as Tanner poured the liquid off the macerated plant matter through a stainless-steel mesh strainer and into a wide-mouth canning jar. When he stood himself next to me, knife in hand, and set the jar near my elbow, I assumed getting my blood was next and extended my left arm.

"I don't think I can watch this part," I admitted, "but take what you need."

Tanner's fingers were strong and gentle. He used the knife to puncture the tip of my ring finger and squeezed, released, and repeated, occasionally massaging my palm. I lost track of time, pictured bright red liquid flowing from the golden tip of a calligrapher's pen, and was relieved when Tanner declared he had enough.

I peeked at the jar. Wispy streams of liquid life hung suspended in the cloudy, brownish water. Pride—or something akin to it—rose in my chest.

"I forgot to grab a Band-Aid for you," he said.

"I can get one," I assured him.

"You're not going to faint?" he teased, topaz eyes sparkling under a fan of lashes.

I pressed the tender fingertip against my thumb and snorted. "I'm the mother of sons. I don't faint, and I always have Band-Aids and antibiotic ointment on hand."

Standing, I made my way to the bathroom and fought an unexpected wave of wooziness. My day was catching up with me and I wanted my bed, but I wanted to watch Tanner more.

"Will this do?" I handed over the first-aid supplies and an old makeup brush I'd found in the medicine cabinet.

He nodded, bandaged my finger, and started toward the front door.

"This is meant as a temporary measure only, but it should last a few days." Once on the porch, he looked me up and down. "Follow behind me. We're going to start at the end of your driveway and loop the perimeter of your property clockwise."

"Okay."

"It'll be an uneven line—we'll include the trees and bushes closest to the house."

"Can I bring a flashlight?"

He shook his head. "Trust your senses. Ready?"

"Ready."

"Stick close. Stay quiet."

We walked in silence to the end of the short driveway. Tanner surveyed the paved street, crouched, and dipped the brush into the jar.

"Wait. Tanner," I whispered. "What should I do?"

"Your feet are bare?"

"Yes."

"Keep your hands free and feel through your feet. See if you get any feedback from the ground and alert me if you sense any changes."

He began to chant in French, dropping into a crouch every few steps and brushing a signet-like shape over tree bark, bushes, and the occasional patch of grass. Cool fingers of night air stroked my ankles and wrists and even the exposed skin at my belly, and the less I could see in the ambient dark, the more my other senses attuned to the surroundings. Our feet crushed leaves and needles, releasing more scents into the air. I stepped closer to Tanner's back, curled a finger through one of his belt loops when we pushed through tangles of underbrush, and paid attention to every swoop of his brush.

The timbre of Tanner's voice drew me along, and without knowing when it happened, I became a participant in the dance of words and intentions and the herbal allies blended with my blood. Tanner may have been the architect of the wards, but a tangible part of me was in the mortar. Tree bark became my skin. Sap blended with my blood. Tree limbs became my legs and arms; leaves, my fingers and toes; blossoms and fruit, my skin.

If Tanner and I had been lovers, I could have offered him an apple or a pear from one of my trees and felt his teeth on my thighs and breasts. Before I could linger any longer on that evocative thought, we were back to where the driveway met the road and retracing our steps to the house.

Warding the interior meant painting the same watery ink on every threshold and windowsill, which took longer than our walk through the woods. My shoulders sank away from my ears once the ceiling-mounted trapdoor to the attic space was inked. Tanner carried the emptied jar to the kitchen sink and methodically rinsed the brush and washed his hands before following me to the living room couch.

Leaning forward with both elbows on his knees, he threaded plant-stained fingers through his hair and massaged his scalp. "I've been thinking about the orchards. Each grow heirloom trees, none of them have reported missing employees to local authorities, and the land has been in family hands for generations —so what's the underlying motivation to murder?"

Greed? "Land's a valuable commodity," I posited. "Just look at how property prices have risen in the past five years. It wouldn't be the first time someone was murdered so that someone else could have access to their land." I continued, "One set of people taking land from others is woven deep into the history of this island, into most every inhabited square foot of land on this continent."

Tanner hummed in agreement. "Most of my ancestors arrived as explorers. Or as indentured beings."

"Humans and druids?"

"And other things."

"Other things?"

"Have you ever met any shifters?" he asked, pulling his hair back again. For a moment, aspects of his ancestry shimmered across his face.

My cheeks warmed. Had I met any shifters..."I met two were-cougars online and went on a couple of dates."

A low sound vibrated deep in his chest, setting whatever was hanging around his neck to swinging against his shirt. "At the same time?"

"What? No!" Really, Tanner? "I picked one werecougar, we had two dates, neither of which went very well. Why do you ask? Can you shift too?"

"Druids can take animal form." A pained expression rippled across his face, shifting his features once more. "What are your plans for tomorrow?"

"Are you changing the subject?" I asked.

"Yes."

"Why?"

He pressed a hand to his sternum and clutched his shirt. For a moment, his eyes were unveiled. "The story of my life and how I got here and why I am having issues accessing my animal forms would take far longer to tell than we have tonight."

"Will you tell me another time?"

"If you're still interested in knowing more about me, yes, Calliope, I will answer all your questions."

"Good." I sat up and extended my arm. He let go of his shirt and shook my hand. "So, tomorrow I want to research the deeds to the Pearmain's property and...wait, what am I supposed to do with that bat-thing?"

"I'll deal with it in the morning."

"But Harper will want to see it when he gets home." And he'd never forgive me for letting it go without him saying goodbye. Was there a way to stay in touch with magical creatures?

I leaned forward and mimicked Tanner's posture. "July twenty-fourth is going down as one of the oddest days of my life. I found the heads of two murdered beings in a freezer, I came out to my sons about being a witch, and I'm having a sleepover with a druid." I glanced over at him. "I'm overwhelmed and exhausted, and I'm going to bed."

He covered one of my hands with his. A torrent of sensation accompanied the weight of his flesh pressing against mine, anchoring me in place. I reached into the maple floorboards, sought the dank soil and bedrock underneath the house. Instead of receiving a calming, connecting rebound, flickers of desire scuttled over the surface of my skin, like someone was trailing the tips of their fingernails—or the end of a branch—over my forearms and up my legs.

Tanner's pupils dilated; the hand on mine pressed heavier, and he brought the other one to cup my jaw. Unexpected heat flooded my inner thighs and prickled against my sex. I followed his unspoken suggestion as he rose, brought his other hand to my face, and stared.

"What are you doing?" I whispered. "Are you trying to spell me?"

His entire body went rigid. He shook his head. Didn't speak. His arms, bent at the elbows, lifted me until my toes scrabbled to stay in contact with the floor.

This was not my idea of foreplay. "Tanner!"

I grabbed his wrists, thick with rigid tendons, and yelled his name again. Boards creaked, my house trembled, and the sensation I'd had outside earlier—of cool fingers of night air wrapping my waist—returned. This time the invisible digits were thicker, colder, more insistent. More embodied, as though they were trying to separate me from Tanner.

One loud snap from the edge of the woods and the golden light in his eyes flickered out.

My heels hit floorboards, the walls groaned, and I tried to wriggle away. But he kept hold of my face, bringing his forehead to mine.

"What the hell?" I demanded.

"She's coming."

"Who's coming?" I squeezed his wrists again, tried pulling his hands off my face so he'd get the message and let me go. His skin was fiery hot and slicked with sweat while mine self-armored with scattered patches of goosebumps.

He kept his forehead mashed against mine as though he could bore his way past skin and bone, inhaling and exhaling slowly even as he relaxed some of the intensity of his grip. His over-heated fingers slid past my ears and rubbed at my scalp.

I shook my head, finally able to disengage from his touch. "Tanner, *who* is coming?"

CHAPTER 6

The vibrations from another subterranean snap echoed from below the concrete foundation. Tanner dropped to his hands and knees, pushed away the wool rug, his movements frantic.

"I need something to draw with, Calliope, something..." His gaze was wild. He sat back on his heels, patted his pockets, and drew out the pocketknife he'd used earlier. Stabbing at his thumb, he gestured me to join him. "Sit. Hurry."

I shook my head. "No way, not until you explain this."

"No time," he whispered, his voice ragged. "No time." He dropped the knife, grabbed my thigh, and pulled me down. "I have to make a circle. Now. Before she finds your house."

That was enough for me. I joined him on the floor, pushing away the table and a basketful of books and abandoned mending. "What do I do?"

Tanner granted me a two-second assessment. "Build the strongest ward you can around your sons then around this house, especially the ground directly below this room."

He re-cut his thumb, turned away, and began to chant.

I ignored the bloody lines and squiggles appearing on my pale maple floorboards and concentrated on picturing Harper and Thatcher and encasing them in a bubble of rosy pink light. Fierce, protective, maternal light. My hands heated, and I deepened the color, thickened the circle, and let the bubble surround them in their sleeping bags.

Tanner was halfway through completing his circle. His scrabbling mussed up the rune-like marking in a couple of places, but pointing that out to him seemed silly. I had equally as important wards to place and less time to place them.

"Calliope, *move*," he said.

I moved. Taking the carved bone handle of Tanner's knife in my left hand, I followed his lead and sliced my right thumb, let blood slick my fingers, and began to draw my circle within his larger one.

"You shall not pass. You shall not pass..." The entire *Lord of the Rings* movie trilogy was a favorite of my sons. I had no idea what other words or phrases I could have used on such dire notice. Every time I repeated those words, I made an X, put a circle around it, and drew a line to the next one.

All using my blood.

My thumb throbbed. I drew the final circle, connected it to the first, and sat back on my heels. Tanner finished a few seconds later. There was blood everywhere, even on his face.

"Record time," he said, grunting as he hugged his knees to his chest and checked our nested wards. "Where's my knife?"

I wiped it on my shirt. "Let me wash this and..."

"Stay." Tanner grabbed my wrist. "Do not leave this circle." He continued, "I can tell you about her now, if you'd like." Using his knife, he sliced into his shirt, tore off a strip, and another. "Bandage up. You first."

I showed him my thumb. He pinched the sides of the cut together and wrapped the bit of cloth around three times, ripped the end in two, and tied a loose knot. He handed the other piece of his shirt to me and extended his thumb. He'd cut himself pretty deeply. Glancing side to side, I could see the symbols he'd drawn required much more blood than my simple Xs and circles.

"It all began with Idunn, the Norse Goddess of Spring and the keeper of the apples of immortality," he started.

"So, we're going way, *way* back," I said, letting out an exhausted laugh and releasing some of my built up stress—some. Not much.

"Yeah, we are," Tanner said, letting out a matching huff. "The myth goes that Idunn was kidnapped by Loki, the trickster, and though Idunn was returned, safeguards had to be put into place to ensure, should she be kidnapped again, or worse, the gods of Asgard would always have access to the apples. Centuries go by, humankind spreads over the Earth, and apple seeds and cuttings are one of the agricultural items they take with them. But what humans don't know is this: the potential to produce Idunn's apples lies within the seeds of each of the ancient varieties. Growing viable trees from those seeds, however, requires magic and rituals few know how to perform properly."

He took a deep breath. "And pesticides, genetic manipulation, global warming and other things are destroying the old varieties, which means…"

"Which means," I interrupted, "it's of utmost importance that we protect those ancient varieties and the people who continue to safeguard the stock. Like the Pearmains."

Tanner nodded. "Exactly."

"But how could a commonly grown apple tree produce the apples of immortality?"

"That's where the Apple Witch comes in."

"And is the Apple Witch the reason for all this?" I asked, sweeping my uncut hand across the area in front of us.

"Yes," Tanner whispered, "and I am so sorry."

I didn't know if I wanted to thank him for presenting an opportunity to learn or yell at him for endangering me, my sons, and my house. "Tell me more."

"The earliest caretakers of the seeds of Idunn's apples were culled from her female followers, and in return for safekeeping the lineage of the fruit, this group of thirteen were gifted with the ability to change their form."

"Like shifters?"

"Not exactly." Tanner returned to his self-soothing habit of threading his hair between his fingers and tugging it tight to his skull. Every time, his features shifted slightly and another layer of who he was came into focus and disappeared again. "The females can transform into trees—apples trees—and most of the early safekeepers chose to make that change just once, as their human lives were ending. While one of the Keepers was making her final change, a younger one was beginning her initiation into their ways. This allowed the thirteen to stay constant.

"Fast forward a few generations. The Keepers had to look farther and farther for women willing to commit to the rigors and responsibilities of their role and work harder and harder to keep them. A handful of the younger ones decided to experiment with changing back and forth while they were still in their fertile years. They discovered that as long as they bled monthly, they could shift between human and tree, thereby keeping a semblance of a normal, human life. But even with this development, their numbers dwindled until only three of these women were left. They began to eat the apples, which they were warned never to do..."

I snorted softly. "Because isn't that how so many fairy tales begin, with someone being warned not to do something, which they promptly do?"

Tanner nodded. "You could probably finish the story for me at this point. The Keepers' DNA had begun to morph into a hybrid of human and tree. Which meant they could bear human children, and some of those humans carried the capacity to bear the apples of immortality." While he spoke, he'd released his hair and begun caressing the pouch he wore around his neck. The leather

—at least, I assumed it was leather—was burnished to the color and sheen of a chestnut. "One of my first druidic teachers was one of these women."

And things just got even more complicated.

"Have you eaten the apples?" I asked. *Please say no.*

His unbandaged thumb slowed its circling. "Somewhat willingly—out of curiosity—and somewhat against my will."

"Are you immortal?" July twenty-fifth, though barely two hours old, was starting as strangely as its predecessor had ended.

"Not exactly."

"How old are you?"

He shrugged. "Eternally thirty-seven?"

I tucked his admission away for a time when I wasn't so tired that 'eternally thirty-seven' didn't sound so perfectly plausible. "And I'm going to venture a guess that you do the work you do, so you can have access to apple growers. And the apples."

"Yes," he agreed. "But only in part."

"So how does this explain what happened half an hour ago?"

Tanner groaned. "My teacher had a daughter—all three of those Keepers had daughters, who themselves grew up as Keepers. They had no say in it, given the dire straits, and my teacher's daughter and I became lovers for a time. And then we parted ways."

"Is this daughter here, on the island?"

"If not here, then she's close."

"Why the strong reaction?"

"She wants something from me I can't give."

"Why?"

"She's become corrupted." There was more. I could see it in the way the corners of his eyes tightened. His features stopped shifting and hardened into the Tanner I'd met at the Pearmains'.

"Do you think *she* has something to do with the catatonic orchardists and the severed heads?"

"I'm not willing to rule out her possible involvement."

"You have to admit it's an odd coincidence."

He nodded. "I agree. It is. But jeopardizing the orchards also works against her, so..." His words drifted off into the far corners of my sleepy house.

"Tanner? I need to be able to trust you." I was desperate for my bed.

His eyes looked genuinely wounded that I even questioned his intentions. "I'm not here to hurt you, Calliope. We've known each other what, twelve, thirteen hours? Every instinct I have is to protect you and this house and your sons. There's more I can do to shield all of us from her influence—and I'll do it, I promise."

We leaned against each other and lapsed into silence. The story of Idunn and her apples and the Keepers was a lot to absorb. Add in the parts about women morphing into trees and Tanner's old girlfriend being the jealous type...

I shook my head. I needed to sleep.

"Do you think we can go to bed now? I haven't felt a thing since you started telling me that story." I closed my eyes, sank my awareness deep into my land, and came back knowing the wards we'd cast had cloaked our presence.

Tanner must have performed a similar scan. "I think we can. Would you mind if I showered?"

I shook my head and clambered to my feet. My knees didn't want to straighten, and a hot shower would be a godsend. "Go ahead. I'll check all the locks and..."

"I'll do it with you." Tanner rested his arm around my shoulders and kept me at his side as we stepped over our circles. Whatever had been here earlier didn't appear to notice—or care—that we'd left the confines of the protected space. My house was in its nighttime cycle of deep, steady breaths.

Together, we checked the locks on the ground floor doors and windows. I left Tanner at the bottom of the stairs with a feeble goodnight and mumbled instructions for where he could find clean bedding and towels.

Dropping my clothes on the bathroom floor, I gave thanks to the marvel of modern plumbing and scrubbed the blood off my body and out of my hair. I left the bottom half of my bedroom window open a couple of inches and wedged a section of wood in the top half to prevent it from being opened further.

Not that anyone or anything would try to get into my house through the windows. That would be too much for one day. Too, too much. I did, however, lock my bedroom door and wedge a spindle chair under the knob.

Wednesday morning— after asking Tanner to please clean up the dried blood and stopping to grab breakfast and a coffee on the go—I had my assistant Kerry research the Pearmain property while I downloaded images from the day before off of my cell phone.

"Here's everything I could find." Kerry stepped into my office clutching a stack of files to her chest. "It's not much, but from a cursory look, I'd say the orchard has been in the family at least two hundred years."

I rotated my office chair and gestured for her to leave everything on my desk.

"Be careful handling the older papers," she warned. "I noticed the newspaper clippings are crumbling at the edges."

I stood and brought the stack to the work table set alongside one wall. A cork board was mounted above the chair rail; maps of the island and the region covered most of its surface. The repetitive motion of removing the pins and separating them by color into little boxes helped me begin sorting the past twenty-four hours.

Pull. *I'm not pregnant.*

Drop. *Hallelujah.*

Pull. If I wanted access to my magical potential, I had a lot of catching up to do. And I had to accept guidance. *Drop.*

My sons had nascent abilities, ones that needed magical mentoring, as it were, *pull, pull*, and look who showed up.

Drop.

Scratching the back of my head, I shook off my body's suggestion about what other kinds of magical mentoring Tanner might offer me. Turns out there was a complicated man under the Provincial agent's orderly exterior. And the man had some heavy baggage. Heavy, *old* baggage.

I switched tasks to stabbing at the cork board, pushing a red-flagged pin into every apple-grower's location. There wasn't an obvious pattern in their placement, but I didn't need the obvious right now. I just needed information. "Kerry? Can you get me a breakdown of the varieties of apples grown on the island?"

"You trying to drive me and the growers nuts?"

"No." I dropped one of the pins and crouched to pick it up. The stiff fabric of my jeans pinched and poked at my belly roll, further irritating my old tattoo. "But I know how obsessed most of them are about their apples. I'm grasping at straws a bit here, but see if they'll tell you which varieties they grow the most."

"You got it."

"Oh, and ask if they have any rare or endangered trees. And get a list of their year-round workers and seasonal workers."

"How many years back do you want me to go? Three, five?"

"Three should be fine."

My phone buzzed with an incoming text message from Tanner. "May I use your office?"

I glanced at my wall, prepped and ready for the Pearmain investigation with its anonymous complaints, severed heads, underground tunnels, enigmatic druid, rogue witch, and who knew what else. Sure, Tanner could share my office. Why not? We were already unofficially working together. Heck, just hours ago, we were bonding over blood wards and true confessions.

"Okay," I texted. "When?"

"How about today? Now?"

I chuckled. "How much money you got?"

No silly emoji, only, "Have you called Rose?"

Nosy man. Of course I hadn't called Rose.

"Call her. See you soon."

I puffed out my cheeks. I hated to be hurried along by anybody, especially when they were right. If my training was time sensitive, of course it would be better to speak with the witches, find out what it was I was supposed to do, and do it. As long as it didn't involve travel or elaborate rituals and dress codes, I was open to whatever was required.

After texting with Tanner, I closed the door to my office and called Rose.

And Rose gave me an earful.

"Well, Calliope," she began, "since we have no idea when your next period is coming, I'm going to put you on daily doses of tinctures of blue and black cohosh and see if that will jump start your cycle. In the meantime, pack a bag—I'll put together a list of what you need—and be prepared to meet me on the west side of Vancouver Island. I have to speak with the rest of the coastal covens, but I think we'll reserve the sacred grove for the coming full moon and get this ball rolling."

"Bossy," I muttered, hanging up.

Kerry knocked before poking her head into my office. "There are three men out here," she whispered, making a funny face. "And they're asking for you."

"Does one of them look kind of grouchy?"

She nodded.

"And does one of them have bright red hair?"

She nodded again and giggled. "Friends of yours?"

I beckoned her in and shut the door. "The tall one is Tanner Marechal. He's with the Ministry of Forests, Lands and Natural Resources. He's going to help with the Pearmain investigation, and since his agency doesn't have an office on the island, I said they could work here."

"So...I'm working for them too?"

I stared at the closed door, one hand fisted at my hip.

My phone buzzed with another text. "What's going on in there?"

I showed Tanner's message to Kerry. "Let me know if they become high maintenance. You don't fetch coffee, you don't pick up lunch orders, and if I'm not here to answer questions, your word is law."

She looked relieved.

"But," I continued, "you know how to find everything in the office and who to call and cajole when we need stuff, so if you do any of that for them, I'll see their agency pitches in."

"Deal. Any idea whether any member of the Terrific Trio is single?"

"Tanner is, that much I know." *And I have first dibs, but honestly, don't go there. He's too complicated.* "No idea about the other two. I'll let you sharpen your investigative abilities on answering that question."

Kerry winked, tightened the belt of her empire-waist summer dress, and opened the door. "Ms. Jones will see you now."

Adding three men to my already snug office space would not work well long term, but for the day's debrief, we'd make do. If they needed more space, they could...I glanced around the room. There was no more space.

"Kaz, can you ask Kerry where the extra folding chairs are stored and bring in two?" I asked.

He nodded and left the door open behind him.

Tanner closed it and turned to me. "Is Kerry trustworthy?"

"Mostly. But I'd much rather details like frozen heads and missing bodies stay between just us for now."

He nodded in agreement.

"Kerry's an asset," I added. "She knows practically everyone on the island, and if she doesn't, someone in her family does. There are a lot of ways she can help, so don't hesitate to ask.

Conversely, given that she and the rest of the Pippins are *related* to half the island, keeping things tight should be SOP."

Kaz walked in with the chairs and unfolded them across from the wall with the maps. He and Wes were settling in when Kerry knocked while opening the door.

"Calli?" she said. "There's someone here with a delivery for you, says she has to give it to you in person?"

"Tell her I'll—"

"Calliope Jo-ones?" A very round, sunny woman with a sing-song voice sidled Kerry out of the way. "I am Belle. Belle de Boskoop. Rose sent me."

Belle floated through the doorway, dressed like a bouquet of wild yellow cowslips. She lifted a crisp paper bag by its handles and made a show of offering it to me just as her attention snapped to Kaz—and his, to her.

He plucked the bag from the tips of her fingers, handed it to me, and offered Belle his hand. "Kazimir Wickson. At your service."

Matching splotches of blush graced their cheeks when he straightened from his slight bow, and I remembered where I'd seen and heard her name before. Belle was one of the three witches recommended by Rowan. "I'm Calliope. And these other two are Wessel Foxwhelp and Tanner Marechal." I commandeered the paper bag, looped an arm through Belle's, and turned to the men. "I'll be right back."

I steered us past Kerry's desk, out the door, down the stairs, and into the alleyway beside the small office building. A trio of males stared out my office window.

I turned our backs to the snoops. "Dr. Renard recommended I speak to you about becoming more of a witch."

"Rowan? I *love* that girl and bless her, always looking out for us, but anyhoo, I'm here because Rose sent me. I am a Plant witch, and I specialize in tinctures and extracts and such and she said you needed help moving things along. You'll find *exactly* what you need in the bag, along with instructions and my contact information if you have any questions or concerns or if you just need to talk."

"Belle, thank you. *So* much. I'll take a look at everything later this evening."

"Rose wants you to start taking the herbs tonight. She filled me in on your case, and I want to assure you I've had success with worse."

Curiosity got the better of me. I unrolled the top of the bag and peered in. Three stoppered bottles and a roll of paperwork. "What do I owe you?"

"Nothing right now. We'll settle up after the ceremony."

"I'm not going to have to take out a loan, am I?"

Belle fluttered her finger. "Heavens no, but if you need reassurance, the prices are on my website right there in black and white. Or maybe it's pink and white, I'm not sure, but—"

I stuck out my hand. "Thanks again, Belle. I've got to get back to work."

"Handshake, pancake, give me a hug!" She enfolded me in a floral-scented embrace before holding me at arm's length and beaming. "Put in a good word with that adorable Mr. Wickson, would you please? Or better yet, direct him to my workshop. I have the perfect potion for what ails him."

"Is he sick?"

"No, but he's going to feel *very* out of sorts if he doesn't come in for a sample of what Ms. Belle has to offer." She pursed her plumped, rose-pink lips into a moue and blew a deliberate kiss in the direction of the one man still standing at the window.

CHAPTER 7

I re-entered my office and stashed the bag of drops. "Did you catch Belle's message?"

Kaz's blush was far redder than I would have guessed, given that Wes had the red hair. "I did. I assume you have her contact information?"

"I do, with clear instructions to pass it on to you."

"Well, then, I'll take that number, please," he said, holding out an open palm.

Tanner cleared his throat. "May I remind you all we have severed heads to discuss?"

"And I have a witch to woo." Kaz feigned indignation and tried to make himself as tall as Tanner.

"Point taken." Tanner laughed, lifting both palms.

This lighter-hearted version of the government agent was good to see after the weightiness of what happened earlier, but what I really wanted was everyone on the same track.

"Who here has connections in the Fae community?" I asked.

Tanner snapped to attention. "When did we conclude the heads belong to the Fae?"

"I believe the pointed ears and elongated noses are consistent with garden trolls, what my aunt used to call the hidden folk." I had consulted a compendium of magical creatures and seen the resemblance between the frozen faces and those carved into the picture frames. I saw no reason to add the compendium was my childhood coloring book and the consultation occurred while my eyelids were struggling to open.

"I didn't even know we *had* a troll community," Kaz muttered in Tanner's direction. "I hope those heads weren't the end of it."

"The end of dead trolls?"

"Well, yes. Not the end of garden trolls as a species. Those tunnels were rather small. I suppose it does make sense they would be the smaller versions."

Time to take charge. I turned my back to the map and raised my voice. "Guys. Is there a network of magical beings we can tap into? A registry of sorts, maybe online?" Brilliance flashed on the inside of my forehead. "What about using a dating app to try and connect?"

The men stared.

"Oh, don't tell me you don't know about ShiftR. Or MagicalMates?"

All three shook their heads, the looks on their faces varying degrees of the same expression: mild shock.

"Trolling for trolls." Wes elbowed Kaz, seemingly pleased with his quick wit.

I gave Tanner a silent plea for mercy. What was it with his cohorts?

He stood and took over. "There is a directory. I'll share it with you, but it's obviously not up to date, as Calliope's name isn't listed. I'll also arrange to have Kaz or Wes revisit the other two sites where the catatonia spell was active. Calliope, I'll stay on the island with you. There's the giant bat to have another look at and…"

Wes did a double take. "Wait, did you say giant *bat?*" He went from slouching to sitting straight. "When can we see it?"

I had to rein in this circus of tangents.

"Why don't we all have dinner at my house tonight?" I directed my question at the ringleader. I noticed he hadn't gotten to the part where he shared that a spurned lover was stalking him.

"Dinner's a good idea," Tanner said. "Kaz and Wes are leaders in the mentorship programs too. And I'm not a bad sous chef, so you can put me to work."

"Did you just make the assumption I'm cooking for all of you?"

Guilty.

"I have a grill," I informed them. "Stop at one of the grocery stores or farm stands. Pick up whatever you feel like cooking and drinking. Be at my house around six-thirty, seven o'clock."

Kaz's hand went up slowly. "Calli, lass. Would you happen to have an extra bed?"

Three-ring circus. "Are *all* of you in need of housing?"

"It's the middle of the summer and you know how hard it is to find a place to stay," Kaz said. "When we came over to help Tanner, we weren't planning to be here more than one night, let alone two. Or three."

"My sons have camping equipment. I can bribe them into sleeping in the living room or under a tarp in the yard or... We'll figure it out." I turned and faced the map. The afternoon was marching on, and this band of merry men needed to focus. "Tanner, could you please put pins in the locations of the other orchards? Use the red pins. The ones with little flags."

I left Tanner and company at my office. My car choked at the foot of my driveway. I stuck my head out the window and yelled, "Honey, I'm home," even though my sons were at work and there were no other vehicles in sight.

An invisible barrier dropped, the front wheels bit into the

gravel, and I was delivered to the base of the porch steps. Stepping out, I toed off my shoes, sniffed the air, and pivoted to assess what I could see of my property. Nothing seemed amiss above ground, and when I peeked through the shed window, I found the bat—every bit as oversized and otherworldly as I remembered—hanging upside down, wings enfolding its body and face.

My garden gave a gentle tug on our bond. I tickled back. Instead of prepping for a houseful of hungry males, I threw on a summer dress and laid claim to my favorite chair, with its chipped and faded turquoise paint. My toes quickly found their way under matted stems of low-growing chamomile, the connection to soil easing my exhaustion. Canes laden with raspberries and blackberries arched over my shoulder, tumbling fruit into my upturned palm. I popped the berries one by one into my mouth, tugged my dress high enough to expose my legs, and let the sun on my skin and the juice on my tongue make for a delicious midday treat.

This garden had nurtured me as a child. After I moved back into the house, fixed the fence, shored up the raised beds, and amended the soil, we picked up where we'd left off.

The plants had things to say about the creatures moving through the soil at their roots, starting with their daily vermiculture report. They added vague whispers of larger creatures on their way to my island, creatures that carved through rock, flew through the air, and swam the waters. But given my plants' loose relationship with the concept of time, I didn't know if the creatures they spoke of had been here for decades or were more recent arrivals.

I fought the urge to stand and run. Moments from yesterday flashed across my eyelids, from the frozen heads to the oily presence at the marina to the symbols drawn in blood over my walls and floor. I pulled my plants closer, asked for more stories, and returned to floating along with the rootlets below and the bees above until the arrival of a car and distant voices roused me from my late-afternoon stupor.

"Mom!"

Harper, his girlfriend, Leilani, and Thatcher stomped across the grass, the tops of their backpacks visible behind their heads. I hugged the kids and sent them in to shower and unpack.

Close on the heels of the three teens, a pickup truck loaded with two bright yellow kayaks drove past the entrance to the driveway, stopped, and backed up. Wes's hair shone garnet red in the slanting light when he stuck his head out the driver's side window, waved, and skillfully maneuvered the vehicle onto the grass. Tanner unfolded himself out of the back seat and reached back inside the car for an armload of shopping bags.

A few minute later, Wes and Kaz were bickering in front of the outdoor grill, Leilani was apportioning bread dough while she chatted with Harper, and Thatch hustled through the kitchen, gathering plates and utensils.

"Dude," Thatch said in his brother's direction, "grab that end."

Harper leapt to help reposition the oak table, adding a long bench to one side and enough chairs to accommodate seven diners.

"We're *starved*, Mom," Thatcher said. "Haven't eaten much more than instant oatmeal and those homemade power bars Harper's been experimenting with, y'know, the ones that taste like tree bark."

"Hey! I'm working on it!" Harp tossed a stack of cloth napkins at Thatcher's head.

Thatcher ducked and laughed. I dreaded the day their bantering no longer echoed through the house.

"And Mom," Thatcher added, sidling next to me, "those guys with Tanner? They are *so cool*."

The ultimate compliment from a teenager.

Twenty minutes later, food was on the table: two platters of grilled vegetarian sausages, a cutting board of fresh-baked focaccia and three styles of goat cheese. I poured ratatouille into a ceramic bowl, tucked in a broad serving spoon, and took my seat at the head of the table. Tanner chose the chair next to mine.

Once the scraping of chairs and bench legs had ceased, Wes tapped his beer bottle with a fork and cleared his throat. "Begging everyone's indulgence, I would be pleased to offer a blessing before we eat.

"Mother Earth, Father Sun,
  Bless these bodies, All and One.
  Bless the soil, rain, sun and air,
  The hands that toiled to bring us this fare.
  So Merry Mote and Blessed Meet,
  Grace is done, and it's time to eat."

He lifted his head when he finished and grinned. "Dig in!"

"Can you hand me the bread?" I asked.

Tanner had longer arms and was closer to the board. He set it between us. I ripped off two chunks and handed him one. Leilani had topped the slabs with rosemary and fleur de sel. My mouth watered, and I groaned—quietly, but it was definitely a groan—as I chewed.

Sun-ripened wheat, ground into flour, formed the body of the bread. Nimble fingers had pressed and pulled the dough into shape and coated it with olive oil. Those same fingers acted as a conduit to and from a youthful heart, one filled with promise and the shy desire to please, and be pleasing, and to nurture.

I glanced at Leilani. She was feeding a bite of bread to Harper.

"Do you sense anything?" I whispered to Tanner.

He stopped chewing and surveyed the table. Everyone was absorbed in passing platters and filling. "No."

I pointed to the bread. "Take another bite. Chew slowly. I think she's a witch too."

He did as I suggested, studying Leilani while he chewed. Both his eyebrows were raised when he turned to me, nodded, and gave a quick thumbs up.

Now, what do I do?

Instinct. I trust my instinct.

"Leilani, this bread is delicious. Did you add anything special? Any secret ingredients?" I asked, doing a bit of seat-of-the-pants planning on how I could steer the conversation toward magic without completely freaking out Harper's lovely girlfriend.

"When I'm in the kitchen, I just do what feels...natural," she said, "what feels right. Although I do talk to the ingredients when I'm working and I can never follow a recipe exactly."

"It tastes like you put a lot of love into this batch of bread."

She blushed and lifted her shoulders toward her ears. Harper slipped an arm around her waist and tugged her closer.

"My dad always tells me I work magic when I'm in the kitchen," she confessed.

I couldn't have asked for a better lead-in. "Have you ever considered that what you're doing when you're preparing food is a kind of...magic?"

Leilani's cheeks turned an even brighter pink, and her gaze darted to Harper.

He kissed her nose and turned to me. "Mom. Tanner. I kind of let it slip to Lei-li about the bat..."

"And then I told her about the raccoons," Thatcher piped in, "oh, and the river otters..."

"River otters?" Wes reached across the table and grabbed Thatcher's forearm. "You've got an affinity with them too?"

Thatcher nodded then shot me a guilty look. I threw up my hands.

Here goes nothing.

"Leilani." I regrouped, poured a fresh glass of water from the pitcher, and forged ahead. "I'm a witch. Kind of a lapsed witch, you might say. But since I was a very little girl, I've experienced a strong affinity with earth—literal earth, as in soil—as well as with plants and trees, anything that has roots."

"Is that why Harper and Thatch can communicate with animals?" Leilani's eyes were round as a pair of vintage Bakelite buttons.

"Yes, magical abilities are inherited."

"My Papa—his name is Mal—is a sorcerer," she admitted, "and I was never, ever, *ever* supposed to admit that to anyone. He's a good sorcerer," she added, spreading her fingers and pressing them against the tabletop. "And a good man."

"Mal, as in Malvyn Brodeur?" asked Wes. "He's also rumored to be very good with other people's money."

Leilani nodded. "He is," she agreed proudly. "And my other father—my Dad—is James."

"The rest of our guests have magical abilities too. Would you like to hear about them?" I asked, hoping this wasn't all too much for one night.

Leilani nodded quickly and snuggled more into Harper.

Wes cleared his throat and set down his knife and fork.

"I follow the druidic path, as do Kazimir and Tanner." He shifted in his seat, looking slightly uncomfortable. Kaz shoved another bite of sausage in his mouth and chewed while Wes explained. "Druids are similar to witches, but there are significant differences. Witches can choose to have animal familiars. Druids can take multiple animal forms."

"Any animal form?" asked Thatcher.

"No. The bond is very specific. One by water, one by air, one by land."

"What can you become?"

Wes smiled. "Both River and I count otter as our land form, though as you well know, they also spend much of their time in the water."

Harper broke in, "I was probably around seven when I realized what I felt toward anything with wings wasn't normal." He wrapped his arm more tightly around Leilani's shoulders and spoke directly to Tanner. "Like, I could see out of their eyes, feel them in flight. But I never experienced anything like what happened with that giant bat, the feeling of bonding. I couldn't stop talking about it. Ask Thatch."

Thatcher nodded his head. "Oh, man, and every time we passed one of the really big trees on the trail we were cleaning up, we had to stop so he could check it for bats."

"What about you, Thatcher?" Tanner asked.

My sixteen-year-old grinned. "Mom knows I've always liked four-footed, furry creatures. Squirrels. Feral cats. And I *always* wanted to go looking for mountain lions whenever one was spotted on the island."

"But what about the raccoon?"

Thatcher fidgeted with the food on his plate. "I must be a late bloomer because it was only like, two summers ago, maybe, that I started following random animal trails. I got pretty familiar with this one raccoon and then her babies, and then one of them bonded with me. Her name is Pokey." He ripped apart another hunk of bread and used it to sop up the last of the ratatouille on his plate. "Not sure how it works exactly, but if I think about them, the raccoons, they just...show up."

"What about you, Leilani?" Tanner reached for another piece of focaccia and refreshed the puddle of oil on his plate.

"Growing up, I spent a lot of time in Dad's greenhouses, but mostly I just love making food for people. It makes me happy."

I touched Tanner's thigh and spoke before he could. "I...*we* suspect you're imbuing the food you make with your own kind of magic."

"That makes total sense," she said. "My dad's kind of like you, Mrs. Jones. He talks to plants." She rolled her eyes. "A *lot*."

"Have your parents given you lessons, trained you how to expand your magic and use it for different purposes?" I asked.

"I'd say they teach by example," she said, a shy smile turning her cheeks into apricots. "Dad grows food. Papa grows money."

"Tanner says we're all going to magic school," Thatcher announced, beaming.

Leilani gave him a quizzical look. "*Magic* school? Like spells and stuff?" She turned to Tanner. "Is that something I can do too?"

Tanner cleared his throat first. "Yes, you can."

She looked at her lap, the muscles in her upper arms flexing as she worried at her napkin. "Mal and James have always said I was special," she whispered, "but I figured that's what all parents say to their kids."

"I'd like to meet them," Tanner said.

Leilani lifted her head. "I would be happy to introduce you. When does magic school start?"

"Mid-September. We hold retreats on the mainland one weekend a month and have weeklong events in January and early July."

I scanned the table. Plates were mostly emptied, and all the food was gone but for bread crumbs and juice from the cooked tomatoes. "Did anyone pick up dessert?"

Silence.

Leilani raised her hand. "I can make a lemon poppy seed cake, if anyone's interested."

"I think we're *very* interested," I said. "The kitchen is yours. Harper and Thatcher, you two are on dish detail."

"I'll scrape the grill," Wes announced, starting to stand. He leaned across the table and poked Kaz. "You comin'?"

"I have to go see a witch about a potion." Kaz's eyes beamed. Tanner picked up his plate and the empty bread board and walked them to the counter.

"Before you do," he said, speaking to the older men, "can I get you two to check out the bat with me?"

"Business before pleasure, boss."

"Harper, coming?"

I begged off participating in the Q and A I was sure would follow the introduction to the mysterious flying creature hanging in my shed. Thatcher tagged along, assuring me he would be all over dish duty on his return. Leilani looked like she wanted to join in but returned to squeezing lemons and portioning out the ingredients for her cake.

"Did you want to go with them?" I asked.

"I'm a little overwhelmed," she assured me. "Baking calms me down."

A 'little bit overwhelmed' explained my current state too, and being in the kitchen with Leilani was calming. "Did you find everything you need?"

She nodded and poked around in the spice section of one cupboard, withdrawing a jar of poppy seeds, a shy smile on her face. "I know your kitchen pretty well, Ms. Jones."

"Which means it's time for you to start calling me Calli," I teased.

Leilani smiled more confidently and twisted her hair into a messy bun atop her head. The oven pinged it was up to heat, and she returned her attention to measuring and mixing.

I took my refreshed water glass to the deck and tried to make myself comfortable on the swing. The cushion under my head had the consistency of a paving stone. I ignored the discomfort and let the low thrum of male voices guide me past the lumps of hardened pillow stuffing into a half-dozing, half-floating state.

Sweet, lemon-scented air wafted through the screen door.

A metal utensil clanged against porcelain.

Someone lifted my head and sat, adding their weight to the swing and tipping it in their direction. My head came to rest on something softer than a paving stone but not as soft as my bed. A car started then another, the hum of engines trailing off until silence blanketed the property. I was close to falling fully asleep when fingertips rubbing my shoulder alerted me someone wanted an answer to their question.

"What did you say?" I mumbled, wiping the corners of my mouth.

"I think you should go to bed." Tanner shifted his weight and moved his hand off my body.

"But I didn't get any cake."

"I saved you a slice."

I groaned and sat up, shifting to rest on my other hip.

Tanner handed over a dessert plate. "I thought dinner went well."

I popped a bite cake into my mouth and murmured agreement. I was about to say more when the full effect of Leilani's inner workings hit my tongue. "Wow, there is a *lot* of lemon in this." The cake was dense, delicious, and intensely tart. I chewed another bite, poppy seeds crunching between my teeth. "Either she wasn't paying attention when she was measuring or she's having a strong reaction to our dinner conversation. Or to something else."

Tanner murmured his agreement.

"Who's here?" I asked, placing the dessert plate on the side table. "I thought I heard both cars leave."

"You did. Kaz is off to woo his witch, Wes and Thatcher are playing a video game upstairs, and Harper took Leilani home."

"Is she okay?"

"I think she'll be fine," he said, pressing the tines of his fork onto the last of the cake crumbs.

"What did Kaz and Wes have to say about the bat?"

"We put a tracker on it. Harper's disappointed we let it go, but he understands. And I don't think that's the last we'll see of the creature."

"You released it?"

"We try to do what's best for the animal in these situations. Didn't seem to be in a hurry, though. Either that or it was groggy from the twenty-four-hour spell, but yes, there is no longer a bat in your shed." He leaned forward and glanced around the periphery of the treeline. "But I don't think it's left your property."

"Did Pokey make an appearance?"

Tanner chuckled. "Thatcher was hoping the raccoon would stop by so he could impress the guys, but he needn't worry. They're already impressed. With both of your sons."

I popped another bite of cake into my mouth, ready this time for the heavy dose of tart lemon. "Did you learn anything new after I left the office?"

"Clifford and Abigail are doing better. Rose and River brought them out of the catatonia spell, and now they're recovering. They're willing to sit for interviews around lunchtime tomorrow."

A comfortable silence settled between us. I wrapped my fingers around the sensation of being in the immediate vicinity of a man I was attracted to and let go of the sharper edges accompanying said man. "I've gotten backed up on a couple other complaints I need to follow up with. Nothing that appears related to the Pearmains. But I'll give you a set of spare keys to the house and the office. Kerry knows to expect some combination of the three of you for as long as this takes."

"Wes will head off the island tomorrow and go straight to the other orchards. He and Kaz will probably go for a paddle first thing in the morning. They like to check on local otter populations whenever they travel."

I listened to Tanner's voice, zeroing in on its texture and rhythm more than the words coming out of his mouth. He'd stepped into my life a little too fast, a little too neat and had a little too much baggage. Ancient baggage. And we hadn't touched upon the blood wards or the Apple Witch at all.

"I've got other cases to update too," he said. "Go to bed. I'll see to whatever needs doing."

CHAPTER 8

Thursday morning, delivering fresh-squeezed orange juice seemed as good an excuse as any to grab a private moment with my boys. Inside the tent, Thatcher was still asleep, but Harper was awake and chafing to talk.

"Mom." He swirled the juice with one finger and kept his voice low. "I can't believe you never told us you were a witch. All these years of you saying to me and Thatch that you'd support us no matter who we loved or what we did and you didn't even tell us what *you* really are."

"Doug asked me to keep quiet," I said, my stomach going sour. My son made a good point, and I was grasping at straws. Never a good place to be with a teenager.

"But is Dad a witch? Or a druid like these guys?"

There had been whiffs of magic in the shadowed corners of the Flechettes' palatial estate. But Doug's parents weren't the warm and fuzzy type, and they made it clear I wasn't going to be the daughter-in-law representing the family on the various boards they cycled through. When Doug's mother put him in charge of all the realty offices on the Gulf Islands, I was relieved to be out of their daily orbit. Until the move began to feel like an isolation tactic.

"I don't recall ever seeing Doug call on magic," I admitted. "Only denigrate mine. And the little bit my aunt used when you two were babies."

Oh, this was so much for my child to process. And the more Harper was feeling, the more his face went blank. "Why would Dad do that?"

"I assumed his parents had been the same way."

"But why didn't you insist, Mom? Did you even try?"

I could only shake my head and try to not cry. Of course I had tried, until trying and failing dried up my self-esteem. Years ago, I'd stopped asking myself why I wasn't more insistent, and eventually the pain of staying silent dulled until it was small enough I could wrap it up and pack it away.

"Letting go of my magic seemed less important than keeping our household running smoothly and keeping your dad happy. We were young when we got together. We both changed after we were married and after we had the two of you. Changes which had nothing to do with either of you." I made it a point to plant a kiss on Harper's troubled forehead.

When he asked me to elaborate, I cut him off. I hadn't forgiven myself for the neglect, and the sourness in my stomach was spreading to my heart. "He's my ex-husband, but he's still your father. We're both to blame for our marriage not working out."

Harp took a long swallow of the juice, a challenge in his guarded eyes. "You're not going to forbid us to explore our magic, are you?"

"Absolutely not. Your skills and talents are yours to develop as you're ready, and I will help you in any way I can."

"And you're going to study too right?"

"Absolutely."

He nodded. "I'm glad. For all of us. What do you think about Tanner?"

"I only met him two days ago. I like him so far."

"I do too. I'm excited and a little scared and..."

I waited as my oldest struggled to articulate.

Thatcher was awake and listening, ready to jump in with the brotherly thought-sharing and sentence-finishing they'd been doing their entire speaking lives. "And we shouldn't tell Dad, right?"

I handed Thatch his glass of juice, extended my legs and crossed my ankles, and waited for the voices from both sides of the fence to flood my head in one...two... "I think we keep this amongst ourselves while we're figuring it all out."

Both nodded their agreement and dove in to speculating about how their magic might manifest and what they could do to boost their abilities. The phrases they tossed back and forth sounded like they'd been pulled from a discussion of their favorite online multi-player game. I scooted backward out of the tent, my work for the moment done. Overhead, the aged crabapple tree's leafy branches carried a smattering of misshapen fruit. My older cousins and I had played battle games with the apples we found on the ground, and the trunk and lowest branches were already gnarled when my mother and I first arrived at the house.

Mama.

Moments of intense mothering left me wanting a mother of my own. I ran my fingertips over the nearest fruit. Tears blurred my vision, and I gave in to the invitation to step closer and closer still, until my sternum fit snugly over the place just below where the trunk separated into two main branches. I rested the side of my face against the bark and reached my arms up as though to partner in a dance with this steadfast friend.

The Old One had a lot of life coursing under its scabby surface. And it had a heartbeat, slow, so very, very slow. The dappled sun warmed my back, and my feet reached below the uppermost layers of sod and found a groundwater aquifer—sandstone and siltstone; shale and conglomerate, glacial sediments, fossils and mudstone.

I hugged the crabapple more tightly, close to full-on crying. My breast bone became spongy, like living wood. The whoosh of blood through my veins matched the capillary-like action taking place beneath the bark, a drawing up of water from the roots all the way to the leaves and fruit.

Interspersed with those same, nourishment-seeking roots was a whole other network. I followed the mycelial layer past the boundaries of my property, coursing faster and faster, to other apple trees and orchards until I crash landed at the base of one of the oldest trees in the Pearmains' orchard.

A laugh—rich, resonant, and feminine—rolled through the flexible underground plexus and flooded the porous spaces in my bones.

"Mom."

I ran. Or I tried. But my feet and toes were rooted to the ground at the base of the ancient tree and my arms were wrapped around the crabapple's trunk, and every morsel of awareness was caught somewhere between the far section of Cliff and Abi's orchard and my lone *malus Rosaceae* companion, miles away.

"Mom!"

The worry in my sons' voices, helped along by firm hands shaking my shoulders and gripping my wrists, gave me a route back. Honing in on the beacon of their touch, I crashed into my body and slumped to the ground.

"*Mom.*"

"I'm okay," I whispered. "I'm okay."

I wasn't okay. Whatever valve or switch that regulated the flow of my magic, the one that had clicked to the on position two days ago, was now dialled to four. Or maybe five. The bottoms of my feet tingled, while liquid echoes of the connection to the Pearmains swam up the connective tissue in my legs and swirled around the bowl of my pelvis to gather at the base of my spine.

"Just let me lie here for a sec." Why was there so much internal movement through my hips and belly? Sharp pains pinged from side to side, like I was ovulating from both ovaries and having menstrual cramps at the same time.

Harper and Thatch kneeled on either side of my torso. "Do you want us to get Tanner?"

"No." The disturbance on the left side of my belly included itchy skin near the tattoo. I shielded my eyes from the brightening sun and scratched over the layers of my underwear and pants. Rolling my head to the side, I said, "Let me catch my breath. Do you know what you want for breakfast?"

Thatcher let out an exasperated sigh. "Mom, we can get our own breakfast. We should be asking what do *you* need?"

My body returned to normal in the spaces between a handful of breaths. Harper brushed off whatever bits of grasses and leaves had collected on my back and helped me to stand. As soon as I relaxed from my neck and arms down, my fingers unclenched, and I dropped the short, thick section of branch I must have grabbed as I fell. I bent to pick up the stick.

It was straight, tapered, and the perfect length for a wand. My old one, held together with duct tape and sentimental attachment, was more than ready to retire.

I tucked the length of crabapple wood into a back pocket and hugged my sons. "I think what I need most is to get over whatever just happened. And get myself to work."

Inside the house, the *tap-tap* of a toothbrush hitting the rim of the sink beat out the rhythm of a normal morning routine. I was walking toward the bathroom from my bedroom at the end of the hall, where I had placed the branchlet on my neglected altar until I could strip the bark and sand and oil the wood.

"Tanner, are you planning to go to Cliff and Abi's with me?" I asked.

Tanner had experience with the two other sets of growers, but the incident occurred in my jurisdiction. I wanted to collect soil and water samples, as well as bark, leaves, and fruit from the older trees.

"I'd prefer to have you come along or meet me there," I added.

He stepped out of the bathroom, a towel around his waist. There was nothing underneath the swath of white terrycloth except skin, and the man had gorgeous legs to go with his beautiful feet.

"Now?" he asked, his toothbrush gripped in the side of his mouth.

Sure, Marechal, drop the towel, and let's go. No one'll notice the naked provincial agent in my car.

It took every ounce of willpower to direct my gaze above his waist. But then I saw his chest up close and the pouch nestled between his pectorals, and I turned and practically fled back to the sanctuary of my room. "I need to stop by the office first to grab our collection kit."

"Give me ten minutes."

Eight minutes later, Tanner was fully clothed and stretched out in the passenger seat of my car. He levered his seat all the way back before we left my driveway and kept his eyes closed the entire ride, even through the stop at my office.

I parked outside the Pearmains' gate and cut the engine. Tanner shifted his hips and tapped my wrist as I prepared to step out.

"Calliope." He was almost supine and turned his head slowly to face me. "I don't think I've said thank you enough for your hospitality and your generosity. Thank you."

"You're very welcome." I ducked and stopped. "And thank you for cleaning up the...the blood."

He nodded and tugged on the lever, readjusting his body to face in my direction. One arm draped over the back of his seat, and the other rested on the dashboard. His body had that *there's more I want to say* coil to it, but the interior of an electric car wasn't big enough to hold the conversations waiting for us. I slid away, tilted the driver's seat forward, and grabbed the evidence bag from the back seat.

"I can carry that for you," he offered, looking up at me through eyes shaded by an errant lock of hair.

I shook my head. I'd been hauling bags across fields in all kinds of conditions since my first day on the job. The weight centered me. "I've got it. You deal with the gate. And pay attention to anything that feels off. I'm already apprehensive."

Big conversations with my kids and out-of-body experiences first thing in the morning did that to me.

Tanner murmured his agreement, his attention on the fence and yard. All traces of the salt circle were gone, as was the collection of assorted trinkets. He pushed and held the gate open and followed me in, stopping to peek into the windows of an older model four-door sedan.

"Do you think that's River's car?" I asked.

"River's. Or Rose's. I'm not sure. But one or both have been with Clifford and Abigail since they got here on Tuesday."

No one greeted us as we rounded the curved path to the front entrance of the farmhouse, but classical music wafted on air currents and a peaceful sensation patted my worry down to a mild case of neighborly concern. I was debating whether we should enter the house or continue around when a man with short, salt-and-pepper brown hair opened the screen door and stepped onto the porch. Seeing Tanner, River bounded down the stairs and took him into a back-thumping embrace.

"I'm very happy to see you both. Our patients are doing well, all things considered." Deep brown eyes met mine as he offered me his hand. River's mouth was framed by a closely trimmed beard shot through with white around his lips and over his chin. "Rose is with them on the back porch. And there's something I want to show you, but it can wait."

We followed him past the formal sitting room with its collection of photographs in unique frames and out the kitchen door to the rear portion of the wraparound porch. Clifford and Abigail were in their rocking chairs. Rose occupied a third.

"Hello, Calliope." Age and hard physical labor had shrunk Clifford Pearmain. He wasn't as hale and hearty as he'd appeared at the anniversary celebration in May, but his cheeks had better color compared to the last time I saw him.

I embraced the still-imposing farmer in a quick hug and turned my attention to the more frail Abigail, whose shaking fingers picked at a tissue. I crouched on the floor near her rocking chair. "Hello, Abi. It's good to see you."

"It's good to see you, too, dear. Who's the handsome fellow you've brought?" A bit of preening accompanied Abigail's question. The hand at her temple patting flyaway gray hairs hinted she had her wits about her. Plus, Tanner was hard to miss.

He bent to offer his hand and took hers gently. "Ma'am. Tanner Marechal. I was here on Tuesday when Calliope found you."

"Pull up a chair and sit awhile, Tanner. It's a lovely day, and River's made us lunch."

I eyed the platter of tea sandwiches, noted the absence of deli meats, and reached for a small triangle for politeness's sake. Cucumbers and fresh dill with a mayonnaise-based spread. A perky, optimistic energy zipped from my tongue to my belly. River or Rose had added a little something extra to the food— and Leilani would find at least one ally with a similar gift in our new circle of magical contacts.

I turned my attention to the small talk, now peppered with

comments about the summer weather and other perennial farming topics. Once the sandwich plate was emptied, River brought out butter cookies and a pitcher of iced herbal tea.

I reached into my backpack for my cell phone, a notebook, and a pen. "Abi, Cliff, do you two feel up to answering some questions?"

They exchanged glances, Abi's worried and Cliff's more settled resignation.

He patted his wife's knotted fingers and brushed at the front of his short-sleeved shirt. "We are."

I prepared to record the conversation, placing my cell phone next to the plate of cookies and positioning the table between Clifford and Abigail's legs. "Do either of you remember anything about this past Tuesday, July twenty-fourth. Or even Monday the twenty-third?" Faltering, I waved both my hands. "Let me rephrase that. Did you have any appointments scheduled on Monday or Tuesday here at the house or the orchard? Were there any unexpected visitors?"

Abigail signaled she would speak first. "Sundays we go to church. And we have a late lunch. It's a day of rest, Saturday being the Farmer's Market, and you know how exhausting that can be, Calliope."

I agreed. "So, there was nothing unusual this past Sunday. What about Monday?"

"Now, wait a minute, Calliope," Clifford interjected. "We didn't say there was nothing unusual. I like to have a walk in the evening, helps with my digestion."

Abigail nodded at her husband and continued her slow rocking.

"I checked on the new stock," he continued, pointing over my shoulder. "Those trees we planted earlier in the spring, and I would have walked back to the house but I felt like stretching my legs a little further. So I went the long way 'round to the oldest section of the orchard." He gripped the curved ends of the armrests and peered at me, his wild, steel-gray eyebrows lifting. "You familiar with that section, Calliope? Those trees might look like they're done an' ready to be chopped down and hauled off for firewood, but there's life left in 'em yet. They're kind of like old friends you just can't get rid of. Know what I mean?"

Everyone on the porch hung on Clifford's recitation, and everyone nodded at his question.

"So, I went around the back, just stood there, looking at those old trees. Thought about their lives and my life and everything this land has seen." His rheumy eyes stared past the crowded porch toward his beloved orchard. "Something told me it was time to make amends."

"Amends for what, Cliff?" I asked, leaning into the moment.

He kept rocking, his gaze on the hidden horizon. My question hung in the air unanswered.

Tanner went into the house and returned with a handful of framed pictures. "Clifford. Abigail, we need to ask you about these."

"Those are family pictures, Agent," Cliff said. His hands gripped the armrests and relaxed. "Been around for years and years."

"It's not the photographs. It's the frames," Tanner specified. He handed one to Abi and one to Cliff. "These are hand-carved."

"Yes, they are."

"There are faces in the corners. We think they're the hidden folk, perhaps a type of garden troll."

"You would be correct in your assumption," said Clifford, his lower jaw trembling. "When my ancestors arrived on this island, these hectares were seen to by trolls, and they didn't take kindly to newcomers showing up and imposing their will on the land. Took both sides an entire generation to figure out how to share. And then it took my great-grandmother falling in love with one for it all to fall apart." He smoothed his fingers over the carved faces. "Abi and I been tryin' to set things right. The two grandsons who're taking over? Their troll ancestry has reasserted, and we're thinking this might be the best way to protect them and keep the two sides who love this land united."

Tanner cleared his throat and pressed on. "Trolls are magical beings. Your story affirms local legend that says they have an affinity for orchards. But legend can't explain why we found two severed heads in your freezer. And why you both were under a very powerful spell when we found you."

Abigail worried the edge of her apron, a different one, similarly aged and patched as the one she was wearing when we found her on Tuesday. She picked up where her husband left off. "Clifford found them in the orchard, back by the oldest trees, the ones that haven't been doing so well. We considered tearing those trees out, but then we decided the boys could make that decision, once they get here." She continued, "There were no bodies, just the heads. We didn't know who to call or what more to do so we decided to store them until we could figure out our next step." Tears streamed down Abigail's face, and her thin voice had begun to waver. "We did not kill those poor souls. We've lived with them on this land for as long as I can remember. Peacefully. They like the trees, and the trees like them."

"Did you find the tunnels?" asked Clifford.

"We found three under older trees that look to be healthy and producing apples," I said. "Are those the ones you're referring to?"

Clifford nodded. "Did you explore 'em?"

"One of our colleagues went down the ladder," Tanner answered, "but didn't go farther."

"When I was younger and more agile, I'd stick my head down, check things out. Bring food." Cliff looked at Abi and smiled. "Trolls liked my wife's goat cheese. They took good care of the trees. And we left them in peace."

Abigail's hands began to shake even more. "Clifford, tell them the rest. Tell them about why we maintain the tunnels."

"Those tunnels are meant to be places of refuge and safety for whoever needs them. The Pearmains have done their best to keep them open and passable for over a hundred years."

"When you say, whoever needs them," I interrupted, "what do you mean?"

"I mean those tunnels have sheltered more'n trolls. They're part of a network that runs through this island. I know of two other orchards that connect to ours."

Rose came off her chair and stood protectively in front of Abigail. "Tanner, Calliope, I think these two have had enough questions for one day. River and I can stay until tomorrow. Then I have a date with Calliope over the weekend."

Her stern voice and withering look conveyed that she would not be argued with, about either point, yet I was surprised to hear my weekend was spoken for. I hadn't started taking the herbal tinctures Belle had given me; even if I had, it was far too soon for results. Or maybe I didn't need to have my period for this particular ritual.

"One more question, Rose," I said, lifting my hand like I was back in grade school, "and then we can call it a day." Clifford looked to his wife and they nodded in agreement. "You returned to the house after your walk Sunday evening."

"That's right. Went to bed around ten."

"Did anything unusual happen on Monday?"

"The realtor that pesters us about selling stopped by, like she does most every Monday. Said she had a new client who was very interested in acquiring orchards. I stuck her card on the side of the refrigerator, underneath one of those big magnets from the hardware store."

"Can you describe what she looked like?"

Cliff turned to Abi. "You have a better eye for that sort of thing."

She nodded. "She always dressed in a skirt and jacket. Short, dark brown hair. Not what I would call a soft woman, all angles.

And not very amiable, considering she wanted our business. She never once stayed for tea."

"And after she left?"

Cliff and Abi exchanged confused glances. "Next thing I remember was waking up with Abi lying next to me. And an awful headache."

CHAPTER 9

"What's your take on all this?" Tanner asked when River returned from helping Rose escort the older couple into the house for a rest. "You've been with them for two days. Have they mentioned anything else?"

The two men and I headed to the newer section of the orchard with the intention of looping around to collect water samples from the three ponds before finishing with the section of trees that housed the tunnels. Tanner took over labelling the individual vials and bags as I handed them to him.

River placed marks on a map to indicate where the samples had been taken. "Neither of them mentioned the realtor before today," he said, digging into a back pocket, "but the business card was stuck to the side of the fridge."

He handed the card to Tanner, who passed it to me.

"I don't recognize her name, but she works for my ex-husband's family," I said.

When I flipped the card, the familiar tingle of magic prickled along my skin and the printing on the front disappeared.

"Tanner, quick, write this down." I recited the name and

phone number and handed over the piece of paper. "Bag this too. It might be useless, but I want to keep it just in case."

"Will you look at that." Tanner examined the now blank business card and swore under his breath. "Clever."

Clever—not a word I would use when describing Doug. But his mother? The mounting connections to the Flechette family were putting me on edge. I stuffed back my discomfort to mull over later. "River, want to check out the tunnels? Plenty of light."

"I'm game."

"I want to go down too," I said. If staying front and center in this investigation meant I had to confront old fears, I was ready. Mostly. Maybe it would help knowing Tanner and River didn't seem the types to toss taunts down the ladder and refuse to help me if I freaked out underground. After Cliff's story, and this morning's wild ride, I needed to see and experience the tunnels for myself.

"I wonder if Cliff has a map."

"Bet he does."

We looked at each other before mutually deciding to forego the map.

"Shall we each take a tree?" asked River.

Tanner shook his head and crossed his arms over his chest. "One of us should stay above ground. You two feel free to explore."

"Fair enough. You might be a little on the long side anyways. Calli, do you know where you want to start?"

I smiled at River's reference to Tanner's height and closed my eyes. Sniffing at the sun-warmed air led me to the grass, beyond its roots, and into what lay below the field and rocks. I shifted my weight, opened my eyes, and pointed to the tree tugging at my pant legs. "That one, the second one in."

River strode past. "I'll take the farthest. See you in a bit."

"If you were investigating this alone," Tanner asked, once River was no longer within earshot, "what would you do?"

"Create a grid, take samples of plant matter and soil like we've been doing, and photographs too."

"What else? What would you do, as a witch?"

I laughed. "I'd take off my boots and read the ground and the trees."

"So do that." He slipped his feet out of his flip flops and waited at the edge of the path for me to do the same.

"I think I want to keep my feet in my boots during my first foray underground." I waggled my fingers in his direction. "These should be enough for now."

Tanner smiled. "Okay, partner."

Reassured, I detoured off the curving path to where I'd heard the humming the day before, the loud thump-thump in my chest a clear warning I was about to step out of my comfort zone. Way out. I had something to prove to Tanner and River—and myself. It was time to bring my magical talents to the forefront.

Clifford said the tunnels were places of refuge. I swept my flashlight's beam over the interior of the tree trunk before directing it down the ladder.

Here goes nothing.

After a twist, a wiggle and a push, my feet met solid ground on the third or fourth rung down. I gripped the vertical beams of the ladder and paused to remind myself to breathe. At the bottom, carved walls bowed outward, giving the appearance of a barrel-like antechamber. The tunnel went off in one direction only, giving me no choice where to go; I just had to choose my method of locomotion: crawling, crouching, or scuttling sideways like a crab.

I chose a modified scuttle, directed the flashlight's beam in front of me, and left the fresh air and weak light at the bottom of the ladder.

Sound was muffled underground. Rocks and roots bumped out of the walls, giving the surface a rough finish. I inured myself to the few crawly creatures I could see in the beam of my light and went deep into denial about how many more I might be missing. Progress was slow. My heart rate and breathing were slightly accelerated but steady. Mostly. When I stopped, musty air irritated my nostrils, and I sneezed twice, almost knocking my head against the wall to my left.

And that was when the presence inside the tunnel made itself known.

A creak and a pop and another pop went off, like a membrane stretched to the breaking point, between me and the ladder.

I flared my nostrils and inhaled through my nose, using my connection to the earth entombing me to keep me calm as I pivoted and dropped my butt to the ground. *Tender. Green. Fresh. Curious.* This was similar to the presence I had encountered earlier in the day.

I planted my left palm to the packed earth, fear and excitement flooding my muscles, and pointed my flashlight's beam at the wall to my right. Little rootlets, three or four inches long, sprouted out of one of the exposed roots. I scrabbled closer, intrigued.

Not rootlets. Branches, with tiny stems and glossy green leaves. I went to touch them with a fingertip.

Mine.

The voice reverberated through the earth, shaking loose bits of dirt and pebbles embedded in the archway over my head.

Mine.

I dropped the flashlight and fisted both hands against my chest, the seared skin on my fingertips burning like lemon juice on paper cuts. The voice was terrifyingly close, and my legs wouldn't obey my brain's command to move. I retrieved the flashlight with shaking fingers. Dirt crammed under my fingernails, and flashes of my aunt's dank cellar mingled with the stale underground air. Overwhelming claustrophobia and the voice, with its warning, possessive message, suffocated my curiosity.

"Calli, what's wrong?" Tanner's concerned face met my dirt-streaked visage once I made it to the base of the ladder.

I threaded one arm through the closest rung, my legs shaking.

"Panic attack," I huffed. "I thought I outgrew a certain childhood incident. Guess I haven't."

Next time—if there *was* a next time—I'd come prepared, with one of those big, black police flashlights. And maybe a hard hat with a headlamp so I wouldn't have to pick bits of bugs out of my hair. And knee pads and leather gloves and a counter-spell to prevent that voice from chilling me to the very marrow in my bones.

"You okay to come up on your own, or do you need help?" he asked.

"Give me a sec to get my legs back under me, and I'll be fine."

His head and shoulders disappeared, along with the light from his cell phone. I clung to the ladder, rested my forehead on my hands, and sneezed again. The dull thud of Tanner moving about overhead provided a lifeline to freedom.

"Tanner?" I called. "I'm coming up."

Three closely spaced rungs rose above my head. Getting up the ladder and out of the tree's innards entailed twisting the upper half of my body, ducking my head, and not caring at all how dirty my shirt was about to get. I didn't stop moving until I'd crawled out from under the shade cast by the tree's wide reach and dropped onto a patch of sun-warmed grass.

Dry stalks prickled the back of my neck and arms, but at least I could breathe. My knees gave silent thanks before they finally gave out.

Tanner crouched beside me and nudged my hip. "Have some water."

I rolled to my side and cracked open one eye. The lukewarm water was like nectar. I drank half the bottle. "Save the rest for River."

Tanner chuckled. "River's in his element down there. He may not emerge for a while."

I hung my head and shook out my hair, struggling to sit cross-legged.

"Hold on a sec." Tanner screwed on the bottle's cap, dropped it on the grass, and positioned himself on his knees in front of me. "You've got an assortment of..." he began, eyeing my hair.

"Don't tell me what's in there." I held up my palm, pressed my fingertips to his chin. "Just get it out. Please."

He laughed softly. "I thought you earth witches loved dirt and crawly things."

"I do love dirt. And I love the crawly things most when they stay in the dirt and out of my hair."

Tanner breathed steadily through his nose, tugging at strands of my hair and proceeding methodically, section by section, all over my scalp. The soothing rhythm of his fingers wove a wordless familiarity between us. I couldn't remember the last time anyone had touched me in such an oddly intimate way.

When he finished, he brushed off his hands and sat back on his heels, tipping my chin up with two fingers. When had his eyes gone from golden brown to a startling topaz? "I think I got them all," he said. "See anything interesting down there?"

I nodded, still enamored with the gem-like quality of his eye color. "I was mostly fine. Then I heard these odd noises, and when I went to touch these little things that had sprouted out of the roots, I heard a voice. All it said was, 'Mine,' which completely spooked me, and that's when my fear of tight, dark places took over."

While I was talking, a halo-like light suffused the air around his head and shimmered off the hairs on his forearms. The cord looped around his neck pulsed in time with the beating of his heart, which made my heart rate ramp up again.

Leaning in, I imagined stroking the shadowed patch of skin

revealed by the undone buttons of his shirt. Instead, I reached for the woven leather cord and pulled.

Tanner grabbed my wrist, his thumb sliding into my palm, applying pressure to my smaller bones. He didn't move my hand away and the compression didn't hurt, not a lot, but the message in the gesture was clear.

"I'm not ready to share that with you," he whispered.

"What *are* you ready to share?" I kept pulling, prodded into bold behavior by the impatient layers of accumulated desire rumbling in the rich earth below. But the *mine* on the tip of my tongue and the laughter burbling deep in my chest were coming from me, not some ghostly entity that liked to inhabit tunnels and apple trees.

Tanner brought his face close enough I could see his individual eyelashes, the pulse at the base of his throat, and the sharply edged curve of his full lower lip—the one that looked wine-stained. Or bruised. I stared at that lip, pulled harder on the cord in my hand, until he lowered me onto a hillock of grass.

His upper body followed the arc of my descent and his mouth came into high relief. He slid one, strong hand to the back my neck and lifted, exposing my throat. "I want to share a kiss with you."

The ground below me lifted in response, forcing my back to arch until my breasts met his chest. I unfurled my legs and nodded consent, never loosening my grip on the cord.

Tanner angled his head and kissed one corner of my mouth, and the other corner, and when the crush of his lips met mine, dark cherries ripened to perfection burst open and flooded my tongue. Bottled water slaked one kind of thirst. Tanner's kiss invoked a wholly new need to drink and get drunk and never get up.

I invited his juiciness to pour into me and through me and feed the land at my back.

He hovered the full length of his body over mine, supporting himself on elbows and forearms planted to either side of my shoulders. His hands cupped the sides of my face, and his thumbs explored the contours of my cheekbones and eye sockets while his lips continued to conquer and cajole, offering bribes by way of an endless supply of over-ripe cherry and hints of mint.

Tanner released my lips and bit my chin, trailing his tongue from the edge of a collarbone as he followed the taut edge of a tendon, over my jaw and back to my mouth. The line he left burned below my skin, melting any residual resistance.

I bent my knees and pressed my heels into the backs of Tanner's thighs, urging him to give me more of his weight, insisting he meld his body with mine.

When he broke the extended entanglement of our mouths, arousal connected the landscapes of our chests and bellies, leaving little room for discerning who ended where. Even the tree branches, furiously weaving a protective canopy overhead, seemed invested in us continuing to kiss.

Until Tanner suddenly peeled himself away, leaving the front of my body bandage-ripped raw. He stood like a toppled tree springing back into place.

A tremor, rising from behind me, pushed at my back. I took the hand Tanner offered and joined him, unsteady in the double whammy delivered by the unexpected kissing and the end of the unexpected kissing. He brushed the dirt and dried grass off my back, and when he finished, he grabbed my elbows and faced me.

Despite the strength of the afternoon sun, the earlier glints of golden light that radiated off his body had disappeared. A cloud settled across his eyes, the gem-like clarity disappeared, and a denseness claimed his body. He pulled me into a hug and spoke into my hair, sounding more like a government agent delivering a summons and less like a man who'd initiated and followed through on a series of succulent kisses.

"I should not have done that, Calliope. I won't do it again, I promise."

My voice was muffled by his armpit. "What if it's okay with me? What if I want you to kiss me again?"

"I…"

My arms circled his waist. A few minutes earlier, the man lying between my legs had pulsed with desire, need, and sexual power. The man who helped me stand was as wooden as a coat rack. The Tanner who held me tight in this moment and nuzzled my hair was somewhere in between, and whatever was going on in his body—and maybe his heart or his soul, I didn't know—was big enough to split him into pieces.

Mine. The voice was muffled, and I finally understood what it meant.

The voice didn't want the old tree in the other section of the orchard or the tender green leaves popping out underground. The voice wanted Tanner.

I hugged him a little tighter and a little longer until his heart rate slowed. His arms and legs relaxed against my body.

A shout from River startled us apart.

Tanner took a step back as the other agent jogged into view.

"Hey!" he yelled. "Find anything interesting? Calli was just debriefing me on her adventure." He squeezed my hand before he released it. Nothing in my body reassembled in its right place.

River wasn't even breathing hard when he plopped onto the grass and helped himself to what was left in the bottle of water. "I think we need to come back with full spelunking gear, more lights, more help. The tunnel's a marvel of engineering and magic. Or magical engineering. Anyways, count me in when you're ready to explore further." He drained the refillable bottle and handed it to me. "And you?"

I blew out a fast breath and shook off the sensation of Tanner's mouth consuming mine. "I'll frame this by confessing I'm not fond of tight, dark places."

River chuckled. "You were right at home, then, hey?"

"Not exactly," I said, joining him on the grass. "But something magical's alive in this section of the orchard, and I connect with it."

"Me, too," Tanner murmured, although he didn't look as blissed by the connection. Or any other connection.

I reached into my bag and pulled out a container of dried fruit, tearing a piece of pear in half for a needed boost of sugar. River's interest in my story piqued when I got to the part about the voice saying *mine* in the tunnel.

Tanner paled slightly. "Was it male? Female? Other?"

"Female. -Ish?" I picked at the other piece of pear and thought about it. "Definitely female. Any thoughts? Either of you?"

"I didn't hear anything underground," River said, "but I get an overall sense of well-being when I'm amongst these trees. Or maybe it's that Rose and I have gone twenty-four hours without irritating each other." He laughed to himself. "Speaking of my favorite sister and witch, I should get back to her. We're hoping we can leave the Pearmains to their own devices." He flopped onto the grass and sighed before he bounded onto his feet and extended his right arm. "Calliope Jones, it has been my pleasure to begin to get to know you."

"River, same here. I'm sure we'll be in touch."

He released my hand. "Tanner, what's your plan?"

"I'll head to Calli's house when we're done and likely hop a ferry to the mainland later tonight or first thing tomorrow."

River nodded. "One more thing. I removed all the charms hanging off the front gate when I fixed it. They're in a sack, which I'll leave at your car. Take a look at what's in there. Might have something to do with the spell they were under, might not." He set off down the path, his walk loose and relaxed. "Keep me in the loop," he shouted before a turn in the path took him from sight.

Tanner crumpled onto the grass beside me.

CHAPTER 10

"I like him," I said, "I like Kaz and Wes too. And Rose, but she's..."

Rose's focus was the health of her patients. My contact with her thus far had been perfunctory.

I tried not take her lack of warmth personally.

"Rose is complicated, Calli, but she's the best herbalist I know and she's dedicated to keeping her lineage going. And if she lives long enough, she'd like to see it expand and thrive." He shifted closer to me then changed his mind and reclined on the ground, folding in on himself as though the kiss we shared had never happened.

"Tanner, you feel it, don't you?" I was unwilling to chalk up everything about our physical encounter to an invisible force, but I needed to hear his take.

He crossed his arms over his face. "Why don't you explain what you mean?"

I pressed my palms onto the grass and closed my eyes. Well below the surface, a palpable presence rolled and stretched, pleading with me to shed my clothes for an afternoon of naked sunbathing and apple-sampling and kissing. More and more kissing.

Releasing the connection, I turned to face Tanner. "Close your eyes. And tell me you don't feel desire."

Tanner shook his head and scrabbled to stand. "Calliope, I…"

"Come here," I said. He really was going to fight me on this. I rolled onto my hands and knees and crawled the three feet that would bring me within reach of his ankles. I grabbed the bottom of one of his pant legs and tugged. "Come. Please."

"I believe you."

"Then why won't you relax and *feel* it with me? Aren't you an investigator? Isn't this what you do?" I licked my upper lip and sat back on my heels, thighs parted. The ground below my legs warmed and softened. I wanted Tanner to get over his resistance and crawl over to me.

Feline in its desire for touch, the ground agreed. I spread my knees wide, arched my spine, and offered Tanner a silent invitation.

He stared. Stormy weather clouded his eyes and put a damper on my otherwise lovely afternoon. "Calliope, get off the ground."

I refused. I sprawled on my back and rolled my head. *No.* The little rocks underneath me didn't hurt at all. The welcome bites of pain reminded me I was ripe and ready to rumble. Two buttons on my shirt popped off. My fingers curled into the grass. Desire forced my legs apart, and I almost ripped down the zipper of my pants.

This was not *my* desire.

"Tanner," I pleaded, bound in place, "help."

He grabbed a wrist, wrenched me to my feet, and hurried us both to the path.

I bent over, dropped to my hands and knees, and retched. "What the hell just happened?"

Tanner kneeled in front of me, wiped my mouth, and cupped my face in his wide palms. "Everything you just felt was an extension of whatever inhabits this orchard, and I'm starting to think it's connected to her."

My knees almost buckled underneath the weight of that idea. I whispered, "Everything?"

"Almost," he said, offering a slightly pained smile.

I plunked my forehead against his chest, inhaled the musk and mint scent of him brought to the surface by the heat. His hands slipped from my face as his arms circled my shoulders. "How are we going to run an investigation," I asked, "if everything we feel or everything that happens is potentially influenced by her magic?" I lifted my head and looked into Tanner's eyes. "It is the Apple Witch, isn't it? Or is it something else?"

He shook his head and offered no answer.

I looked around. Sparrows flitted from branch to branch, their calls filling the air with avian banter. Sunshine warmed the apples' skins, releasing sweet scents. It took a Herculean effort to extract myself from the soporific influence of our surroundings, slip from Tanner's embrace, and gather my things into my back-pack. My buttons were casualties of our encounter. I accepted his hand as he urged us away from that section of the orchard.

"Now I know how sailors feel when they hear the sirens singing," I muttered.

Tanner glanced at me and grimaced. "Exactly. And I've known a few good men who've gone down."

I swallowed. I was joking about sirens.

The porch was deserted when we came within hollering distance of the Pearmains' house. Rose must have been alerted to our arrival. She exited the back door, closed it deliber-ately, and waited for us to get closer.

"Calliope," she began, her voice softer than before, "we need to hurry. I heard from the other witches, and they want us to meet them tomorrow on the Blood Moon. Which seems a good omen considering your Blood Ceremony comes next after this ritual of initiation."

My knees shook. This was getting real. I reached for Tanner's wrist.

"I can drop the boys at the Fulford ferry," he volunteered, "or they can take the one later tonight out of Long Harbor."

"I don't even know what I need," I stuttered.

Ms. Petite and Formidable gave me the once-over. Her waist-length hair was absolutely striking, its dark silver and white strands patterned like a wild checkerboard starting at her roots. I couldn't tell if the pattern was natural or dyed, and I wasn't about to ask.

"Here." Rose paused on the lowest step and handed over a book with a folded piece of paper tucked inside. "I made a list of supplies you'll need to bring. Call me if there's anything you can't locate. And don't forget to read the book. All of it."

Lucky for me I was a fast reader.

Tanner's steadying hand left my lower back when he stepped from behind and made his way to the stairs. "Rose, are Cliff and Abigail all right to be left alone?"

She nodded, turning to the screen door and leading us into the house. "Come say your goodbyes. They have plenty of food, and they don't appear to have any residual physical discomfort. I had Clifford drive their truck to the road and back, and he did just fine." Rose lowered her voice, leaned into Tanner, and whispered, "Him being cranky is a good sign."

I crested the last hill before the center of town. Tanner spent the entire ride from the Pearmains' staring out his open window. My insides were reeling from the effects of kissing him. Not knowing how much of his past had arrived to haunt, influence, or seduce him, I wasn't sure I wanted more of his company. If I dropped him in town, he could figure out how to get to my house, maybe commandeer a hefty stick and fashion it into a mode of transport.

I didn't realize I'd snorted out loud at the image of Tanner astride a makeshift witch's broom until I realized he was looking at me oddly.

"Something funny?" he asked.

"Not really. Do you want me to leave you anywhere?"

"I'm fine going to your house, if you're fine having me there."

Fine. I focused on the road ahead and the ever-present clusters of gawping tourists. Tanner could have a time-out in the car while I shopped. Rose's list included items stocked at the natural foods store, and I was in and out in a few minutes.

"I have to make one more stop before we head home." After the incident at the orchard, I wanted to add another herbal ally to my garden, and there was a well-stocked nursery on the northern tip of the island. Tanner grunted, re-folded his arms across his chest, and returned to staring out his window.

I parked. He elected to stay in the car and paw through the bag of trinkets River had left on the back seat. Shrugging my bag over one shoulder, I ignored the feeling Tanner was tracking me through the rear view mirror. Once I located the rows of potted herbs, I lifted one after the other to my nose. I crushed a few leaves and petals between my fingers until I decided two pots of motherwort would fit in nicely with my other herbs.

"Got what I needed." I tucked the pots behind the passenger's seat. Once I buckled myself in and started the engine, I gripped the steering wheel with both hands and turned to look at my passenger.

The air around him was cool, like he'd withdrawn every bit of heat and curiosity into himself. Maybe he wasn't the one raising the fine hairs across my back and up my neck.

"Did you feel anything just now or when I was shopping in town?"

"No. Nothing."

I backed up, shifted, and drove to the road. An SUV with tinted windows was parked in the pull-off area by the bank of rural mailboxes. The sign on the driver's side door declared it property of the Flechette Realty and Development Group. With at least six offices on the lower mainland and Gulf Islands, it was inevitable I'd see my ex or his fellow agents out with clients, but I didn't recognize the citified woman behind the oversized sunglasses.

"Tanner. What was the name on the business card left at the Pearmains'?"

He scanned his phone. "Adelaide Dunfay."

Bingo. I would bet my two pots of motherwort Ms. Dunfay's presence on this sparsely-populated road was anything but coincidental. "Can you keep an eye on the car behind us?"

Moody one moment, alert the next, Tanner repositioned the back of his seat and adjusted the mirror on his side of the car. "What's up?"

"Not only is that one of my ex's SUVs, the name on the door matches the business card from the Pearmains. And I haven't seen a single For Sale sign anywhere on this road."

That solidified his attention. "Any reason to suspect Doug or his family would send someone to follow you?"

"Well, no," I mused, signaling the upcoming right-hand turn with my blinker. "But the boys are supposed to spend the weekend with him, and they mentioned he's bought a new condo in Vancouver and I'm curious, that's all."

The SUV's left blinker went on. The driver peeled away and accelerated up the winding road toward the other side of the island.

"Should we turn around and follow her?" I asked.

"No." Tanner flipped his visor up. "How long were you two married?"

"Twelve years."

Three or four kilometers passed before he spoke again. "He involved with anyone now?"

"No idea."

"Are you?"

I negotiated the final set of tight curves, pulled into my driveway, and chuffed out a breath. "Nope. I have mysterious troll heads and missing bodies to occupy my time."

Harper and Thatcher were eager to talk about the mentoring program. Tanner offered to drive them to the Fulford ferry, which would give them time to ask questions and me time to start packing.

Rose's note included a meal plan for Saturday dinner and Sunday breakfast. I held the list with both hands, circled my kitchen for inspiration, and settled on homemade granola. My version was so laden with nuts and chunks of dried fruit it could double as a snack and best of all, I had everything I needed on hand.

I gathered the ingredients, set the oven to a low temperature, and measured, mixed, and tweaked. Once the baking trays were in the oven, I set a ten-minute reminder and settled on a stool to read the book Rose provided.

Underneath the list of camping supplies were the objects required for the ritual: Wand. Athame. Bowl. Red dress. Yarn or ribbon, at least three yards.

Shit.

I marked my place in the book and scrabbled off the stool. Somewhere in my bedroom closet or the attic crawl space was a collection of sewing notions and unfinished craft projects, bits and pieces that had belonged to my aunt and my maternal grandmother. Or so my aunt said. Surely, I could cobble together the needed length from those remnants.

The timer dinged. I dashed to the kitchen, stirred the granola, and returned to my closet. I located one rubber band-wrapped shoebox that harbored a small stash of holiday ribbons, but very little of it felt nice to the hand or as though it could last through a ritual—even though I had no idea what the ritual entailed. I would check the attic after Tanner returned.

He was returning, right?

I reviewed our last conversation, the hurried bits as the boys stuffed clean clothes and toiletries into their backpacks after pulling out the smelly stuff from two nights before. Yes, Tanner had reiterated, he'd stay another night—if I was willing to again provide a bed—and figure out his next move after we debriefed.

Better to keep reading and lower the risk of burning the granola, and ask for help getting into the attic.

C ar lights swept across the kitchen, and the familiar rattle of the Jeep settling to a full stop brought me out of Rose's book. The granola had cooled, and I was completely immersed in reading about the many stages of a woman's life, be she Magical or human, and the rituals meant to herald us into each stage.

Turns out, at the tender age of forty-one, I lacked fully one-hundred-percent of the suggested minimum rituals needed to help grow and sustain my magical gifts. It was a wonder I'd managed to keep my hands working under such dire straits. The weight drawing down my shoulders pooled in my heart and the bottoms of my feet. Maybe the couch could just swallow me whole.

"How are you?" asked Tanner, stepping into the kitchen. He brought his face close to the cooled granola and inhaled. "And this smells delicious."

At least I could cook. "Thanks. It's my culinary contribution to my upcoming journey deep into the realms of witch magic. Which, according to this book," I lifted the paperback and waved it in the air, "I lack. I'm going to need months to catch up, if not years. It's a wonder my magic even works anymore."

I tried a dramatic sigh.

Tanner responded with a short laugh and a more serious assessment. "Perhaps your ability to sense through your hands and feet as well as you do speaks to the power you've managed to keep alive."

"Perhaps. I rarely wield my wand, but I am making a new one." I pulled myself off the couch and joined him in the kitchen. The granola was cool enough to pour into glass containers and add to my growing pile of supplies. "Thanks again for driving the boys."

"I enjoyed talking with them," he said, scooping a handful of oats and nuts and doling a bit into his mouth. "They're curious. And I think they'll benefit from being around peers, as well as the adult mentors."

"Did you eat?"

He nodded. "I checked in with River, and we had a quick dinner with Kaz and Wessel. And I filled your tank."

My gaze shot to his. I wished I could accept everything helpful and attentive about him at face value. But that kiss earlier in the day, at the orchard? "Could you help me with one more thing tonight? I need to get into the attic, and the pull-down ladder is stuck."

"Sure. Let's do that now." Tanner needed ten minutes of muted swearing to figure out the problem was rusted hinges. "When you get back from the ritual, you might want to have someone take a look at your roof before the rains get here. Could be a leak." He held the sides of the lowered ladder and jammed the resistant hinges into place. The lone attic lightbulb, covered in grime, gave off a faint yellow glow. "Got a flashlight?" he asked.

"Right here. And thanks." I started up the rickety steps and paused, sweeping the flashlight across the beams and floorboards until I spied what I was looking for.

When I first left this house for married life with Doug, my aunt had given me the child-sized steamer trunk packed with mementos: a few of my mother's books, pieces of costume jewelry and glass vials of crystal beads, bundles of velvet and silk satin ribbons. A shoe box tucked into a bottom corner held squares of fabric, pinned together and ready for quilting. Tiny blood-colored spots dotted the bits of cotton where the pins had rusted.

I went through the trunk's contents with reverent hands.

One day, I would bring the trunk to my room and go through everything, piece by piece. Read every book, page by page. And hope something more of my mother would reveal itself. Because there was an empty place in my chest no one else had ever filled and questions I still wanted answers for. When all the magical happenings settled down, I planned to contact my cousins and ask whether my aunt had left any old photographs or scrapbooks with them before they moved her to the eldercare facility.

I sat back on my heels. If only I could take the contents of the trunk and make something beautiful to wear out of the fabric scraps, take apart the jewelry and…

I pivoted, attic dust swirling around me like a cascade of fairy sparkles, and yelled for Tanner. "Can you come here?"

The folding ladder squeaked with every step.

"What do you need?" he asked as his head and shoulders appeared through the rectangular hole in the floor.

"Could you help me get this down to my room?"

"Sure."

My gaze swept the tent-shaped space and honed in on the low book shelf. "And those books too." I slid the trunk to the opening. "Watch the straps," I cautioned, pointing at the cracked leather strips tacked to either end. "One broke and the other looks just as fragile."

"I can take this myself. Where do you want me to put it?"

"My office. The room across the hall from the ground floor bathroom."

While he maneuvered the trunk down the ladder and stairs, I scanned the books. Childhood favorites, vintage cookbooks, and a set of binders from *Good Housesweeping*, all with faded spines and covered in fuzzy, brownish dust. Better to haul up my vacuum cleaner and clean them off first.

Tanner stepped to the bottom of the ladder and held the sides as I descended.

"On second thought, I'll get the books later." I blew drooping strands of hair out of my face. "We can close this up now."

Stepping off the lowest rung, I pulled the long string hanging from the ceiling and listened for the click of the lightbulb turning off. Tanner's chest was to my back, both his arms raised as he guided the slightly warped attic door closed. He quickly lowered one arm, wrapped it around my shoulders, and let go of the door.

I tamped the urge to pivot on the balls of my toes—a dusty ballet dancer in dirty khakis and a snap-front shirt—and burrow my nose into his breastbone.

He turned me to face him with his free arm. "Calli?"

I got my wish. A cluster of curly chest hairs tickled the tip of my nose. My mouth went dry, and my lips likely tasted of old attic. I slipped my arms around his waist and waited.

If inanimate objects could hold their breath, then the walls and floorboards of my little A-frame were doing exactly that right along with me. I was safe. Buffered. And we were the only ones in my house.

I was safe—*we* were safe—from the presence in the orchard.

Tanner stroked his hands down my back and tugged at my shirt, slipping warm fingers between my skin and the sweaty patch of cotton. I shifted my hips when his fingertips asked permission to slide below the waistband of my pants. Tilting my head back, a cool blue light from the waxing moon washed over one side of his face.

He scanned the periphery of my neck, cheeks, and jaw before settling on eye-to-eye contact. "It would be so easy to court you, Calliope Jones."

I lifted my heels off the floor and kissed the left side of his mouth and the right side.

"It would be so easy to be courted by you, Tanner Marechal," I said, giving his name the French inflection that could make even a packing list sound sexy. "But I'm not ready."

CHAPTER 11

The drive to Carmanah Walbran Provincial Park was bumpy and dusty and felt interminably long. I was glad for the use of Harper's Jeep, which provided high clearance over the jumbled rocks and wash-outs that punctuated the logging road. I had to pay attention to what was directly in front of me, rather than run fantasies of what it would have been like to toss every caution and warning to the four directions last night and invite Tanner into my bed.

At one point, I stopped the vehicle and pulled over to stretch my legs and back. With the engine off, the only sounds were bugs and birds, and though I could have reached below the manmade surface of the road, I didn't. I was afraid of what I might uncover in these logged-out, clear-cut areas of once magnificent forest, and without the support of the ground, I wasn't equipped to explore my feelings for Tanner.

I could, however, acknowledge the rootlets taking hold in my heart, tender shoots of self-discovery that had nothing to do with being attracted to a man and everything to do with nurturing my witchy leanings.

Cleaning my hands on a disposable wipe, I got back into the

Jeep and continued, and when I finally pulled into the park, I was ready to embrace my destiny. Mostly. Being in a vehicle by myself for five hours on my way to face a ritual of unknown proportions had shown me the humor in my situation. Plus, I always held the power to say no.

There were a dozen or so trucks, SUVs, and campers in the parking area. I slid off the front seat, opened the back door, and gathered my things. Only one path, marked by government-issued signs painted a familiar shade of brown, led out of the parking area and into the woods. Following an overlapping chorus of voices, I located the correct campsites. Bright orange and royal blue tents were visible behind a privacy fence of trees, along with small picnic tables loaded with coolers and propane cook-stoves. Eclectically dressed women bustled around the tables and benches.

At a site further down the path, a woman poked her head out from between the trees and waved. "Are you Calliope?"

"Yes."

"I'm Busy B. C'mon, we're making dinner and getting dressed. Oh! And I brought a two-person tent so if you'd like to share, I have room."

I was fine with sleeping in the same tent as any of the other witches. Except maybe for Rose. Her imperial air would guarantee I got no sleep.

"So, do you know all the women here?" I asked, twisting the cap off the input valve of my self-inflating camping pad.

"Yes and no. I know all of them cozily and a few of them more intimately, seeing as how we're in the cluster of covens that include the smaller Gulf Islands but not Vancouver Island. Including every witch at every meeting would be too much. Most of the women who're here are the more senior ones from their covens." Busy tapped my shoulder and crawled closer before she sat and tucked her voluminous skirt around her tiny feet. "It's a big deal," she whispered, leaning in, "this thing they're doing for you. I don't think I've ever been to a ritual where we have to take the initiate through so many stages all in one night."

"Should I be scared?" I asked, mostly joking.

Busy's honey-colored softness gave way to a hardened amber appraisal. "A little." She gave a curt nod and continued, "Once we start, we can't stop for anything. I've heard of women fainting. Never heard of anyone actually dying…"

I choked on my water and spit a mouthful across the top of my sleeping bag, "Dying?"

"I'm kidding, Calliope," she giggled, slapping my knee and softening. "I'm *kid*ding."

The clang of a wooden spoon hitting the bottom of a pot saved me from hearing any more details, truthful or teasing, and brought both of us out of the tent and onto the pathway connecting the campers. Curious faces greeted me when I ducked under low-hanging branches and into a double-sized site, with two fire pits, two picnic tables, and eleven women. Thirteen, once Busy and I made our way through the branches and stood side-by-side.

"Hi." I waved at the cluster of witches. Most of them looked to be in their late thirties and up, with no one younger than twenty-five. They were witches, though, so I could have been off by a few years. Or decades.

"This is Calliope Jones, everyone," said Rose, pointing at me with a chef's knife. "Let's fill our plates. Then we'll introduce ourselves after we've all had a bit to eat." She turned to me. "We have our given names, and we have our self-chosen ritual names. And for the purposes of ceremonies such as the one we are creating tonight, we give ourselves the option of adopting a name that is personally symbolic, thereby amplifying our iden-tity—or the role we are playing within the sacred circle." She lowered her voice for my ears only and emphasized her words with tight flourishes of the knife. "This Ritual of Initiation is not held often. Rarely have I ever come across a witch so ill-trained, yet so obviously in touch with at least a modicum of her powers."

I gulped down my nervousness. Rose had given me a back-handed compliment—I thought—by acknowledging the truth I was both a neophyte and a potential diamond in the rough.

"Busy, would you please start us off?" Rose asked.

Busy nodded, handed her plate to the witch to her right, and stood. "My name is Busy B. I am here to represent the Daughter in the form of Astrea, virgin goddess of innocence and purity."

She sat, reclaimed her meal, and smiled at the young woman with the freckled, fine-boned visage to her left.

"My name is Cordelia. I am here to represent the Maiden in the form of Artemis."

The next woman to stand, another of the younger ones, had a mischievous glint in her eyes as she welcomed me. "I am here to represent the Blood Sister. My name is Sapphos Star."

The witches continued, and though I tried to remember everyone's given name and Goddess aspect, I couldn't, except for those I'd already met: Belle the herbalogist and, of course, Rose. When she stood, the women in the circle quieted their chirping.

"My name is Rose de Benauge. I invoke the name of Kalima, and I represent the Dark Mother." When she finished, she silently acknowledged every woman in the circle before she turned her attention fully to me. "And you, Calliope Jones, are here as Priestess."

After introductions were finished and dinner plates and bowls were emptied, Rose stood, rising to her full five-feet-four-inches, and spoke. "If your role is to set up for tonight's ritual, you are exempt from clean up. Plan to meet me at the trail-head in ten minutes. Everyone else, pay attention. Those of you on kitchen detail can put all foodstuffs—and I mean *all*—into the trunk of Belle's car. Make certain there is *nothing* left out that would interest bears. Once we're good to go here," she added, gesturing to the tables, "and while we still have some light, gather your ritual objects, change into your dresses, and I shall see you at the trees."

The other women shooed me away from the eating area with the excuse that, as the star of the night, my time would be better spent in preparing myself. Power emanated from every one of them. Even Busy and Belle, who I'd met earlier, had taken on a kind of gravitas the closer my watch ticked to the start of the ritual.

Back at the shared tent, I brushed off my trepidation and shook out the knee-length red dress I'd brought per Rose's instruction. Next, I washed my feet at the water pump and slipped a fresh pair of lightweight wool socks over clean toes before re-donning my boots. All I had to add was the length of ribbon, my athame and my wand, and the poncho my aunt had assembled from black-and-white squares crocheted by my mother. At least, that was the story my aunt offered. I had enough skill with a needle to keep the garment mended and would to do so until the end of its days or mine, whichever came first.

"Ready?" Busy stepped through the row of trees that provided privacy to each campsite. Her smile infused me with sweetness and strength.

"Ready," I replied. "Should I go to the trailhead?"

"Sure. Or wait for me if you'd like company. I want to wash the smell of scallions off my fingers before I put on my dress."

"I'll wait here." I gestured to the bench at our picnic table and tucked my dress behind my knees, avoiding the greasy spots as I sat. I parted my lips and exhaled a soft breath. The humming sensation that accompanied Busy was oddly comforting.

"Don't be nervous." My roomie returned smelling of soap. The tent swayed as she rifled through her things. "You're in very good hands, Calliope Jones."

"I know. I trust Rose."

Busy unzipped the flap and crawled out, clutching the skirt of her white dress to her belly. She stayed in a crouch as she closed the entrance to the tent. "Don't want any bugs or critters joining us tonight."

Dropping her hem, she stood and wiggled her curves into place.

"You look radiant!" I was amazed at the transformation. Busy's honey-gold hair floated away from her face, catching every last bit of light. "It's like you're a...a goddess!"

Busy beamed. "We're all goddesses," she assured me, "and tonight, we're here to celebrate you. No pressure, of course."

I giggled. "Let's go meet the others before I totally chicken out."

CHAPTER 12

The walk to the sacred grove was mostly awe-filled and peaceful. I had to keep my gaze to the ground, what with tree roots making random appearances and loose footing where winter's snow and ice had deposited a tumble of river rocks. Even the raised boardwalk, with its rotted or missing slats and loose nails, called for caution.

Ahead of us, Rose's group had tied strips of cloth to head-height branches, marking the turns with a luminescent wave whenever the path split. And when a section of boardwalk dead-ended at a washout, we hiked up our skirts and dresses and scrambled along a narrow ledge. The drop to the shallow river below was less than six feet, but it was straight down and I had no intention of needing any kind of a rescue before, during, or after the ritual. Once the path resumed, I followed it around thigh-high clumps of ferns to where the others waited.

My nighttime sensors took in the depth of quiet in the old growth forest. Pausing, I gazed upward past the lacy tips of branches to witness twilight settling its sheer blue-black cape over the massive Sitka spruces ringing the ritual area. These trees had stood for hundreds of years, some for over a thousand, and I could feel the weight of their ancient presence.

The witches spaced themselves into a rough circle within the clearing. Once I was at my designated spot, I unlaced my boots and bared my feet. I needed to root down to find a place of inner calm, one that wasn't worrying about leaf mold-loving critters or spiders and other bugs. Especially not the bugs with hundreds of squiggly legs running up and down their sides.

I wasn't in the basement of my aunt's house. No one had forgotten me. I was fine. I was in a circle of powerful women, and it was my night to be initiated into the mysteries of modern day witch-hood.

A ripple moved through the women.

Rose spoke. "As we prepare to enter this ritual of initiation, does anyone have anything they wish to say before we begin?"

Heads, illuminated by the light of the rising full moon, shook slowly.

"Very well. Calliope, as you are a witch who is new to ritual," she continued, everyone's attention settling on me, "there is one thing you must understand. Rituals do not always take hold in the way we hope or intend. There will be moments tonight when you will be asked to trust this place, to trust the women around you, and to trust me. I will explain every part of our ritual as it is happening. As you follow my voice, as you feel that trust build, know that hardest of all will be the moments when you must trust yourself."

Rose's words hovered in the air between us.

"L'Runa will assist me."

L'Runa's skin glowed like polished walnut. Long, skinny braids of hair bleached white hung from either side of her head down to her waist. Hawk feathers formed a wing-like fan at the front of her crown, with miniature ears of blue corn to either side. The power circulating through her almost sent me to my knees. I refocused on Rose's words.

"If everyone would take a few steps toward the center of our circle so that L'Runa doesn't have to trample the plants, we will start with grounding and purification."

Cloth rustled against ferns and bushes of low-growing salal as the women drew closer to one another.

"We ground ourselves, to be present to the work we are doing and to be present to our connection to everything around us. Find a comfortable stance, close your eyes, and connect to your breath. Relax your throat, your belly, your knees."

I followed Rose's voice, and while night moths of anxiety and anticipation still fluttered about, I eventually found a steady source of support in my bones. I pictured them holding me up much like the sturdy beams anchoring my beloved house.

"Send your awareness to the soil below your feet and deeper, and deeper still, through stone, through water, to the fire at the center of our planet."

I followed Rose's voice down and back up, opening my eyes with care when instructed for the next step of the ritual.

L'Runa untied the bundle of herbs and feathers hanging from the strips of white leather girdling her hips and turned to Belle. She dipped her bundle into the water-filled chalice and sprinkled Belle's head and shoulders. I caught a soft whisper of words, a repeated chant that grew in texture and breadth as each woman added her voice when L'Runa stood before them and repeated the motions.

When the tall witch paused in front of me, she offered a quick smile, one that softened the angles of her face and called my attention to her ice-blue eyes. L'Runa raised the volume of her voice and slowed her cadence enough so I could hear the exact syllables of the chant.

Words—soft with blessing, sharp with warning—penetrated my skin and created a netting below the surface. The sensation was simultaneously odd and familiar, sticky and viscous, generating spider web-like connections between me and the other women and every living thing around us.

I let my wonder be and surrendered any search for an explanation.

L'Runa handed the chalice and bundle to Rose and went to one knee, allowing the petite leader easier access to her head and shoulders. When L'Runa stood, she placed the ritual objects in the center of the circle and took her place between Elphane and Belle.

"Now, we cast our circle," Rose said.

Every witch turned to face the same direction. A quick scan of the night sky informed me we were facing North. Rose turned her left hand to face the ground, raised her right arm, and drew a pentacle in the air. I couldn't hear the words she spoke, but when we turned as one to the right—East—I could hear her brief invocation to Fire, the next turn to Water, and finally, to Earth.

She paused when we returned to facing North, pivoted clockwise to face the center of our loose circle, and pointed her right arm to the ground, informing us the circle was cast and we were now between the worlds.

I would be lying if I said I didn't feel a palpable difference in the air around me, in myself. I ran my hands up and down my outer thighs, just to feel the solidity of my body, and made certain to listen for my heartbeat echoing in my ears.

"I will now call in the cardinal directions and the elements and invoke the Goddesses." Rose lifted her hands, palms forward and fingers spread, and began to speak. The glow from the moonstone rings decorating her fingers brightened. "Powers of the East, please be present. Bless us with words that lift our hearts. Teach us to embrace clarity of mind."

A breeze played with the hem of my dress. Goosebumps flitted up my legs and arms. I held my breath.

Rose released her words, the moonstones faded, and she made a quarter turn. "Powers of the South, please be present. Bless us with the transformational power of fire, teach us the promise of renewal held in every day." I watched in open-mouthed awe as flames flickered over the hearts, bellies, and foreheads of the witches across the circle from me. A warm tickle drew a gasp from my throat; I was similarly aflame, until Rose made another quarter turn to invoke the next direction. "Powers of the West, please be present. Bless us with waters that nourish and cleanse. Teach us the power of the steady course."

A mist arose, coating my forehead and cheeks. I brought my fingertips to one side of my face to make sure I hadn't imagined the cool drops.

"Powers of the North, please be present. Bless us with depth in our connections to one another. Teach us to honor our Mother Earth."

The ground underneath my feet rose and fell in time with my breath. I stopped shaking and started trusting.

Next, Rose opened her arms to the sides and began to move in a circle. The bottom of her lace dress flared out as she spun, sending ripples through nearby plants. "Elemental air, soaring over mountains and across flatlands, carrying our words, present in our every breath, elevating our minds and opening us to learning, please be present. Bless us with cleansing winds that soothe our wounds and imperfections. Bathe us in silver energy."

A moment later, a tiny flame appeared in Rose's palm.

"Elemental fire, who dwells in the dark at the center of the Earth and lights our solar system, please be present. Bless us with your gifts of action and creativity, your purifying flames and golden energy."

She turned in place until she again faced West and lowered both hands into the chalice at her feet, dowsing the flame. "Elemental water." Rose stood, raised her cupped palms, water coursing down her arms. "Falling from clouds, rising from our springs and wells, flowing through our streams and rivers, abiding in the depths of our lakes and oceans, nurturing our emotions, please be present. Bless us with the tides of courage and change and bathe us in blue energy."

Rose stopped moving as she finished speaking. Her dress, glowing with silvered flickers of light, settled against her slender form. She took a wider stance, bent slightly at the knees, and turned her palms to face the ground.

"Elemental earth," she said, gently tamping her feet in place and pressing the air with her hands. "That which is everywhere underfoot, grounding and abundant, please be present. Bless us with the dark of your caves and the green light that grows within everything planted."

The lights on Rose's dress faded, and my vision sped outward, past the wide trunks of the trees and into the consuming dark.

The spruce and the fir absorbed the lingering wisps of Rose's words. "Our intention as we gather here amongst these ancient trees, on this sacred ground, is to guide our sister, Calliope Jones, through the stages that bring her to Priestess. Calliope, are you ready to receive?"

"Yes." I waited, expectant.

Sounds filtered into my awareness, rising from the ground and closing in from the surrounding trees. It took me a few stuttered breaths to understand the women were creating the sounds, using drums, a rainstick, fingers clicking, soft clapping, voices trilling. A chant began, and as the words gradually became clearer, I joined in, silently mouthing and following along as the voices got louder and louder.

The moment I thought we had reached a crescendo, voices went silent as if one. Women's arms floated out and up. White sleeves slid toward shoulders to reveal skin: bared, tattooed, adorned. Muscled, plump and lean. Fingers wiggled, and the sounds of nature at night gradually replaced the women's voices.

I almost giggled. I stopped myself as the women around me lowered their arms in slow motion, bent their knees, and took hold of objects they'd left by their feet. One by one, they placed wreaths—or maybe they were crowns—on their heads. A couple of the women bent again and retrieved other objects. L'Runa adjusted her headpiece, made her way to me, and offered a simple circlet of braided wire decorated with alternating metal leaves and round mirrors the size of silver dollars.

"For me?" I whispered.

She nodded. Her glowing braids swished against her body. "Yours to keep, Calliope Jones."

I tucked my chin as L'Runa placed the circlet on my head and stepped away. I straightened, touched my fingertips to the metal, and gently adjusted the fit until it sat secure.

Busy was next. She lifted the length of ribbon draped behind her neck and placed it across my uplifted palms. Little blue flowers were braided into her crown. "I am Daughter. I offer Calliope Jones the gift of play and the power of innocence."

She stepped back, and Cordelia stepped forward. Her crown was decorated with arrowheads and bits of antlers.

As Cordelia spoke, she lifted one end of Busy's ribbon and joined it to the one she offered. "I am Maiden. I offer Calliope Jones the gifts to be found in the fertility of your mind and within this earth we inhabit and the power inherent in joining this community of women. May it be a place of solace and insight."

"I am Blood Sister," said Sapphos Star, "and I offer Calliope Jones the gift of knowing and embracing her deepest self and making the time to run with Her as she finds her pack. I bless you with the power of unfettered truth." Sapphos repeated the step of joining her ribbon to the prior one. The scent of apple blossoms and nectar wafted up from her headpiece of carved fruit and flowers.

I inhaled quietly; my nerves calmed.

Airlie stepped forward, her lush curves visible beneath an almost transparent gown. Roses and downy white feathers interlaced with pink ribbons formed her headpiece. She smiled at me as she tied a knot in the lengthening ribbon and recited her pledge. "I am Lover. I offer Calliope Jones the gifts and powers of death and rebirth."

"I am Mother." I would have recognized the throaty laugh in Belle's voice whether it was fully dark or I'd been blindfolded for this event. "I offer Calliope Jones the gift of nurturing, be it others or your own creativity, and the power of trusting your body."

Belle's ribbon was a wide, silk velvet, and her crown was adorned with gold-painted sprigs of wheat and other grains.

The next woman walked toward me with a centuries-old dignity. Rachel, that was her name, and I recognized her from Dr. Renard's office. The tiny torches in her headpiece lit up like fairy lights, and in between each was a reclining female figure with a rounded belly. "I am here to represent the Midwife. I offer Calliope Jones the gift of nurturance beyond the circle and the power of the Gatekeeper and the Storyteller."

Her ribbon consisted of many intertwined lengths of yarn.

Ivy danced forward, her smile lighting her face. She was another woman I hoped would be part of my growing social circle. "I am Amazon," she sang, her trill accompanied by the tinkling sounds of metal pieces bobbing against one another. "I offer Calliope Jones the gift of self-determination and the power of inspiration as you focus on your passions."

As she leaned back to remove the cord draped over her neck and down her chest, I spied an arsenal of miniature weapons circling her head: a bows, arrows, conch shells, shields, javelins, and even a noose.

If Ivy was joy-filled, the next woman was ageless and formidable. Tonatzin, the Mexican goddess. Over the required white dress, Justine wore a green cloak decorated with stars. She loosened the dress's black belt and tied it to the growing length of ribbons puddling at my feet. Seashells and frogs, attached to short bits of springs, sprang from her crown.

"I am Matriarch," she said. "I offer Calliope Jones the gift of self-knowledge: of your strengths and your weaknesses, of your many blessings, harvested from your life to date. I challenge you to find the power inherent in the conservation of your formidable energy and success in directing it toward that which is truly deserving. And may you share the abundance of your many blessings."

Rose stepped into the circle and turned to face me.

I already felt taller, stronger, bigger.

"Calliope Jones, you are here as Priestess. It is especially fitting that we initiate you at this stage of your life. Behind you," she said, sweeping her arm to the half-circle of women who had already spoken, "is an accumulation of power, a wide circle that places you on the precipice of descent into the deeper aspects of yourself, a descent made possible because you have chosen to align yourself with the company of women gathered around you tonight.

"This ritual marks the start of your vision quest. It is perhaps the first of many, and in this turning of the self upside-down, you shed that which no longer serves you. You will go beyond that which you know and make room for that which is coming. As you travel—alone but supported—may you come to know the union of power and compassion such that you extend it to others along the way. May you call upon your Circle to help you remain grounded as you rise into realms of knowledge, perception, and leadership opening to you in this very moment."

While Rose spoke, my eyes closed. All the muscles in my face relaxed. My spine arched—heart lifted skyward—and my heels rose off the moss-covered mound until only the tips of my toes held me connected to the ground. The sticky net I'd felt earlier kept me suspended.

Memories swarmed across my forehead and filtered into my facial bones. My mother's face came into focus, fingertips of both her hands stroked my cheeks.

Mama, too, wore a crown and a white ceremonial gown. A dry section of my heart plumped with the drops of maternal love radiating from her eyes. I arched farther, basking as I was cradled, wanted, and loved.

Other images moved across the movie screen of my forehead —some of them were definitely my memories; some of them were snapshots that could have been from my life, or my mother's, I couldn't tell and didn't need to know—until I came to a moment I remembered all too well. The scramble to pack what belongings we could fit into a dented Volkswagen Bug and the long, long drive from the coast of Maine to the coast of British Columbia and our arrival at my mother's sister's house.

My mother's death.

A crack zig-zagged horizontally across my chest. The flames that earlier had danced so pleasingly over the front of my body now branded the muscles between my ribs. I gasped and arched further in an attempt to flee the pain.

Mourning. Going to school. My first period. High school, band of girlfriends. Dating. College. Environmental studies. Meeting Doug. The sense of inevitability around our courtship and marriage. Being forced to choose him rather than continuing my studies into graduate school and greater activism.

My magic shutting down.

The burning sensation across my chest turned to ash.

Mutual abandonment. The births of my two boys. The joy. My job. Finding my way. Autonomy. Becoming respected. The boys growing up. Doug and I growing apart. Divorce.

My determination to find my way.

The little bright and shiny bits and pieces I kept tucked away. The simple joys and pleasure of being with my plants. The compulsion to connect with living, growing green things.

Living, growing, green things.

Plants sprouting, seeding, dying, becoming loam for their offspring. Cool moss at my back.

The lightening sky that presaged dawn. Soft voices. Careful whispers, sent in my direction, pull me back into the circle.

"I am Sorceress. I offer the Circle the gift of time out of time and the powers of alchemy."

"I am Crone, the old one. I offer the Circle the gift of listening and the power of divination."

"I am Dark Mother. I offer the Circle the gifts of solitude, retreat and hibernation, and the power of destruction as it leads to rebirth and letting go."

"I am Transformer." L'Runa—I knew that voice. "I am the source of All. I offer the Circle the gift and power of fear as an ally, the power of courage as we embrace change. I am the Carrier of the Cauldron. I am the Cosmic Womb and the Oracle. I am Shakti, and I am breath."

That final word—*breath*—lingered, repeating itself over and over in my awareness as I came more fully awake. I heard Rose open the circle. In unison, the other witches affirmed the ritual was over and that the door to the other world had closed. I was offered sweetened tea from a thermos, and many hands helped me to sit then stand. The whispered reminder to breathe buoyed me during the long, slow walk back to the tent and acted as a pillow for my heavy, empty head. Busy—I knew it was my tent-mate because of the gentle hum—placed a lightweight blanket over my chest and throat before zipping me into my sleeping bag. Before she left the tent, she also placed a heavier, folded blanket over my legs and belly. The added weight sent me over the edge and into sleep.

CHAPTER 13

I awakened to silence, slightly disoriented and unvisited by
dreams. A few whispered greetings, a metal bowl of
steaming oatmeal and a refreshed thermos of tea, and I was
back in the Jeep and on my way home.

The logging road out of the park was gouged with ruts, and
the chances of blowing a tire or being run off by a logging truck
offered an ever-present danger. I didn't have a moment to
process the ritual until I hit the packed dirt road ringing Lake
Cowichan. My fingers finally released their death grip on the
wheel. I relaxed into the seat back and opened the windows for
fresh air.

Did I feel different? The tattoo on my belly was itchier,
reminding me I really should look into getting it removed or
altered. Loosening my zipper so I could give it a scratch, I darted
a glance to the passenger seat. I'd tossed my things, including the
length of joined ribbons and yarns, into a canvas boat bag.
Perched atop my wrinkled red dress was a crown. I was going
home a princess.

No, a *Priestess*. What was it Rose said? *This ritual marks the start
of your vision quest...*

For the rest of the drive, I stayed alert to anything that could be construed as a sign or an omen. Aside from the occasional kettle of vultures circling overhead, I found no auguries in the sky, trees, or on the ground, nothing beyond the hyper-bright light of a cloudless summer day. I made my ferry, napped on the quick thirty-minute ride, and backed into my empty driveway.

I positioned the Jeep close to the outdoor hose, my hair and skin every bit as dust-coated as the exterior of the vehicle. A bubble bath followed by a slathering of moisturizer was foremost on my mind as I tramped up the stairs and deposited my load of gear on the floor. I had just taken off my boots and was getting ready to peel off my dirty clothes when a scuffle on the front porch alerted me I had visitors.

Harper and Thatcher stood in the doorway, the screen section opened wide and distressed looks distorting both their faces. My ex-husband stood behind them. He was shorter than our sons, and his eyebrows, forehead, and receding hairline rose like tufted hillocks in the space between where the boys' shoulders met.

"Doug?" I half-expected him to jump up and down in a bid for attention.

Instead, he elbowed the boys apart, stepping between them and across the threshold to my home. The old A-frame and I shuddered as one.

Technically, Doug was connected to Harper and Thatch; there was no reason for the wards to keep him out, even though I'd jokingly asked Tanner to add my ex to the Thou Shall Not Pass list. I would address that oversight as soon as Doug said whatever he came to say and left.

"What are you doing here?" I kept my back to the living room and stood my ground, an act I appreciated with even greater clarity after the ritual.

My inferred refusal to give in to Doug's attempt at bullying forced him to jostle our sons farther apart. It was an uncomfortable moment for all three males.

"I had some very interesting conversations with my sons this weekend," he sputtered, "and I think you owe me an explanation."

"Dad..."

Doug wheeled around, grabbed Harper by the T-shirt, and shoved him toward the living room. Thatch hesitated before following his brother. Their gangly legs and soured attitudes took up the entire couch.

I moved to stand between my sons and their father, a wave of protective energy flowing up my spine and down my arms. "Doug. This is *my* house, and I'm saying this *once*—hands off and sit down. Or else."

"Or else what, Calliope?" he spat out. "Or else you'll call your boyfriend?"

Oh, so *that* was what had Doug's knickers in a twist: Tanner, and likely his offer to mentor the boys. And Doug's resistance to all things magically inclined as well as his litany of the missteps I'd made during our years together.

"Why are you here and what do you want?" I asked.

He stood wide-legged and crossed his arms over his chest. The pronounced paunch he'd developed in the final years of our marriage was gone. In its place was a more tapered waist, muscular arms, and a meanness in his attitude I hadn't seen before.

Or hadn't wanted to see.

"I am here to tell you there will be no magical training for Harper or Thatcher, by you or anyone else. Period."

"Dad, you have no—"

Doug glared at me before he turned his torso and addressed Harper, grinding his words between his teeth. "I. Am. Your. Father. I have every right, legal and otherwise, to act as I see fit. And I see fit to hustle your two sorry asses off this island and into a decent school system. Someplace where discipline and order mean something, so right now, you keep your ass on that couch and shut the fuck up."

Two teenaged jaws dropped open, and two sets of eyes went round as Doug punctuated every other word with a pointed finger wielded like a tool for punching holes. A red flush crept across both boys' faces.

Stunned into silence, I planted my knuckles on my hips and mentally thumbed through the spells I'd memorized, looking desperately for something that would blast Doug out of the room and off my property.

Before I could latch on to any one spell or hex or incantation, long pent-up words burst out of me. "Douglas Ingraham Flechette, this is my house and you will not speak to *any* of us that way."

My fury must have triggered…something, and my raised palm reinforced my resolve.

Doug flew backward, knocked the screen off its hinges, and tumbled to a landing at the bottom of the porch stairs. Tanner, who was walking toward the house, swerved around the heap of arms and legs and waved at me.

"Trouble?" he asked, stopping on the grass.

"Tanner, meet my ex," I replied, still shaking from the effect of whatever I had just unleashed. "Doug Flechette, Tanner Marechal."

Doug ignored the hand Tanner extended and stood, gathering his legs under him before he came to his full height of five-feet-ten-inches tall. The agent had a few inches on him and embodied a way of moving that broadcasted restrained power.

My ex appeared unbothered—or unawares—poured his weight into his back foot, and slugged Tanner in the midsection.

Tanner grunted, bowed into the blow, and shot out his left hand. He grabbed Doug by the neck, straightened them both, and pulled his opponent's face in close. Tanner held up his other hand in my direction.

Stunned, I watched as Tanner's back and shoulders undulated

under his short-sleeved shirt. Whatever was happening with his face had an effect on Doug. My ex went from raging to a quiet whimper. Tanner's body returned to its normal size, and he let go.

To his credit, Doug didn't back down. "What makes you think you can walk in here and interfere with my sons' lives?"

"They are smart young men, fully capable of making decisions regarding their education," Tanner answered. "I merely informed them they had options outside of public school."

"You're forgetting something. They are my sons—*mine!*" Doug yelled, spit flying. "And no other man can replace me."

I'd had enough of Doug's bottled-up anger years ago, and watching the two of them posture on my driveway was more than a newly anointed witch with a Priestess's crown and a wealth of untapped potential should have to bear. I turned the handle on the outdoor faucet, grabbed the end of the deck hose, and sprayed the back of Tanner's bare legs and the front of Doug's chest.

The look on my ex's face was priceless.

Tanner laughed and spun around, his face split by a broad grin.

"Perfect timing," he said, his turned back a dismissal to Doug. Tanner took the stairs in two steps, ruffled my hair as he passed, and muttered his intention to locate a towel.

I turned the faucet to off and dropped the spray nozzle and the hose. "Do you think you can be civil? Or am I going to have to insist you leave until you've cooled off?"

Doug plucked at the soaked front of his form-fitting T-shirt. The muscles in his face fought for dominance until a forced version of a polite smile won out over the ugliness seething underneath. "I'm leaving. I have a ferry reservation. But mark my words, Calliope, this is only the start."

"You at least going to say goodbye to Harper and Thatch?"

He glared at me over his shoulder and continued to march

down the driveway, making it a point to slam the door to his SUV and accentuate his departure with a squeal of tires.

Men.

Twelve hours ago—was it only twelve hours?—I was in a tent, asleep next to Busy, surrounded by trees and birdcalls and other witches. I heaved a bone-deep sigh. I was exhausted from the excursion, in a good way, and now I had to deal with Doug's shit. Again.

"Mom?" Thatcher's quiet voice teased its way into my tiredness. "Tanner's got us helping with dinner. Can I get you anything? Water? A beer?"

I turned and hugged my youngest son, a grateful heart rising and expanding in my chest. "I'd love a beer. And a snack. I'll take whatever you can find," I said. "Oh, and Thatch? I'm going to sit in the garden for just a bit. Your father—"

"I know, Mom. Dad can be an ass hat."

He waved me off and went back into the house. I stepped off the deck and followed the footpath around the house and down the slope to my garden. The motherwort appeared to be settling into its new home, spreading inquisitive roots and sending up stalks.

I settled onto the old chair and scratched at the tattoo.

Thatcher appeared with my beer and a bowl of cheese puffs. "You okay, Mom?"

He stretched out on the narrow strip of trimmed grass running between the aisle of raised beds and crossed his arms behind his head.

"I'm really good, sweetie." I popped a crunchy puff into my mouth and let it dissolve on my tongue. One day—probably later rather than sooner—I'd be comfortable with this swinging back and forth between the magical and the mundane. Until then, I would treasure moments like this. "I had a wonderful weekend. What about you?"

"Mm...Harp and I had a good conversation with Tanner on

Friday, when he took us to the ferry. And we should have listened to you when you gave us that whole 'don't tell your Dad' spiel because we did. We told him we have magic—or at least, it looks like we have magic—and he lost his shit, Mom. He also hit Harper."

My blood came close to a simmer. I suspected something like that had happened, but to hear Doug wasn't able to manage his anger around our sons...that was bad. "Did Harper hit him back?"

Thatcher rolled his head in the grass until he could look back at me. "He wanted to," he replied. "I could see that, but Harp's a lover, not a fighter." He pulled at the dried grass and let it flutter from his fingers. "It hurt though. Emotionally, not so much physically. It's fucked up, Mom. Dad's fucked up."

"Did all that happen Friday night?" I held the cold beer bottle to my face to cool my cheeks, took a long swallow, and then let the bottom of the bottle rest on the irritated section of my belly.

"Naw, we had a good time on Friday and most of Saturday. Dad's got this sweet condo in Vancouver, and he took us out for Chinese after we finished moving his stuff. They got in the fight this morning when Harper found an injured bird on Dad's balcony."

"Does the condo have a lot of glass?"

"A ton, Mom, and it wasn't the first bird to end up hurt. Dad said other ones crashed before and he just tossed them over the railing. Harper lost it."

I sipped at the beer. Both sons were tender-hearted. Toward four-footed and winged creatures and to each other and to me. I prodded Thatcher's shoulder with bared toes. "Then what happened?"

"Harper spilled. Told Dad about you and Tanner and what *he* does. I think Dad assumed you and Tanner were dating or something, and then he lost it."

"I'm sorry."

"Not your fault, Mom," he said, turning his head so he could look at me. "Want to know the good news?"

"Sure."

"The bird lived."

A series of piercing whistles ended our conversation.

"It's too beautiful to eat inside." Tanner yelled, gesturing to the deck. "Harper and I put everything out here."

A fter the four of us ate, I curled into a corner of the porch swing, nursing my second beer. My body continued to hum, hours after the ritual. I was very much in the processing stage and not quite ready to talk about it.

I had questions, though "Tanner, can the wards keep Doug out now? Because after that display, I really don't want him near me, the house, or the boys."

"Mom, we can handle ourselves," Harper insisted. "Tanner showed us how. And once we're in the program, there's going to be so much more we can do."

I took one last draw of my beer, placed the empty bottle on the deck, and eyed Tanner.

"Uh oh, I recognize that look. You're about to get your ass handed to you," warned Thatcher, waving his fork at the man in my sights. He wasn't doing a very good job of hiding his urge to laugh. Neither was Harper.

Tanner adopted an exaggerated look of innocence. "What'd I do?"

"Tanner Didier Marechal."

"Whoa! She used your middle name. Good luck, buddy," Harper teased.

I tried to stay serious. I appreciated Tanner wanting to step in and provide my sons with a magical education in addition to the one they received at the excellent high school on the island, but there were steps to gaining my trust. And he wasn't taking those steps in any kind of approved order.

Tanner's face had paled slightly. "How do you know my middle name?"

I shrugged. "It just came out. I don't think I knew it before I said it."

He swallowed. "I think the ritual worked, Calli. Naming's a latent skill, and it's not used lightly."

"Does that mean I can control you now?"

Why was I flirting with him? And why was I fluttering my hands in the air like a puppeteer?

"Yes. No. It's complicated."

Harper and Thatcher appeared to be enjoying this exchange.

"Let's leave that discussion for another time," I said. "My point is, before you go filling their heads with everything this mentoring program could be, I'd like you to fill *me* in." I looked at my sons and back to Tanner. "And tonight's as good a time as any, unless you two...?"

"Mom, no, we're good," Thatch assured me. "And I agree, you need to know. And then maybe you can tell us what *you* did this weekend."

Boys. I still wasn't giving them enough credit for how well they knew me. "Deal," I agreed. "Tanner?"

He folded his napkin and dropped it on the table. "The program was formed about ten, twelve years ago, in response to a growing need for teens and young adults to have a place they could go for answers to the changes happening in their bodies. For some, it was the very first time they had any kind of explanation for what they felt or perceived or could manifest.

"What we've discovered—actually, what's been confirmed—is that individuals with magic who *don't* have a strong family or tribal unit, or a coven, have a much harder time harnessing their magic when it begins to show up. The most challenging years appear to be between ages fourteen and twenty, twenty-one."

I waved my hand and interrupted. "As an aside, why do you think Harper and Thatcher's predilections didn't show up until now?"

"I'm going to make a stab in the dark and suggest it's due in part to their bonds with you. As you embrace more of your magic, theirs will grow stronger and more differentiated."

"That sounds pretty cool, Mom," said Thatch.

"And we've recruited adults across a variety of disciplines, for lack of a better word," Tanner added.

"You mean different branches of magic?" I asked.

"That, and from clans of shifters. We've set up a system of checks and balances, been attentive to the potential for abuse or manipulation of any kind."

"I'm pleased to hear that."

"And when something unusual or rare occurs, we have others around the world we can call on for consult."

Toward the end of Tanner's explanation, the itchy tattoo on my belly began to burn. I discretely pulled away the waistband of my pull-on pants to see if I'd gotten a bug bite or worse during my hours in the forest. All around the edges of the faded black ink, my skin was reddened, and the area was puffy, like I was having an allergic reaction. I touched it with my fingertips. The spot was hotter than the surrounding skin.

"Can you hand me some of that ice?" I pointed to the pitcher of mystery drink the boys had concocted.

Harper reached in and dried the cube on his tee shirt before handing to me. "What's up, Mom?"

"My tattoo, it's getting kind of itchy. Painful itchy."

"May I take a look?" Tanner asked.

I stood and rolled my pants to the widest part of my hips, lifted my shirt with one hand, and pressed the other to the soft part of my belly.

"Anybody got a flashlight handy?" Concern raised my voice a quarter of an octave. I was getting more uncomfortable by the minute. And staying self-conscious enough I kept trying to suck in my abdomen.

Tanner blew out a low whistle. "Othala," he said. "It's a rune."

Thatcher scooted the table holding the remains of our dinner out of his way and kneeled in front of me.

Harp joined us. "What's happening to our mom?"

Tanner cleared his throat and sat on the swing. He patted the cushion next to him. "Calli, I think you should lie down in case the pain gets worse. Harper, go get a washcloth and a bowl with clean pieces of ice. And Thatcher, if you could bring me my back-pack, I might have an ointment in there that'll help with the itching and the pain until we can deactivate the spell."

"This is a *spell*? What the f—" I flopped onto the cushions, my belly exposed to the trio of curious males, and stared up, way up, to the darkened beams at the top of the A-frame.

The night sky beyond wasn't as sparkle-filled as the remote provincial park, but it was beautiful. And calming. And right now, I needed to stay calm, because pathways in my brain sizzled at the implication that the tattoo my ex had insisted we get— together, designed by him—was actually a spell.

A fucking mystery of a spell, inked onto my body without my consent.

Tanner's comforting voice broke into my frustration. "Cal-liope, we can fix this. Runes are a kind of ancient alphabet and a means of divination." He gently folded the bottom of my shirt up and away from the affected area. "This particular rune has a few meanings, and depending on how it's placed, it can impact the bearer positively or negatively. Or the wearer, in your case."

"Tanner," I started.

"Yes, Calli?" he answered, his voice gentle as his fingers smoothed aloe vera gel over the reddened patches on my skin.

"Doug has the same tattoo. Except his is the opposite of mine."

He stopped spreading. His fingers hovered above the mark. "And where on his body is it?"

I pressed my lips together. I was beginning to feel like a fool. And an idiot. A gullible, foolish idiot. "Same place as mine but on his right side. His is a little smaller."

"I think this is a clear indication your ex-husband has access to magic, and right now, I'm most concerned with how to break whatever connection he may still have to you and *your* magic."

I tried to keep my breath steady and not freak out. Or beat myself up. I thought matching tattoos were an indication of... partnership? Of working toward a mutual goal? Love, even?

"Why now?" I mused, more to myself and the sky. My ex's gesture of bonding had become a modern-day, proprietary branding.

"I think it's obvious," Tanner replied. "You're coming into your powers at last, and that means you're going to be able to break free of whatever influence he, and this, have had on your life."

"I feel..." I whispered, again more to myself and the listening trees and stars than to any of the males gathered around me. "I feel violated."

CHAPTER 14

Tanner's touch became gentler. My sons backed away from staring at my belly and sat in the two chairs. I reached out an arm. Thatcher took my hand, held it in both of his, and Harper leaned closer and whispered, "We love you, Mom."

"I love you too." Tears formed under my eyelids, and my mouth watered at the same time. Six days of a heightened emphasis on magic, and I was ready to beg for normalcy. As my mind scrabbled for clues about how my *new* normal might manifest, the pain around the tattoo began to dissipate.

I fluttered my eyes open. Tears glistened along my lashes, and Tanner's hand hovered above the left side of my abdomen. His eyes were closed, and his lips were moving. As he chanted, the pain returned, gathered under his palm, and surged like a scab being ripped off tender skin. Searing pain hit me hard and fast, and I twisted on the hard cushion.

"Tanner, what are you doing?" I managed to get out the words without screaming.

"Removing the tattoo." He glanced up at me. "I really think this needs to come off. Now. Is that okay?"

I ground my teeth and nodded.

"Harper," Tanner said. "Get me a plastic bag, like a sandwich bag, something I can close up tight." He resumed the chant, his voice getting louder, the words tumbling into one long, desperate sing-song. Harper returned with a Ziploc bag.

"Open it," Tanner ordered.

I lifted my head, watching in disbelief as Tanner chanted the tattoo off my skin, onto his palm, and into the bag.

He pinched it closed and held it up to the feeble light shining through the screen door. "Gotcha."

"Guys, I'm bleeding." It wasn't a lot of blood, but the skin was raw and stung in the air and I needed something on the bare wound and fast.

"First aid kit?" Tanner asked.

"Cupboard above the fridge," I hissed between short breaths.

Tanner tucked the bag with the rune-scarred skin into a pocket of his backpack. "Thatcher, stay with your mother. Harper, get the kit. And scrub your hands. Calli, I have to wash up. Then we'll get you bandaged."

He stood quickly. Thatch sank to his knees beside the swing and let me squeeze his hand.

"Thanks, sweetie," I whispered. "It really hurts." The rest of my body began to react to the multiple layers of pain and betrayal uncovered by the removal of the tattoo. More quick breaths in and out through my mouth helped level the spikes of discomfort and keep more tears at bay. "Did your Dad ever make you two get tattoos or anything?"

"No," Thatcher assured me. "But Harper and I will do body checks tonight as soon as we get you fixed up."

"Maybe there's a way Tanner can check," I said, wincing. I tried to roll up to sitting, only to find the swing had started to spin. "I feel really woozy."

W hen I came to, I was lying on the couch in the living room. Thatch had pulled my favorite mid-century chair close and was staring at my face.

"Mom, how d'ya feel?" he asked, one hand resting lightly on my forearm.

I tried the head-lifting thing again. No spinning but a dull ache throbbed across the left side of my belly, into the bones of my pelvis and lower back.

"Better?" I answered. "But do you think I can have a couple ibuprofen or something?"

He nodded. "Be right back."

I patted the sore area. A wide, Telfa bandage crinkled under the slight pressure.

Calli.

I looked around the room. No one else appeared to have heard the voice. And this one was different from the one I'd heard here and in the orchard.

This one was masculine. And familiar. And this voice wasn't resonating up through the ground. It was coming from the woods ringing the back of the house.

CALLIOPE.

Heart thumping, I scrabbled off the couch and fumbled with the sliding doors to the back porch. The exterior lights were off and the wood under my feet and under my hand at the railing was damp in the night air. Closing my eyes, I tried to shut out the conversation inside the house and listen for the whispering.

Calliope, come here.

The voice was creepy, and nothing in me wanted to respond to the command.

"No," I hissed. "*No.*"

Wood splintered and cracked. A different voice, deeper in tone and louder, cursed as another tree, more to the left, rocked like it was having a spontaneous meeting with a sledgehammer and losing. The pain from the tattoo removal had burned like fire; this attack on my woods affected my bones and the timbered infrastructure that gave shape to my house.

What the—

Angry. Whatever was out there was becoming angrier, breaking branches, creating a ruckus outside the bordering line of brush and trees. I gripped the railing, sent my awareness into the ground, straight, like a taproot, followed by short bursts of green light—the wards.

The wards Tanner had placed along the curving circle of woods were keeping something from reaching the house and getting to me. And maybe to my sons.

I spun around too fast and went from standing at the rail to landing sideways on the swing, right onto my throbbing hip. Taking a deep breath, I heaved myself up and reached for the door as a tall silhouette appeared on the other side.

"Mom?" asked Harper. "What're you doing out here, we're…"

"Get Tanner," I urged. "Quick!" I plopped onto the cushioned seat and pressed my palm to the covered wound. "Shh!" I said when they came back, and motioned for them to be quiet. "Listen. Can you hear that?"

A creature—or a human—moved about in the woods. Tanner paused then repeated the same over-the-railing leap he'd performed the first night he was there. He was followed in quick succession by both Harper and Thatch.

I stifled my protest, felt along the wall for the switch to the floodlights, and flicked. Intense blue-white light bathed the backyard, prompting whatever was beyond the edge of the grassy area to let out a low growl. The hair on my body lifted at the sound. I clutched the railing and managed to croak out a garbled, "Boys!" before my vocal chords clamped down. None of them turned at my strangled cry.

Think, Calliope. Protect my house? My land? My sons?

The floodlight illuminated the backsides of my three defenders, all of them barefoot, in shorts and T-shirts, wielding no weapons other than intellect and bravado.

Tanner's shoulders and arms were doing that rippling thing I'd seen earlier in the evening when he'd had Doug by the throat. A trio of adult raccoons, tails fluffed and raised, chittered over to Thatcher and rounded their spines. Winged creatures, at least two, circled overhead, the translucent areas of their wings shimmering. I gripped the rail tighter.

Owls added strident, back-and-forth calls simultaneous to the arrival of Harper's bat friends. Wood snapping in my hands let me know I was squeezing the railing a little too hard.

I know what to do. Startled, I inhaled through my nose and began to chant.

"Ivy wind; Ivy bind. Ivy wind; Ivy bind..." Fighting like with like, I called to the invasive dog-strangling vine, the one preparing to overtake one section of my garden. I called to the barberry vines, armored with thorns, and to the pea shrub a well-meaning neighbor—in love with everything bearing yellow flowers—had planted, unawares it, too, was an invasive species.

I called to these non-native plants, asking they redeem their presence by finding and binding whatever stalked my children, my house, and my very body.

A slithering sounded beyond the reach of the porch light. Leaves fluttered, trees wavered, and the raccoons and bats stayed alert. Tanner's back continued to ripple, even as he leapt into the woods once a series of strangled screams and cries for help rang through the trees.

I let my arms hang at my sides and relaxed my legs. First Doug, then the tattoo, and now this, whatever this was.

"Dad? *Uncle Roger?*" Harper's voice registered the shock I knew he must have felt as he and Thatch rushed to help Tanner drag two vine-wrapped bodies from the woods. Even from the deck, I could see it was, indeed, Douglas Flechette and his twin brother Roger.

I wanted to laugh, a long, maniacal peal that would halt the current weather pattern dropping these unwanted visits from my ex at my door. Instead of laughing, maybe I'd ask Tanner to call in his cohorts and let them deal with the mess. I'd open another beer and watch the circus from the sidelines.

Before I could do either, swirling lights at the end of the driveway informed me the Royal Canadian Mounted Police had arrived.

"Not a moment too soon." Muttering under my breath, I paused at the front door to center myself before sauntering to the end of the drive. "Evening, officers. What can I help you with?"

"Good evening, Calliope. Sorry to disturb you, but we've received two calls about," Officer Jack scrolled through his cell phone and looked at me while he read, "a disturbance in the woods. Have you heard anything unusual this evening?"

I pressed my lips together and shook my head, slow and relaxed, like I really was considering their question. "No, nothing unusual. The owls have been a bit cantankerous lately and I think the mountain lion that hunts up our way might have gotten a deer, but other than that...no, nothing."

Lewis, the other officer, peered beyond the blinding light. It was an honest effort. The communication device he wore strapped to his shoulder crackled with an incoming missive from Gladys Pippin. At least, I assumed it was Gladys. She'd been the nighttime dispatcher, Sundays through Thursdays, for as long as I had lived on the island, and it was clear only death would get her out of her special chair.

"Got a call about drunk and naked hippies on Bader Beach again," Gladys said. "Probably a bunch of those WOOFer kids just arrived from Europe or the States."

"We're on our way." Lewis arched his eyebrows, tilted his head toward their car, and said, "C'mon, Jack, we gotta go."

Jack looked at me and smiled his sweet smile. I'd always liked him. He'd made it clear on a number of occasions he liked me too. "G'night, Calliope."

"G'night, Jack. And 'night, Lewis. Thanks for checking it out, guys. I'll keep my eyes and ears open." Detection diverted, I turned toward my house, my insides quaking.

As soon as the officers drove off in their white mini-SUV, I picked up the pace, hurrying around the house to the backyard and coming to a stop in front of a pile of bodies.

Two bodies, my ex's and his brother's. Lucky for everyone involved, these bodies were breathing. Even in the dark shadows cast by the flood light, I could see Doug's cheeks were puffy and red, with long welts crisscrossing his face and neck, arms and lower legs.

"Get. This. *Off* me," he sputtered.

"Sorry, Doug. I only know how to cast spells. My tutors haven't covered undoing spells," I admitted, more to Tanner than to either of the vine-bound men.

One of Thatcher's raccoon buddies was nibbling at the leaves and berries on his way to mounting Roger's chest. I was delighted to see how uncomfortable the man was under the poking and prodding of the animal's delicate paws.

Harper was visibly upset. I stepped closer and rested a hand on his shoulder. "Harp. Look at me. I want you to go into the house and let me and Tanner handle these two."

He shook his head hard, his hair sticking to his sweaty face. "Mom, something's going on, and I want to know. I'm eighteen. I can handle it."

I squeezed his shoulder and turned my attention to Thatcher. More raccoons, likely offspring of the mother he'd first befriended, had appeared and were clamoring for his attention. "Thatch?"

"What, Mom?"

"Do you want to stay, too?"

He dropped his gaze to his father and his uncle. The two men, still bound by the invasive vines I'd called upon, writhed on the ground. The vines had done their job and showed no sign of weakening. If anything, they appeared to be applying steady pressure on their victims. "I think Harp and I deserve to know."

"Tanner?" I said.

He nodded solemnly . "I'll work on them simultaneously. Do either of you have your phone handy?"

"I do," Harper volunteered, slipping it out of his back pocket.

"I'm about to work a reveal spell. On my say so, take pictures. The images may not show up, but it's worth a try."

My gut clenched, and the raw area under the bandage continued to throb. A moment of truth was coming, and though my bare feet were anchored solidly to my land, toes pushing aside the grass's stubborn roots in their search for soil, I still felt the rise of bile in my throat.

Tanner grabbed Doug by the shoulders of his shirt and dragged him next to Roger. I watched, fascinated and mildly terrified, as the vines wrapping my ex and his brother thickened in places and sent out tiny shoots in others, linking nearby sections in an approximation of fortified netting.

I stepped closer to Harper and slid my arm around his waist. "I'm sorry you have to witness this."

"I'll...we'll be okay, Mom. Sometimes the truth hurts."

"I know, sweetie, I know."

Harper stepped away and readied the phone on his camera. Tanner stood to the side of Doug's midsection and held out his hands, palms facing down. He closed his eyes and moved his lips. Whatever words he chanted were undistinguishable at first, until they became louder and more clearly enunciated. To my ears, it sounded like he was saying the same thing, over and over, in different languages: reveal.

I ripped my gaze from Tanner's face and stared at Doug and Roger.

Their fingers lengthened. Their skin smoothed, all traces of facial hair gone. They were barefoot when captured, and a similar transformation was happening on their feet.

What caused the most confusion was the change in their faces. It was subtle, remaining true enough to the visages I'd known since they were teenagers, but it was there. They were reversing the aging process and becoming more youthful, even as their ears flattened against their skulls and grew pointed tips at the top.

"What the…" I whispered.

The vines I recruited began to snap. Doug and Roger must have felt their bonds loosening, and Tanner appeared so involved with his spell casting he wasn't prepared for Doug's foot as it crashed into the side of his knee and sent him stumbling to his back.

"Tanner!" I rushed to his side.

Harper was furiously clicking away, and Thatcher stared, dumbfounded, as his father and uncle ripped at the vines and freed their legs.

Doug roared as he broke away, scattering leaves and bits of shredded stems. He ran toward the road, Roger on his heels. Tanner was moaning on the grass, his leg at an odd angle, and Thatcher had given chase after the others.

"Harper! Give me the phone and go get your brother. I don't want him anywhere near—"

A scream rent the air. "Dad—*stop!*"

I turned from Tanner and scrambled to my feet. My child was in pain or danger, and every maternal cell in my body hurtled me forward. I rounded the side of the house, my feet hitting the gravel without feeling the sharp edges of the stones, only to see Doug dragging Thatcher toward the road by one arm.

Tanner's knife was in my hands. No time to wonder how it got there. I aimed it at Doug's arm, pictured him releasing Thatcher, and unleashed an entire marriage's worth of fury at my ex.

Doug let go of Thatcher with an ear-piercing scream and pivoted to face me, blood splashing from the knife sticking out of his wrist. His severed hand was still holding Thatcher's arm as he reached the border of my land.

I grabbed the grotesque remnant of the man I'd shared a life with for over ten years and flung it in his direction.

Thatcher dropped to his knees.

"**M**om!" My eyes fluttered open. I rolled to my side and dry-heaved into the tire track next to my face. Sharp barbs of grass poked into my nose and against my cheek. I tried lifting my head higher; shaking fingers held my hair away from my face until I was finished. Both sons were on their knees, to either side, worry firing the lights in their eyes and the determination in the sets of their jaws.

"I'm okay," I croaked, planting my hands and lifting my head. "I'm okay. Help me up."

Thatcher's shoulder was bloody, and he cradled that arm tenderly with his other hand.

"Did Doug get away?" I asked.

"They both did," Harper said, spitting for emphasis, his eyes ablaze. "And we need to have someone look at Thatch's shoulder. I think Da—*Doug* almost pulled it out of the socket."

I turned to Thatcher. "You in pain?"

He nodded, made it to his feet. "You better check on Tanner, Mom. He was out cold."

"Harper, you come with me. Thatcher, make yourself an ice pack and call Kaz and Wes. Tanner's cell phone's probably in one of his pockets or his bag. See if any of them can come and help. Or if they know what we should do." I brushed off my bruised knees and held out my hand to Harper. "Let's go."

CHAPTER 15

Harper was able to assist Tanner up the porch steps, into the living room, and onto the couch. Tanner's face was paler, the brown of his skin a shade I'd never seen on him before. A large, splotchy, red contusion covered the side of the damaged leg. I palpated the area as gently as I could, relieved to see the skin was unbroken and the bones intact.

I hoped.

"Did you call Kaz?" he asked, his voice faint. "Wes is still at the other orchards."

Thatcher piped up from behind my shoulder. "He's coming."

"Good. Listen for him, please." I turned to Tanner and cupped his jaw, not liking the way his eyes were moving back and forth.

"Calli, I don't know what went wrong. I know that spell inside out and in a dozen languages, and whatever he did..." He sighed, wincing when he shrugged. "Whatever he did packed some punch. I should have known. I should have—"

I pressed my thumb to his lips, shook my head, and finally got him to focus on my face. The dazed and vulnerable look in his eyes softened a notch. "I was married to him, Tanner, and he fooled me for fifteen years. At least now we have a better idea of what we're up against. Wait. What *are* we up against?"

"Those two were disguised, probably by a glamour spell," Tanner said. "They're Fae."

I rocked back and sat on my heels. "*Fae?*"

Tanner closed his eyes and nodded.

"Do you think they're mixed up with what happened at the Pearmains?" I asked. Doug and Roger were the most competitive set of brothers I'd ever met. If they were in cahoots, whatever they were doing had to have some powerful reward at the end. As in money. Or land. Or both.

"Considering their strength and the fact that the orchardists have all been under strong spells, I think we *have* to consider that Doug's connected to the..." Tanner left his thought unfinished as Thatch returned with a bag of crushed ice.

"Mom," Thatcher whispered, as I wrapped a dishtowel around the plastic. "We need to see you upstairs."

I shoved a throw pillow under Tanner's injured knee, pressed the ice against his outer leg, and assured him I'd be back. Hustling up the stairs to Harper's room, I ran down the list of possible injuries and came up empty. Neither Doug nor Roger had touched Harper.

Thatch opened and closed the door and moved to stand in front of me, his hands on my upper arms and his chest blocking my view of the room. "Mom, you can't freak out, okay?"

When did my baby become such a tall, take-charge young man? And when did my baby get so good at calming *me* down?

"Thatch, sweetie? After the week I've had I don't think anything could freak me out."

"This might." He held me in place and turned his head.

Harper's eyes were wide and wet along the outer edges. He nodded, took hold of his T-shirt in the front, and pivoted.

"Help me out, Thatch?" he asked, his voice muffled underneath the cotton.

Thatcher released me and pulled the cloth away from Harper's back as he lifted it enough to expose his shoulders.

"What the hell are those?" My knees jellied, and my back slid down the door until my butt hit the floor.

Evenly-spaced bumps ran alongside Harper's spine. The largest were close to the vertebrae, and the vertical parallel lines grew less noticeable as they approached his sides and lower back. I wanted to believe it was a rash, a reaction to the stress of everything happening in our lives, but no rash I'd ever seen rose off the skin in such an organized and purposeful pattern.

Curiosity got the better of me. Harper flinched when I pressed one of the large bumps in the middle of his back. "Gentle, Mom. They kinda hurt."

"Thatcher, get me a light," I said.

A switch flicked, and a beam of white light hit Harper's back. Thatcher said, "Found my camping headlight. You want to wear it, Mom?"

"What I really need are my reading glasses." Fingertips tentative on my son's back, I paused while Thatcher slipped the wide elastic over my head and adjusted the light. Leaning closer, I sucked in a breath. "Sweetheart, these look like feather follicles."

"Feathers, Mom? Really? *Feathers?*"

"I could be wrong, I—"

"Fuck, I hope you're wrong, because...*feathers?*" Harper pulled the T-shirt all the way off and flung it to the floor. The pain in his eyes went right to my heart. "But Tanner said we weren't...I'm not— Does this mean I'm a...a *bird?*"

I shook my head. I wasn't a fan of lying to one's children to shield them from life's challenges, and I wasn't going to start now. But finding feather follicles on my eighteen-year-old's back was beyond my growing but still woefully limited body of magical knowledge.

"We need to show this to Tanner," I said, opening the bedroom door. A not-unfamiliar male voice had added itself to the conversation filtering out of the living room. "C'mon. Kaz's here too."

Harper pulled a flannel shirt off a hanger and gestured to the door. "Lead the way, Mom."

"Kaz, I have another patient for you," I said.

Kaz looked up from where he was sitting near Tanner. "Who?"

"Harper. Can you come take a look?"

We walked closer to the couch, and I motioned at Harper to turn around. Kaz stepped away from Tanner and gave a low whistle.

"Feathers," he said, shooting me a concerned look. "Haven't seen anything like this in a long time."

"But you have seen this before?"

He nodded.

"So why now?"

"It could be a stress reaction," said Tanner, piping in from his horizontal position on the couch. "It could be that Doug's been dampening Harper's abilities through some means and now that his glamour's been lifted, maybe the connection to his son is also loosened—or broken."

"Do they hurt, Harper?" Kaz had him lean over the dining table and scanned his back under the pendant light.

"They itch more than they hurt," Harper admitted.

"Are they only on your back? Did you see them anywhere else, or can you feel anything like this happening on other parts of your body?"

"No, just my back," he answered, his voice muffled by his folded arms.

"I'm going to put a little numbing cream on the bumps and see if we can get you some relief." Kaz opened his medical kit and placed a jar of ointment on the table. "You have any Q-tips, Calliope?"

"I'll get them for you," said Thatcher. He hustled to the downstairs bathroom and returned to hover near the head of the table, seemingly intent on finding ways to get his brother to laugh.

I left them to Kaz's care and turned my attention to Tanner. His face was a better color, and some of the stress lines across his forehead were less prominent.

"How're you?" I asked, sliding a raggedy multi-hued quilt over his bare leg.

"I suspect my knee's wrenched. There's too much swelling to really tell, but I should be okay until I can get an herbal poultice on it."

Shit. That reminded me Belle's bag of tinctures was sitting on my bureau. I had to take my first dose before bed. "No more leaping off my porch deck or chasing my exes through the woods for a while, okay?"

"Probably not until tomorrow morning, at the earliest," he replied, a pale twinkle lighting his tired golden eyes. The same twinkle had been there in the orchard, only much stronger. And if Tanner and I had been the only ones in the house at that moment, I might have kissed him. That's what stress did to me—made me want to kiss strange men.

"What're you thinking?" he asked, stroking my hand where it rested on the couch beside his hip.

"Nothing." I shook my head, clearing the memory of his mouth devouring mine and the way every element of the landscape around and under us had urged me on. "It's been a week for the history books."

"It's not over yet. You haven't said anything about the ritual." He rubbed his thumb over the top of my hand and slid his palm under mine, interlacing our fingers. "But start with filling me in on what's going on with Harper."

"Tanner, I—"

"Calliope." He squeezed my fingers and peered at me from under his lashes. "Something big is happening here, on this island. And it's affecting me and you and your sons and maybe even others like us. I don't want to leave you, and I can't go back to my office in Vancouver after what just happened with your ex." He pulled my forearm across his chest and drew me closer. "I can't pretend I didn't kiss you in the orchard. Damn near every hour, there's some new revelation or incident, and you're too close to—if not directly within—the center of it all."

I left my hand in his and turned away from the intensity of his gaze and the truth in his words. "Harper has feathers. Or what look like enlarged follicles, like what a chicken has after molting and the new feathers are starting to come in." I shrugged. "Not weird, not weird at all. Just another normal daily occurrence in the Jones household."

"Given his affinity to winged creatures, I'm not surprised," he said, his voice soft enough only I could hear. "I think you and your sons have been under Doug's influence for a very long time. For Harper and Thatch, possibly their entire lives. The coming days and weeks are going to be very interesting."

I wiggled my arm from underneath his and leaned away. "You think there're more interesting reveals on their way? Because if you tell me Thatch is going to start taking all his food to the stream to wash it before he eats and might grow a bushy tail and become even more nocturnal, I might lose it. Seriously, Tanner, what more could happen?"

"Nothing you can't handle, especially if you three stick together and allow help from those of us who are used to dealing with this kind of a thing."

Tanner's touch lit the fires of my erotic imagination while his words poked at my indignation. I neither needed nor wanted a man to try to take charge of things right now. Offer assistance? Sure. Take over? No way.

"Are we like your latest case studies?" I kept most of the sarcasm out of my voice. But not all.

"In a purely observational way, yes. But I can't look at you, or them," he said, tilting his head toward the trio at the table, "without it being very personal too. Wessel. Kaz. River. They've become family. There are fewer and fewer of us druids and witches and other Magicals, so when we find others, the tendency is embrace and enfold."

"Except when they're like Doug. And his brother."

"They seem the antithesis of the kind of magical beings Cliff and Abi have been protecting."

I nodded my head. We could agree on that point. "Those two are raising a field full of red flags. The boys were with Doug all weekend, and from what they told me, he appears to have no problems affording a new condo in Vancouver."

"Money's been an issue in the past?"

"Pfft, you have no idea." My attention had been divided between talking with Tanner and keeping an eye on Harper. Kaz straightened and started to step away. I noticed a beat of hesitation before he came over to the couch.

"May I join you?" he asked, pointing to a side chair. He turned to Tanner and lifted the ice pack to examine the injured knee. "How're you doing?"

"Knee's going to be fine," Tanner said. "It's these three I'm worried about."

"I've seen this before, in other teens who're straddling that cusp between puberty and adulthood. They've gone through all those hormonal changes within a relatively small window of time, and now their bodies are trying to settle into the next phase, kind of like they're figuring out who they are while being armed with all this terrific new equipment. That said, I've only seen this feathering phenomenon once before. Up on First Nations lands in the Northwest territories."

Tanner grabbed the back of the couch and shifted to sit up straighter. "I need to hear more. I've had a trip up there on the back burner. Maybe I should move it forward."

Kaz nodded and turned to me. "I think I know a good man for Harper to meet, but I have to speak with him first." He pinched the bridge of his nose and sighed. "I have to actually *find* him first, then speak with him. But this phenomenon is so rare, I think he'll be willing to at least talk with Harper."

"What do we do in the meantime?" I asked. "Can he start school? Is this a full moon-related phenomenon?"

Kaz rubbed his chin. "We just had the full moon, and you had your initiation ceremony, am I correct?"

I nodded.

"So, we have another month before the next one. I think Harper should go about his life, maybe keep his shirt on," he suggested, his smile kind and full of understanding. "I also think he needs to stay open and willing to being closely monitored."

"Hey. Guys. I'm right here." Harper came up on his elbows and pushed his way into sitting on the edge of the table, his wadded shirt pressed to his chest. "This is happening to me, so I'd appreciate being included. And Mom," he added, punching his arms through the sleeve holes. He winced and pulled the shirt off. "I can handle this. I just don't want Dad to come back here. Did you see how he tried to take Thatch away?"

I had temporarily misplaced that piece of the evening's excitement. I looked from Harper's set and settled face to Kaz's. "Kaz? What do you think we should do?"

"Operation Calliope's Fortress," he said without hesitation. "You've got Tanner here. He's weakened, but don't discount his abilities, especially once he's mobile again. If you've got coffee, I can stay the night, add to the wards."

"Can I do that with you?" Thatcher asked. He'd sidled closer as they spoke and was now bouncing on his toes expectantly as he looked back and forth between me and Kaz.

"It's fine with me," I said. "But if there's any hint, even the *tiniest*, that Doug or Roger or anyone else from that side of the family is back, I want you in the house, okay? No heroics."

Thatch nodded and tapped his brother's thigh. "What about you, Harp?"

"I want to call Leilani, see how she's doing." He winced as he gripped the edge of the table. "Y'know, Mom, she's eighteen too. Should she be here?"

I had no idea, but I was already strategizing how to talk to Leilani's fathers about her potential and their plans for furthering her magical education. "Talk to her, see how's she's doing. No one's leaving the property tonight, so no sneaking out. If she's scared, or…"

"Dad knows about her. At least let me warn her." Harper slid off the table, shook Kaz's hand, and let him know he'd be upstairs.

I watched him walk away, shoulders drawn and the skin on his back a splotchy canvas in shades of red and pink. Doug knowing about Leilani could complicate things.

Kaz broke my train of thought. "Thatcher, if you're going to help me add to the wards, we need to get your arm in a sling. Come here."

"**M**om? Where are you?" came Harper's voice.

I poked my head out of my office. I had relinquished my bedroom to Tanner and unfolded the futon in my office to use as my temporary bed.

Harper's feet landed heavily on the last couple of stairs. He'd donned an oversized flannel shirt and left it unbuttoned. "Lei-li's freaking out. And Mal and Jim aren't home."

"Would you both feel better if she was here with you, with us?" I was on my knees, struggling to make a tight corner with a top sheet. The futon was winning.

"One-hundred percent better."

The concern playing across Harper's face sealed the deal. "Let's ask Kaz to pick her up."

He nodded, worry and relief scudding across his face like clouds over the water on a windy day. "And Mom, is it okay if she stays in my room with me? We won't... I mean, we don't..." He pressed the heels of his palms against his eyes. "Fuck."

"Shh, it's okay. Right now, we all need to feel safe. And I trust you and Leilani." I rolled onto my feet and nudged him into the hallway. "And if there's anything either of you need, don't be shy about asking."

My oldest son, the one who'd broken my heart open at the moment of his birth, blushed and drew me in for a hug. "Thanks, Mom, for understanding. And for being amazing. I love you."

While Kaz fetched Leilani, I changed the sheets on my bed for Tanner and left a quilt and a pillow in the living room for the evening's designated triage nurse and chauffeur.

"Remember to put out towels for Lei-li," I called up the staircase.

I was desperate for sleep, but houseguests deserved clean bedding and their own towels, and if the amount of thumping was any indication, Harper was turbo-cleaning his room in anticipation of his special guest.

He called back, "Got it, Mom."

My special guest was talking on his cell phone in the living room. I pantomimed him walking down the hall and sleeping in my bedroom. He nodded and mouthed a thank you.

Bed. Sleep. I ducked into the refuge of my office, rested my upper back against the closed door, and visualized sliding between crisp cotton sheets and seeing this day finally end.

Dammit. The tinctures were waiting, unopened, in their pretty lavender bag in the downstairs bathroom.

I reread the instructions, dropped the recommended dosage into a small glass of water, and drank it down. The smell of Kaz's coffee meandered down the hall and tried to tease my brain into waking up, but my body wisely overruled the temptation.

When I closed my eyes and sank my head into the blessedly soft pillow, sleep came fast.

Mornings arrived early during the height of summer, and by four-thirty or five on Monday, light streamed through my office's uncurtained windows. I lay on my back, covered to my breasts by a white cotton sheet, and contemplated rising before anyone else.

Stretching my arms and legs, I opted to stay in my makeshift bed. My toes found the cool surface of the wall underneath the window, and my fingertips curled around the legs of the old farmer's table I had turned into a sturdy desk. Underneath, a board laid over the foot rest served as a shelf for my rickety wooden flower press and a stack of cigar boxes and photo albums. At one time, before I started high school, I'd wanted to be a botanist. The oldest album held preserved plant matter and my earliest sketches. A few of my mother's sketches were in there too. She and I would sit side by side and make detailed renderings of the flowers I dissected.

I scooted onto my belly and extracted the album from the pile, along with a few well-thumbed books. Piling the stack beside the bed, I imagined the bodies congregating under my roof would be better served if I familiarized myself with my new skills. Speaking Tanner's middle name without knowing it beforehand then causing my ex to fly out the door simply because I raised my voice—and my arm—were two things that would not have happened prior to the ritual.

But I wanted a mug of tea first.

In the living room, Kazimir slept on his side on the couch, a pillow over his head. The coffee carafe was cleaned and upside down on the dish drainer. I lit the flame on the stove and filled the kettle from the tap, careful to flip the cap up so its whistle wouldn't wake the house. Mornings had a sacred quality to them, and I wanted to sip my tea in silence.

And solitude.

I let a pot of Assam steep four minutes and tiptoed a mug of sweet, creamy tea to my office. Settling in cross-legged, the warmth from the mug spreading into my lap, I leaned against the tongue-and-groove paneling and breathed into a scan of my house. Watchful stillness flowed along the floorboards and up, down and across the supporting beams. When I floated my inquiry beyond the shingled roof, there was a lack of anxiety in the air and the surrounding woods.

The wards were holding. They were strong, complex, and palpable without making me feel claustrophobic or imprisoned.

Soothed by the pervading sense of calm, I drew my awareness into the room and under the lightweight cotton of my night-gown, to my skin. I paused. Breathed. Sipped at my tea, placed the mug on the windowsill, and resumed my earlier position on my back.

Limbs akimbo, I returned to those hours I'd spent encircled by ancient, sacred Sitka Spruce. I replayed the walk to the grove, the way the deliberate placing of my feet had expanded my awareness and opened my eyes, ears, and nose. I replayed the gifts the witches offered—the symbolic gestures, the spoken words, the very act of their participation. I wanted to know more about the meaning of each headpiece, and as I dove deeper into my memories, they were overlaid with someone else's.

For one, elongated moment, love flowed toward me, and I knew it was my mother's love, stored away in a place beyond the present, gifted so I would never again need to wonder.

I snapped into the present and stifled a sob. Reaching for one of my mother's spell books, I opened the cover to read the familiar dedication written in her delicate hand.

For my Calliope.

CHAPTER 16

Pressing the aged paper to my lips, I kissed the ink. The tears rolling down my cheeks dampened the page, and where they landed, more words appeared in faint brownish ink.

My heart thudded against my ribcage, grabbed onto curved bones, and threatened to hammer its way out. I moved the book away from my face, afraid I would smudge or forever lose one of the few examples of my mother's handwriting I possessed. I caught a teardrop on my fingertip and trailed it through the spaces between the words.

The salty wetness illuminated more missing letters.

Nurture your Garden
Know your Roots
Watch for the White-Winged Man
Beware the ...
... Water's Edge

I wet my tongue and pressed the tip against the missing words. The page remained blank, the paper thicker than the surrounding area, as though a section had been replaced with a patch. I scraped the edge of my fingernail after the word beware until a scrap smaller than the nail on my pinkie peeled away.

My instincts were right; whatever word or words had come after had been cut away.

"Mom," I whispered. "I miss you." My mouth and chin wobbled when I tried to blow on the damp paper. I used the bedsheet to wipe my face and left the book open to dry, weighted on either side with other books.

I forced myself to finish my room-temperature drink. And for a moment, I was back in the bare-bones kitchen of my mother's grandparents' cottage on the coast of Maine, drinking a luke-warm tisane from blue-speckled enamel mugs. Outside the window, a field of pale pink and lavender lupins swayed in the breeze coming off the ocean.

At the sound of a soft knock at my door, the memory was gone as quickly as it came, sucked back to wherever it was stored.

"Come in," I said, my voice cracking.

"Calli?" Leilani's hand gripped the edge of the door. She opened it enough to stick her head into the room. "Can I talk to you?"

I waved her in. "There's a pot of tea in the kitchen," I whis-pered. "It's not hot anymore, but if you want, you could warm it on the stove."

"I'd like that. I'll be right back." Leilani glanced at my empty mug. "Would you like some too?"

"With cream and sugar, please."

I'm not sure where I went while I waited for Leilani. "Garden" and "Roots" made sense—I was an earth witch and all I had to do was look out the window at the back yard, garden, and the old crabapple tree to know I had an affinity for plants. But the White-Winged Man, the water's edge, and the warning...my mind blanked.

I was just pulling my nightgown over my knees when Leilani returned with two mugs in her hands.

"Come. Sit down," I said, patting the bed coverings. Lei-li's bright nature always coaxed a smile out of me. "How are you doing?"

Her light brown hair had blond highlights, and I couldn't resist pushing a loose strand away from her flushed cheek and tucking it behind her ear.

She shot me a shy smile. "I have so many feelings right now, Calli. Figuring out my connection to baking and cooking and how that works, talking with your friends—with you. It all makes sense, in a weird but comforting way. I want to trust that whatever is happening is what's supposed to happen. Do you know what I mean?"

I nodded. "I agree it's weird. And I agree it all feels exactly... right. Well, except for the things I don't understand." I sipped at the tea, grateful for its caffeinated warmth even as heated summer air wavered at the open window before sliding into the room. "Is there magic in your family, beyond your fathers'?"

"I have an aunt named Busy. We've always called her Busy Bee because she's a beekeeper, and she loves..."

"I met her this weekend," I said, squeezing her forearm. How serendipitous. "She's incredibly sweet. And she's *definitely* a witch."

Leilani's face wavered from delight to concern, with two deep lines appearing between her eyebrows. "How come she never told me?"

"I have no idea. Which of your fathers is she related to?"

"Busy is James's sister. Mal is an only child. Like me." Leilani dropped her gaze to her lap and her straightened legs and then circled her ankles.

After two cups of tea, I was ready to use the bathroom and face the start of a new week. "I see no reason why you can't approach your aunt and let her know we've met and that your baking has some very special, some would say magical, qualities to it."

Lei-li smiled and giggled. "I'll call her today. She lives on Vancouver Island, in the Comox Valley. It's good farmland, and she's in charge of lots of bees."

"Please tell her I say hello."

"I will."

We stood. Leilani gave me a quick hug.

"I'll wash these," she said, taking both our mugs, "and make some muffins. If that's okay?"

How could I say no to those big, brown, hopeful eyes? "My kitchen is your kitchen."

She left, and my chest deflated. I wanted to deny it was the morning after a very intense night, ignore the fact I had a job to show up to, and spend the day thumbing through my mother's books, looking for other bits of her writing I might have missed.

But I did the adult thing: mixed my second dose of tinctures, showered, and tiptoed across the hall to get clothes for work.

The door to my bedroom wasn't latched, and Tanner's back was to me. Getting clean underwear and a T-shirt from my chest of drawers and onto my body went smoothly. I pulled on a laundered pair of cargo pants and reached for the bag of melted ice that had slipped off the bed. Rabbit-sized dust bunnies huddled in the dark below the bedsprings, just beyond my reach.

Ugh.

PMS had been my monthly motivator behind cleaning the house, and because I hadn't bled for two months, my house was suffering. I could ask the witches if there was a motivational spell for household help.

Resolving to do better, I rose to my knees and came face to face with the glory of Tanner's morning light-lit brown skin and a partial tattoo.

Fanning over his lower back, inked in sepia, was the rounded top of a tree. I held my breath, pinched the edge of the sheet, and peered closer at the exposed V of his sacrum. Scattered amongst the tree's outermost branches were small, seed-shaped lumps.

Whitish in color and uniform in size, they resembled the bumps on Harper's back.

"That you, Calli?"

Startled, I covered his butt and stood quickly. "How's your knee?"

Tanner rolled onto his back. He slept naked. *Of course. He's a Druid.*

And the sheet covering him hid nothing, absolutely nothing.

Not his lean belly, the long muscles of his thighs, or his semi-erection. The pouch he never removed rested right below his sternum, and for the first time I noticed the cord that kept it on his body looped around the back of his neck *and* his ribs.

He bent the knee closest to me and winced. I stopped staring at his body long enough to drop my clothes and the empty plastic bag and place my hands around his injury.

"Still painful?" Through the sheet, I could feel the heat generated by muscle tissue repairing itself. I sent an image of cool water flowing from my palms, penetrating underneath his skin and circling through the knee joint.

"Mm..." He turned his head to face me, eyes half open, and tugged the sheet higher. "That feels nice."

"Let me get you a fresh ice pack. I'll be right back." Lifting my hands, I noticed my palms were bright pink and warmer than usual. I showed them to him. "You've got a lot going on under that sheet."

My cheeks went as heated as my hands.

At least my patient laughed. "Calli, I'm going to pretend I didn't hear that."

In the blessedly neutral space of my kitchen, Leilani was peeking into the oven. She'd wound a printed cotton scarf around her head and was humming.

"Smells good in here! What kind of muffins are you baking?"

"Oatmeal, bran, walnuts, and raspberries from the canes in

your garden," she said, beaming. "They need another couple of minutes."

I refilled the emptied Ziploc bag with ice, grabbed a worn linen dish towel, and gestured to the hallway. "I'm bringing this to Tanner. Save us at least two or three, would you?"

"There's enough for everyone to have three." Leilani lowered her voice. "I'll hide a few. I know how much Thatch likes my baking. Harper always snitches extra for him when he's at my house."

"There should be enough eggs for breakfast. Make a list if you think of anything I should pick up in town."

Her eyes went wide. "Am I staying here all day?"

"I'm about to discuss that with Tanner," I said, ducking into the hall. "Once everyone's awake, we'll see what he and Kaz think."

Tanner was flat on his back, knee bent and eyes closed, squeezing and massaging the thigh muscles of his damaged leg.

"I've got your ice," I said, lifting the bundle.

He extended his leg until it was straight and adjusted the sheet over his pelvis. "What I really need is Rose. Or River. He could bring over whatever she suggests, but I think they're both at the lake."

"Did you call them?" I handed him the ice and reached across his torso for the summer-weight blanket on the other side of the bed. Covering him was an act of mercy for me.

He shook his head as I fussed over the blanket and then the pillows. "Phone's run out of charge. You have to go into the office today?" he asked. I nodded. "Could I trouble you to stay with me for a few minutes?"

"Of course. Leilani's getting some breakfast together for everyone, and…"

He shimmied away from the edge of the bed.

"Sit," he said, patting the area beside his hip. "The other day, driving home, remember when we went to the place that sold plants?"

I nodded. Keeping my hands off anything more than Tanner's knee required willpower. I anchored my gaze on his face and folded my hands in my lap.

"And as we left, there was that car you recognized, the one from a realtor's office, with the name of the woman who left her card at the Pearmains?"

"Yes."

"I think we should have a talk with her." He put his hand on my leg. "And how are you?"

"I am *so* many different things right now, Tanner, my head may explode."

Fuck it. I gave in to my need to touch his skin and traced the length of one of his fingers and another. Was there any part of him that wasn't beautifully proportioned? "We should also talk about the Pearmains and the tunnels and the trolls. They've gotten pushed to the side, with me being away over the weekend. And Doug and Roger showing up."

He turned his hand palm up and interlaced his fingers one by one with mine. "You in any pain from where I removed the tattoo?"

"It's not bothering me. But I haven't looked at it since you ripped it off and bandaged me up." I stared at the pattern made by our twined fingers. I couldn't stop myself from imagining the pattern of color and texture if our limbs were similarly wrapped around the other's. Emotions I'd held in check for days swirled up my legs and arms, making them shake. "I don't suppose you know a spell for stopping time so I can take a breath or five and absorb all this...change?"

Tanner curled up to sitting. The leather pouch swung away from his sternum. "You're the one who'll be doling out the spells, Calliope. There's more I want to tell you—"

A banging at the door interrupted whatever he was trying to say.

"Mom," said Harper. "We need you."

"Coming." I lifted my gaze from the bed to Tanner's face, and before I checked the impulse or even checked in with him, I kissed him full on, slipping my tongue under his top lip to draw it more fully into my mouth.

I could have devoured Tanner Marechal as easily as I downed a pint of seasonal berries. And if his hand at the back of my head holding me in place was any indication of his feelings, he could have eaten a box as well.

The kiss lasted less than five seconds. I pulled away and started to apologize, but Tanner bit my lower lip and grinned.

"That was nice," he whispered. "And if there's any more Assam, I would love a mug."

I swatted his arm and grinned right back.

"I can make it to the living room by myself," he added. "Go see what the guys need. And let Kaz know I'll be out when I'm done icing my swollen..." He shrugged and gestured to the lower half of his body. "Knee."

Thatch was waiting at the kitchen table, his cell phone in his hand, a stack of plates and a platter of muffins by his elbow. Harper and Leilani were seated on the bench, heads together whispering to one another, and Kaz was on the back porch, stretching and yawning.

"Dad called," Thatcher stuttered out. "He wants us to go see him in the hospital."

"Did you actually speak to him?"

He shook his head. "He left me a message. He sounded...apologetic."

Ugh. I threaded my fingers through my hair and pressed my palms into my temples.

"And Mom, Harper and I were supposed to be at work at the farm at eight. I called to let them know we probably won't be in today, but we can't miss tomorrow. There's a shit ton of stuff to harvest and rinse for the Tuesday Market. They need us to help with set up and take down too."

I agreed they couldn't miss more work. Their summer jobs at one of the biggest organic farms on the island brought them needed income, and they loved everything about working with the family that ran the operation.

"There must be something Tanner and Kaz can do to keep you guys safe. Or safer," I said. "Let's ask." I didn't add that as long as Doug was in the hospital—assuming that a severed hand warranted a stay of at the least a couple of days—I thought we might have a little more leeway with travelling off our protected property.

Kaz and Tanner entered the kitchen and dining area at the same time. "River's on his way with herbs for your knee," Kaz informed Tanner, gesturing for him to sit.

"And a piece of Rose's mind?" Tanner said.

Kaz grinned and tossed the agent a throw pillow. "I'd imagine."

Tanner limped to the table and adjusted the chair to rest his heel on the bench. I was relieved he'd been able to get himself dressed.

"You still want that tea?" I asked, trying to keep a straight face.

"I'll make a fresh pot," said Kaz, first affirming it was okay with me. "Thatch, can you help me make scrambled eggs for everyone?"

Watching their interactions from the hall gave me a moment to get my bearings. What had happened to the mundane rhythm of my days, those ones that consisted of inspecting orchards, trading bits of gossip with Kerry at the office, and keeping a loose track of my sons' comings and goings?

One shoulder to the wall, I cupped the left side of my lower belly. The raw area remained swollen and tender, as palpable as the anger rising inside—anger at my ex for further distancing me from my legacy; anger at myself for allowing it in the first place; anger that my sons and Leilani and I now had to go through our days living with an unfamiliar and uninvited level of fear.

I puffed out a quick exhale and dropped the urge to castigate myself. Or tried to. People who wanted to teach and support me and my sons had shown up, and it was better to embrace their assistance and move forward than get stuck in the past. And that saying—knowledge is power—was so true. Doug had taken my power; Rose and Tanner and others were offering me the knowledge that would help me take my power back.

Thatcher placed a large platter of scrambled eggs at the center of the table.

I joined everyone gathering for breakfast and directed my first comment to my youngest. "Thatch, I think it would be prudent to respond to your father but to not make any promises until we know what magic he has and what he's up to."

He nodded, his face solemn.

"And Leilani," I continued, "I'd really like to speak to your fathers. Soon. Whatever it is that's going on could affect you too, simply because you're connected to Harper."

Another solemn teenage face nodded at me.

I didn't really like this new role, She Who Sets Limits. "I have an investigation going on, and it's linked to something Tanner's been looking into for months now. School doesn't start for another five weeks, and I think this is a perfect time for all of us," I looked at each of my sons, and Leilani, "to take our training seriously and to start today."

Three faces went from hesitant to excited.

"Tanner. Kaz." I brought the two druids into our family circle. "We need help. All three of these kids have summer jobs, and they can't miss work tomorrow. Plus, my ex texted Thatcher and said he wants to see both him and Harper. Have you ever heard of the... What was the name of the clinic, Thatch?"

"The Grand St. Kitts."

Tanner gave a low whistle. "That's a private clinic for Magicals."

I threw up my hands. "Harper, go get me a thumb drive. Please. And give it to Tanner."

"What? Why?"

"So he can plug it into his head and download everything he knows about the magical sector in our area so I can stop feeling like I have a lifetime of catching up to do."

The two teens looked at each other and made that weird face, the one that says Mom is off her rocker.

"I'm kidding." I turned to the adult males, who looked almost as perplexed. "What can we do to protect these three?"

"I can stay here today with Kaz," Tanner offered, "and get us started on making amulets. I'll heal faster if I'm in direct contact with the ground, and I've been eyeing that garden chair of yours." He swung his injured leg around, stood, and gripped the back of the chair tightly. "Oh, and by the way, Calliope," he said, bending forward and pointing at the back of his head. "There should be a USB port in there somewhere."

CHAPTER 17

After breakfast, I drove into town without any sense of being followed. I was ridiculously relieved to be in my work domain, even with Kerry's heightened concern as she swiped a handful of papers off her desk and followed me to my office.

"I'm not going to sugar coat this, boss," Kerry said. "There's something weird going on with the apple growers on this island."

"But they're usually such a mild-mannered bunch. Did you get the information I was looking for?"

Kerry simultaneously nodded and shook her head. "Yes and no. Most of the orchards rely on the same four to eight popular varieties. About half the growers have their top-tier specialties, which they must have divvied up ages ago." She placed a stack of print outs on my desk and pointed to the one on top. "And while all of this is public knowledge, more or less, getting these guys to give up the goods on what else they're growing is like..." She smirked. "It's basically an impossible task. Unless you're willing to show up at their property with a warrant. Or spy."

"Did you get the topographical maps?" I neatened the edges of the stack of papers and tucked them into an accordion folder.

"I was just printing those out. I had to grab a new set of ink cartridges for the printer." She turned to leave. "Anything else?"

"Keep your eyes opened wide and your ears glued to the grapevine," I said. "And call me anytime. I'm going to drop in on Abi and Cliff. I'll also share this with Agent Marechal and see what he has to say."

"Ooh, any of his cohorts coming in again?"

"I think they might all be spoken for, but I'll see if he has any other dashing single men under his supervision."

"You do that, Calliope. It's in the fine print of my job description."

I chuckled. Kerry and I didn't socialize outside of the office, but she showed up, stayed late when needed, and occasionally updated me on the island's social undercurrents. Keeping her happy was a priority.

"Oh, and another thing," she said, pivoting around her desk and artfully tucking her skirt under the backs of her thighs. "Two other growers said they'd gotten substantial offers on their properties this past month. I marked their locations on your topo map."

As I was reversing out of the parking slot, my cell phone rang. Tanner. I put him on speaker and pulled onto the road, heading in the direction of the southern section of the island.

"I started looking into your ex-husband's family's business," he said without greeting. "Did you know it's been around since the late eighteen-hundreds?"

"I did. They're quite proud of their longevity. I met a lot of his relatives over the years he and I were together. They weren't much into retiring out of the business. Doug and his brother were always tight, but Roger's wife never liked me," I added. "I never liked her much either."

"Is she a realtor?"

"Yes, and it definitely was not her in that SUV. Her name's not

Adelaide, and the woman I saw had dark hair. My ex-sister-in-law is a dedicated bleached blond. And I need to go, but I'll call if anything interesting comes up."

Shit. I forgot to tell Tanner about the other offers on the orchards, and trying to locate the memo app on my phone while negotiating the curvy section of road was a no-no. I stuck my phone down the front of my shirt, nestled between my breasts, and let that be enough of a reminder to text Tanner from the Pearmains'. He could make the calls today, and we could visit the orchards tomorrow.

I looped my bag across my body as I exited my car. The comforting buzz of bugs and a distant lawnmower gave the Pearmain property a sense of life it had been missing a few days ago. I knocked on the frame of the screen door and was greeted by the tang of fresh-picked lavender and melted honey and a short, shadowed form. Abigail's face lightened as she shuffled across the wood floor to the door, and her smile soothed some of the lingering worry from my chest. It was so good to see Abi upright.

"Been expecting you," she said, pushing the door open and stepping to the side. "Cliff's visiting with his trees. Go on out through the back and yell if you can't find him. I'm stirring up a new batch of soap, or I'd offer to sit a spell. We'll have lemonade when you come back up."

This was the Abigail I was familiar with: hospitable to a point and always with something going on in the kitchen. "Thanks, Abi. I'll see you in a bit."

The newer plantings were situated opposite from where Tanner and I had come across the trees with the tunnels. I ventured on to the wider, straighter path, newly mowed to either side and wide enough to accommodate a truck. I found Clifford checking tubular mesh cages protecting the saplings' slender trunks.

"Mornin', Calliope," he called, waving.

"It's almost noon, Cliff," I answered, smiling back. "What's going on over there?" I pointed past this section of the orchard to a gently sloping hill where evenly-spaced posts marched along four rows of bare soil. Mulch was mounded in low rows in between.

"We're planning to try something new," he said. "The two grandsons I spoke about been readin' up on ways to plant more trees per acre. It's called the tall spindle method."

I knew other orchardists were using the method, most with success. It was a wise choice for those with smaller acreages. "Will you be able to maintain your organic grower status?"

"Oh, for sure." He finished refolding the ends of the mesh and pocketed his wire snippers. "And we'll look forward to having you here to inspect us."

"I have no doubt you'll pass." I waited for him to put his hand tools in the ancient canvas bag he carried. "Cliff, if you're ready, I'd like to talk about the hidden folk."

"I suppose it's time." He sighed and studied his hands, his whole upper body seeming to sag under the weight of my request. "I don't remember when I saw my first garden troll, but it must have been when I was a little kid."

"Can you tell me how you came to be in possession of those two heads?" I led us to a weathered slab bench. Cliff joined me with an audible huff, dropping his bag onto the grass at his feet.

"My knees," he explained. "They don't bend so well." He rubbed at his worn khaki pants and cupped a set of arthritic fingers over each knee. A long sigh escaped from the depths of his chest. "I came into possession of this orchard about two hundred years ago." The look on my face prompted the old man to pretend punch my shoulder. "Surprised ya, didn't I?"

"Two hundred years. That explains the wrinkles," I shot back.

"Like your Tanner, I trained as a druid, Miss Calliope. I've lived a long time. But then I met Abigail." He rubbed his knees again and lifted his chin, his gaze flickering over the vulnerable young trees. "Eventually I told her what I was, and although she wanted to join me on the path, she could not withstand the rigors of training. So, I made a decision. I'd had a long enough life, and it occurred to me the best way to honor my love for Abigail was to age with her." He looked over at me suddenly. "We're doing everything we can to make it to one hundred, but we have a pact that if one of us goes, the other will follow."

"That's quite a story, Cliff."

He nodded. "This orchard will be in good hands. Our grandsons know what to expect."

"You're talking about more than what it takes to grow apples, aren't you?"

Cliff nodded. "We sent the boys off to train as druids when they turned eighteen. They're in their thirties now, but I imagine they'll look a good ten years younger. And stay that way as long as they can." He winked at me and rubbed his knees. "All of this will be theirs: the enchanted trees, the tunnels, the burial mounds. And they will share it with the trolls and other hidden folk."

"Burial mounds?" I asked.

Cliff stood slowly. His knees popped and he gripped my shoulder until he stood tall.

"Come on," he said. "I'll show you. They're in the oldest part of the orchard." While we made our way along the path, Cliff continued to speak of the garden trolls. "They never came all the way to the house, least not in my memory, and I was always too tall to follow them into the tunnels. They could cover themselves —glamour, it's called—and work undetected by the neighbors and other curious folk who'd stumble onto the property."

We were in the dry season, so most of the grasses growing around the trees were tan and crunched underfoot. The few apple trees within view were branch-bound, with inedible fruit, but off to the left, between the orchard and ridge of fir trees that followed the shape of the rising mountain, were a series of burial mounds. At least three of them were ringed with local boulders and looked like those made by First Nations peoples.

Two low, conical mounds stood out. They were covered with grass, and the grass was green and well-tended.

"I found the bodies tossed some distance from the heads, but I didn't tell my wife. I felt it would put too much sorrow into Abigail's heart, and I didn't know if she could withstand it. So I came out here myself and buried them in that one," said Cliff, gesturing to the closest conical mound. "They were given full rites and sent off with prayers."

"May I bring Tanner here?" I asked. The solemnly quiet air wasn't inviting further discussion.

"Of course. Any time. No need to ask first."

I took one more long look around before pulling out my phone. "May I take a couple of pictures?"

"You can, but the mounds won't show up," he said. "You're here with me, and I've made them visible to you, but they're invisible to modern technology and the uninitiated."

I tucked my phone back into my bag and took hold of Cliff's elbow. "Thank you for protecting this place."

Cliff gazed at the mounds for a minute longer, made a series of gestures with his hands, and shuffled his feet in a box-like step.

"We can go now." He turned and led me out of the sacred area and along a path that cut through the 'happy humming' ground. The closer we got to the house, the more the air filled with the scent of Abigail's soap.

Clifford stopped us at the bottom of the porch stairs.

"Calliope, there's one more thing." He pulled a blue-bordered handkerchief from one of his pockets, lined up the corners of the fine cloth, and blew his nose. "I used to be diligent about keeping up the protective wards on this property, and I am sorry to admit I've been remiss in my duties—to this land and the hidden folk who've helped us keep the trees safe. I feel…" He lifted his head, and I couldn't tell if his eyes were seeing the land and sky around him or if they were looking back to some other time. "I feel horrible. If I hadn't been derelict in my duties, those dear souls might still be alive." He blew his nose once more and re-pocketed the wadded up square of fabric. "And now I have to live with the consequences of my neglect. If you could ask Tanner and River to come back as soon as they are available, I could use their help fortifying the old wards."

"I will do that, Cliff, and I'm willing to bet at least one of them will be here first thing tomorrow."

After leaving Cliff and Abi, the call of an old roadside cemetery was too strong to drive by without stopping. A wrought-iron railing defined a roughly square plot, and the stones were uniformly splotched with lichen and moss. I pulled over, intent on meandering until I could find words to honor the murdered hidden folk.

For whatever reason, I assumed stones as old as these would be neglected; they weren't. Many were adorned with necklaces of small white shells or garlands of wild flowers and tiny roses. Smoothed rocks, fist-sized or smaller, sat at the base of a few headstones, stick-in-the-ground vases for flowers and votive candles near others. When I'd last stopped at this plot in June, a riot of lilacs had perfumed the air.

Even with the walk through the old cemetery, I returned to my house with a heaviness in my heart. Mourning was both solitary and communal, and Cliff and Abi deserved to have support. They had carried the secret of the Pearmain ancestors long enough. I promised myself I would reach out to them once things at the Jones house had settled down.

Tanner and Kaz had been busy. Bright neon pink and orange surveyors' ribbons fluttered from some of the trees ringing the house. Evenly spaced at five feet apart, more or less, they were close enough that one person standing between two adjacent trees could touch both.

"What's with the decorations?" I asked, pausing at the base of the porch stairs. A table had been set up for what looked like Magical Craft Hour, and my fingers itched to join in.

"Kaz is teaching us to carve runes," said Harper, holding up a slab of wood the length of a dinner knife and about the width of his palm. "We'll attach these wherever he put a marker."

"But Tanner and I will be the ones to activate them," Kaz piped up from the shed underneath the deck.

"And Aunt Busy called. She's so excited that I'm a witch, Mrs. Jo—Calliope." Leilani was beaming. "She's going to visit soon, like maybe tomorrow. And she's bringing ingredients for one of her special spells too. Enough for all of us."

"That's very generous of her, Lei-li. I'd like to see her again," I added. "She shared her tent at the ritual and took very good care of me afterward."

My phone buzzed. The gynecologist's office. "Rowan, hi."

I ran up the steps, dropped my bag on the counter, and slipped into my office for privacy.

"Calliope, I have more good news for you," she said. "You're free of STDs, and the blood test confirms absolutely you are not pregnant."

I plopped onto my old oak desk chair and spun in a half circle. "That's a relief. I was going to call you and let you know I went through my first ritual last weekend. Rose says I am officially in my Priestess stage. I have a pretty crown to show for it, and one of these days, I hope to have a deeper understanding of what this all means"

Rowan let out a modest squeal. "Congratulations and welcome to the Witchy Women's Club! You'll be in a coven before you know it and taking workshops every weekend. Did Rose talk to you about using herbs to get your menstrual cycle back on track?"

"Belle has me on drops of black cohosh, blue cohosh, and one more I don't remember."

"Good. Those are exactly what I would have prescribed. Also, try to stay out of stressful situations."

I couldn't stop the guffaw that flew out of my mouth. "Oh, my Goddess, Rowan, you have no idea what it's been like around here." I stopped spinning and leaned back in the chair. The wheels squeaked in protest, reminding me of Cliff's knees. And the fact that I had news for Tanner. Lots of news. "And speaking of stress, I've got to go."

"Calli, wait."

I closed my eyes, wished I could just give the guys movie money, ask Rowan over for a glass of wine, and have a girl's night on the back deck.

"Let me know when you get your period," she said. "There's something I'd like to do for you, for your Blood Ceremony."

Blood Ceremony. The inevitability of the next step to my magical initiations hit my belly like I'd swallowed a tub of my aunt's tomato aspic. My womb dropped deeper into the bowl of my pelvis, all saturated and heavy.

"Okay," I answered, "but I have a feeling that once I start to bleed and Rose gets the news, it's going to be all hands on deck."

I hung up with Rowan and scanned the familiar shapes of the furniture and knick-knacks in my office, seeing but not seeing. I had to tell Tanner about my conversation with Cliff while I could still string words together.

Curiosity must have tugged at his shirttails. I answered the knock at my door and waved him in.

"How's it going with the amulets and wards and whatever other crafty projects you guys are doing?" I didn't mean to sound flippant, but I was tired. And hungry. And wobbly on my feet.

"Leilani, Harper, and Thatcher have been given temporary protective amulets. I'm sure they'll show them off. And I spoke with Malvyn. He okayed our plan and has offered his and Jim's help."

I nodded my approval. "I'm curious to meet them. I don't know that I've ever met a sorcerer before."

Tanner looked around my office. I was sitting in the only chair, and my futon bed was a tumble of sheets and a blanket.

"They tend to cluster in the financial sector. And auction houses." He gestured to my sleeping spot. "Mind if I join you?"

"Here, you take the chair." I pushed my pillow and blanket against the far wall, and propped myself up. Any more horizontal and I'd fall asleep mid-sentence.

"Thatcher heard from Doug again."

Crap.

Tanner continued. "I think he sees your youngest as the more malleable of the two. He's lobbying hard for Thatch to visit him in Vancouver. And threatening to pull him from school here and enroll him in a private academy in the city."

I covered my face with my hands. "Let me set that news aside for a moment and fill you in on a couple other things." I scrubbed at my eyes and stood. "Would you mind following me to the kitchen? If I don't eat, I won't be held responsible for what comes out of my mouth."

"Like this morning?" Tanner teased, pulling me in close to his chest. "I liked what came out of your mouth when you kissed me."

Oh, God. I tried to bury my forehead inside his shirt, but it stayed buttoned.

"Calli, it's okay. It was a really nice kiss." He slid his hand over my forehead and pressed me away enough we could see each other's eyes. "And it was really nice to kiss you when neither of us was under the influence of the trees or…"

"Or her." I finished the sentence for him. I had been thinking the same thing, first of all questioning if kissing Tanner was solely my desire and if him kissing me back was solely his. I joked, "Kissing was never this complicated before."

"Want to kiss again?" he asked, adding just enough heat to the question that his golden sparks started to go off like flash bulbs.

"I can't believe I'm saying this …" My voice trailed off as I watched the light bounce across his irises. "But I need food."

CHAPTER 18

One half of a fully loaded veggie burger later and I was ready to bring Tanner up to speed on my day. "Okay, first of all, Kerry has it straight from the farmers' mouths that two other orchard owners have received offers on their properties."

"Are these orchards for sale?"

"No. I'll do a follow up tomorrow and get a description of the realtor and find out if they left a card." I lowered my voice. Harper, Leilani, and Thatch were outside with Kaz, but I didn't want them to know about the hidden folk and the frozen heads. "After I stopped at my office, I went to see Cliff. He told me he found the bodies and buried them. And he happened to mention he's a druid too."

"I had my suspicions," said Tanner. "But he's let himself age."

I nodded and chewed and waited to continue until I'd swallowed. "He made a pact with Abigail. They fell in love, he wanted her to train with him, but I guess she's always been frail. They're both in their eighties, and when one goes, the other will too."

He nodded and reached for the slice of pickle on my plate. "I knew another druidic pair who chose that route. It's not common. Did he share anything else?"

"He buried the bodies in one of the mounds on his property. And he wants you and River and anyone else you can gather to pay him a visit and help him strengthen the wards around the orchard. He's dealing with a heavy load of guilt right now."

"We'll go over tomorrow, whether my knee's up for it or not. Do you think you could find the burial mounds again?"

"I'm not sure." I really wasn't. Each time I visited the Pearmain orchards, more magic revealed itself. "Cliff told me he keeps them cloaked, but if you're going over there, have him show you." I added, "I really think he could use a fellow druid to talk to."

M y eyelids refused to open when confronted by Tuesday's overly bright sunrise. Nature was, on occasion, way too perky in the mornings. Fumbling for my phone, I was grateful to see I'd managed three hours' sleep. And while the sting of the exposed skin left by the removal of the old tattoo had lessened, my entire lower belly was out of sorts. I couldn't bear to touch or take pressure on the left side, so I rolled to my right, shoved a pillow between my thighs, and made a stab at falling back to sleep.

Ugh. Doug. The last person I wanted to be thinking about. Divorce papers should be accompanied by a spell. A spell of Unbinding I could alter at will, depending on how much of a jerk he'd been or how behind he was on the child support payments I was now convinced he could easily afford—he wasn't nice enough to sleep his way into owning a condo in a brand-new building in Vancouver.

Or maybe he'd slapped a tattoo on some other unsuspecting person and finagled an upgrade to his housing situation.

Double ugh. Sleep was probably gone for the day.

I reached for my spell book, the one I'd cried on the day

before, and hugged it to my chest. Palm to the book's cool surface, I closed my eyes, shoved thoughts of Doug and revenge out of my head, and willed myself to picture my long-lost mother. I searched for memories, any memory, in the haze of exhaustion coating my bones.

The rough surface of barnacled rocks snugged against my palms. Long hair floated around my face and shoulders and down my back, strands shifting across skin with every ebbing and flowing movement of gentle waves. I released air bubbles from between my lips, turned my head, and spied my mother.

Genevieve nodded, smiled, and blew out answering bubbles in a slow-moving, aquatic kiss. Her body undulated and rolled, her hair similarly unfettered and floating like the long strands of kelp attached to nearby rocks.

My little-girl body was clothed in the bottom half of my favorite two-piece suit, the candy-striped one with the ruffle at my skinny hips. My mother had also shed the top half of her bikini, and I giggled, eyes closed, at the feel of warm salt water and seaweed on my skin. When I reopened my eyes, it was in time to watch my mother's feet and legs disappearing into the deep green waters below where'd we'd been playing. A large, dark flipper waved in time to her kicks.

I released my hold on the rock and floated to the surface.

The bedding was soggy, and my face was wet with tears when I woke again closer to eight. The corner of the book left a red-edged dent underneath one of my collarbones, and my lower belly was suffering through slow waves of cramps. When I pulled the pillow from between my thighs, it was streaked with pale, reddish-brown blood. I flung it behind me and pulled the sheet over my head.

Fuck. Rose was the last person I wanted to see today.

I ignored the tapping at the door and whispered the wish to be left alone. An invisibility spell was beyond my knowledge, but I could always hope whoever wanted me would just go away.

A gentle tug at the sheet was followed by a warm, familiar hand on my shoulder. "Calli, are you awake?"

"No," I answered, my voice muffled by cotton stuffing.

The side of the futon sank. I rolled slightly with the weight of a body determined to take away my covers.

"I know you're awake," Tanner said, "and I know you started to bleed."

I ran my hand over my hip and around one side of my butt in an attempt to tuck my nightgown closer without getting blood on it. "I'm hiding."

"Would you like a cup of coffee?"

I shook my head, pouting. "I want tea."

"Be right back."

Before I could plot an escape route out the window and to… to where, I had no idea, Tanner returned, accompanied by the pungent aroma of a strong batch of Assam. The warm washcloth he put into my hand after setting a mug on my desk broke my stoicism. "Thank you".

He nodded. "Take your time, but when you're ready, you have to call Rose."

"I know."

"There's a towel on your desk," he said, tilting his head to the right. "Harper and Tanner took the Jeep to work, and they'll be back this evening, right after they're done at the market. James is coming to pick up Leilani. As soon as he does, Kaz and I will head over to help Cliff.

"I'll be in touch later." He patted my hip, stood from the crouch, and left, closing the door behind him.

I rolled onto my belly and pressed the warm washcloth to my forehead. Feeling slightly less petulant, I called Rose to give her my good news.

"We'll do the ceremony tonight," she informed me. "I'll text you the location. No, I'll have Belle pick you up. Around nine."

No. No, no, no. "Wait, Rose, tonight is too soon. There's an investigation I'm conducting as part of my job, and there's been some trouble here at my house." I took a deep breath through my nose, let it out slowly. "I have to make sure my kids are safe. Tanner and Kazimir are helping."

Rose took her time responding. "I understand there are times when family comes first, Calliope. And another twenty-four hours does give me more time to extend an invitation to witches who live farther away." Her voice trailed off before she came back and took charge of my calendar with renewed vigor. "Tomorrow night, then. August first. Which is also Lughnasadh..."

Rose disappeared again; all I heard was distant breathing and the shuffle of papers.

"Lugh what?" I asked, hoping to call her back and settle on a plan so I could get myself to the bathroom before I bled through to the futon covering.

"I keep forgetting how much you don't know," Rose harrumphed. "Lughnasadh is one of our eight sabbats. We bring together covens and other practitioners of magic who have a kinship to the festival. We'll just be a little more seat-of-the-pants and prepare for holding your Blood Ceremony first, and once you're in the Mother Tree, we'll continue with the scheduled celebration." She sucked in a sharp breath. "Unless you hear otherwise, Belle will escort you to the ritual ground."

"Is there anything I should do to prepare?" How was I supposed to prepare to be "in a tree"?

"No baths while you're bleeding, only showers. And do not use tampons, only pads." She continued as though reading from a printed list of instructions. "Tomorrow morning, do not eat after breakfast. You may have water and herbal teas only, nothing with stimulants. Wash your hair and oil your skin. Prepare yourself as though you were going on an important date. Try not to get angry or upset, and most of all, rest. It's going to be another long night, and you'll manage better with the after effects if you're rested when we begin."

That didn't sound scary.

"Thank you, Rose," I said, knowing the witch on the other end had hung up. Rose was beginning to remind me of my aunt. I'd make it through today and tomorrow and let Belle nurture me on the drive to wherever the ceremony would take place. I texted Rowan to give her the good news, had more of the tea, and strategized how I was going to get to my bathroom without leaving a bloody trail.

C leaned up and flushed out, with a pad tucked into my underwear and garbed in a flowy, ankle-length cotton dress, I made my grand appearance in the kitchen.

No one was there. I served myself a bowl of sliced pineapple, bananas, and grapefruit, sprinkled shredded coconut on top, and headed to my garden.

If it weren't for the solace offered by an old chair under my butt, warmed soil underfoot, and strong sun already warming my scalp, I wasn't sure I could settle myself enough to be ready for whatever lay ahead, let alone be an open and willing participant.

Waving a persistent honey bee away from the fruit, I spooned another bite into my mouth, delighting in the contrast between cool and juicy on my tongue and the dry breeze feathering over my bared arms. I found it strange to be bleeding again. I'd only skipped two, maybe three cycles, and I had to admit I missed the familiar weightiness in my body and the physical and mental clarity that would come a few days after.

The vines I had called on to trap Doug and Roger broke through my musing, reaching out for affirmation and guidance. I offered the mental image of a flexible fence marking off a space around their invasive stalks, and asked that they confine their activity to a few small spots on the property. Their natural propensity for rapid propagation made it a hard vow to keep, but I gave them tacit permission to assist with future trespassers and thanked the vines again for answering my call. That seemed to cool their roots.

And it was time to go to work.

Kerry was probably wondering what all had gotten into me. I hadn't left her much to do, and she was prone to adding her opinions to any gossip passing through the office. All the men traipsing through the office were giving her plenty of fodder, and I couldn't fault her wanting to self-entertain. Certifying farmers wasn't the most exciting work on the island. For now, ongoing projects and rounds of reviewing applications would have to keep her busy.

I was so tempted to stay home and putter in my garden. My plants and I, and the surrounding trees and undergrowth, were deepening a relationship initiated over thirty years ago. This feeling—that we had just started to settle into reminiscing about the past and making plans for the future—was a hard pleasure to set to the side.

The darkly patterned fabric of my dress absorbed and held the summer sun; the heat soothed my crampy belly and warmed my inner thighs. I dropped the empty bowl onto the bed of chamomile for the bees to explore and gave my mind over to a short replay of the times Tanner and I had kissed.

I could do that again.

And again. I scrubbed the heels of both palms down the sides of my belly and pressed into my thighs. The action plumped my breasts, and through half-closed eyes I could imagine my hands were Tanner's.

Only, his would be broader. And warmer. And he would take his time sliding my dress up my legs.

Arousal kept me hanging on the rise of an inhale and a shudder and a crack from the ground underneath the chair dropped me into fear on the exhale. I looked straight up to see the branches of the crabapple trembling. Tiny, early fruits swayed like baubles on a jeweler's display, and a voice rose from somewhere beyond the edge of the woods.

Mine.

She was here. And I was alone. I gripped the splintery arms of the old chair and pulled myself out of my heat-soaked slouch, feet on the ground and sun splotches blurring my vision.

MINE.

Whatever Kaz and Tanner had worked into the slabs of rune-carved wood made the wards light up. A curtain of shimmering slivers of green and silver wavered from the ground up to the topmost sections of the fir, oak, and arbutus trees that circled the perimeter of the house.

I straightened my legs, not knowing if I should hightail it inside or holler at whoever was out there.

Two steps later, a new sensation rose up the backs of my knees, an invitation to be lifted up and carried on a broad set of shoulders, high off the ground, and I heard young Calliope giggling, felt rough fur gripped in my hands. I rode the memory through one breath, and another, and steadied my feet when the wards flickered off high alert.

I scrabbled to the porch stairs and into my kitchen without falling or bruising any body parts. I even had the wherewithal to pull my phone off the charging stand before I crumpled to the floor.

"Working from home," I texted Kerry. "Call or text if you need me."

"Will do," she answered. "Dead as doornails here."

I crawled to the bathroom and changed my soaked pad. My office, with the cozy futon and a stack of old books, was right across the hall. I could nap, or I could do what I told Kerry I was doing and work.

The phone vibrated against my breasts. Tanner.

"Are you okay?" He was huffing.

"I am now," I answered.

"She was there, wasn't she?"

Oh, shit.

"Calliope?"

"I'm here." I paused. "And yes, I think she was here. Someone —something—was here, and when it said 'mine' it sounded a lot like the same presence saying 'mine' when I was in the tunnel that first time."

Tanner's huffing slowed down. "I think she's found a portal to your property."

"A portal?" This was news to me. "Can you give me a crash course on portals?"

"An object—often a specific tree or rock or even something manmade—becomes a means of transport between two places, and these places can be near one another, they can be a continent apart. They can even cross dimensions..."

"Tanner. Stop. That's too much information. Keep the lecture local, and one of these days, I'll be ready for the global picture. But today is not that day, so..."

"Got it." I heard him suck in air through his nose and chuff it out through his mouth. "You first heard the voice in the tunnel, at the Pearmains', and that's also where we were forced into kissing, so I'm assuming there's at least one portal in the orchard."

I pinched my forehead and lowered my chin. "Actually, the first time I heard the voice was here, Thursday morning. But it was laughter, just laughter. She didn't actually say anything."

Tanner choked on whatever words were trying to exit his mouth first and took in an audible breath through his nose. And another. "I was at your house Thursday morning, and you didn't think to tell me you'd heard a *voice*?"

I was slack-jawed and stuck at Tanner expressing our first kiss was forced, and he was getting hung up on reconstructing a timeline. "At the time, it didn't seem related to the investigation."

"Calliope, what if she's trying to eliminate you on her way to me?"

"Okay, okay. So how do I identify a possible portal on my property?"

"Don't even think about looking for it until I'm there," he said. "Calliope? Did you hear me?"

"I take it you know how to drive those things?" He laughed. Finally. Serious Tanner was one step away from Bossy Tanner, and I wasn't in the mood.

I was getting fed up with his old girlfriend trying to trim my branches.

"Yes, Calliope," he said. "I know how to drive between portals, though it's not called driving. Can you keep your curiosity contained until we're done here and I can join you?"

I nodded, knowing he couldn't see but willing to be obedient. "I've got another project I can work on. I promise I'll stay out of the woods."

"I'd feel even better if you'd promise to stay in the house."

"I promise to stay in the house."

"And one more thing. If you hear the voice again, call me."

I stared up at the edge of the kitchen counter. Where I was seated on the floor, I was blocked from being seen by anyone looking in the doors or windows. Which also meant I couldn't see anyone *at* the doors or windows.

I scrambled to my knees, plugged my phone back in the charging stand, and plopped down. The crumb-covered floor seemed the safest place to be.

Bear fur. Big fish. Herb plants, berry canes, and invasive vines —these were my allies, and though I couldn't remember ever having ridden on the shoulders of an actual bear, I knew I was in the ocean the same time my mother had swum past me and into the deep, hand in hand with a man sporting flippers.

Real flippers, not the detachable kind.

I shook my head. No one would believe me. Well, actually, I'd recently met a number of people who would—might?—believe me. I felt for the Telfa pad on my lower belly and picked at the

Band-Aid doing a half-assed job of protecting the cut on my thumb.

I had to do something.

I came out of my crouch slowly, circling, scanning the rooms and the areas outside of the windows and doors. Everything looked normal. The wards were off high alert. Cars and trucks passed by just as they did every week day, and I knew if I listened hard, I'd hear prop planes buzzing overhead on their way to the harbor.

Sliding my feet along the floor, I turned the lock above the handle on the front door and continued on, closing and locking every window and door on the ground floor. I kept repeating, *This is my house; this is my house,* and after I extracted my new crown from the jumble of things I hadn't unpacked from the weekend, I owned the words the next time they issued from my mouth.

This. Is. My. House.

I giggled and wedged the crown more securely atop my head. Forty-one years old and still playing dress-up.

Bear fur. Big fish. The trunk with my mother's things was in my office. I kneeled in front of the dusty thing, lifted the top section of the latch and the lid, and surveyed the contents before I pawed through them.

There! I parted two stacks of pinned-together quilting squares and felt for my mother's Witchling sash, the one I'd seen her wearing proudly in photographs displayed on my aunt's mantle. I smoothed the faded fabric, straightened the rows of round, enameled pins, and brought the entire thing into the kitchen.

I snapped a photograph so I wouldn't forget the order in which the pins were arranged; I had no idea if it made a difference or not. I didn't know if the Witchling Way still even existed; my aunt had signed me up for the human counterpart, the Canadian Girl Guides. But the once-colorful pins were grimy, and I wanted to wash and polish them and imagine my mother's pride as she worked toward collecting as many as possible.

Because the sash was so filled with round reminders of magical milestones, I decided my mother would have been the accomplishing kind—maybe even a little competitive—and she would have placed each pin onto her sash very, very carefully.

There were creatures on the buttons, along with trees, leaves, and flowers; esoteric symbols; and tools of the magic trade.

Three pins kept rolling away from my cleaning operation: a bear, a seal, and an apple.

I dried the pins, stashed them in an empty sweetgrass basket, and placed the basket and the sash in the trunk. The three errant buttons stayed in my palm until I placed them on the altar in my bedroom, next to the branchlet from the old crabapple tree. I slipped the crown off my head and placed it on the altar with my new wand and the three pins inside its circumference.

What was I doing? I glanced at what little I could see of my reflection in the mercury glass mirror. Its usefulness had ended decades ago, but my aunt and my mother and maybe other female relatives, other witches in my lineage, had searched its oxidized surface for signs of their own hidden beauties or latent skills.

Pressing my palm to the cool glass, I whispered the words again: *This is my house* and then added, *And I am yours.*

CHAPTER 19

A car pulled into the driveway, fast, splattering gravel. I made it to the end of the hallway as Tanner peered in the front door and jiggled the handle.

"I'm here," I called, waving. "I'm here." I flicked the lock and pulled the door open. The screen door that had taken the brunt of Doug's flight was leaning against the side of the house.

"I can fix that," he said, giving the splintered frame a glance before stepping over the threshold. "Are you okay?"

"Yes. Very." I took a couple steps back, my at-home dress swirling around my lower legs.

Tanner was suddenly next to me, wrapping one of his hands around the back of my neck and clutching me against him.

"I was worried about you," he said, his words muffled by my hair.

He kissed the side of my head, his thumb rubbing the back of my skull.

"I locked the house tight, even the windows." Barefooted, I closed my eyes and rooted down, and down further, searching for her presence.

"I was still worried."

Nothing. I opened my eyes, caught the green light of the reinforced wards draped like emerald-dusted netting over the trees.

"I don't feel her below, Tanner, but the wards. They're shimmering again."

"Those are the new wards settling in with the old ones," he said. "I threw them a little test on the way in."

Tanner wore a faded cowboy-style shirt, the kind with snaps for closures. The fabric was so soft it barely provided coverage between his chest and my cheek. I hadn't moved closer on purpose; Tanner's hand was the likely culprit. He was still cupping my head, massaging me with his thumb, and whether I was aware of it or not, I had taken it as an invitation.

"The lights are beautiful," I said, letting my curves find their resting places along his more angular planes. I liked that Tanner wasn't overly muscled, at least when he was being regular Tanner, not extremely angry or irritated Tanner.

"I could kiss you right now." *The wards are up. The boys won't be home until close to seven.*

"Then do it," Tanner murmured. "Kiss me, Calliope."

All I had to do was pivot on the balls of my toes and lift my heels.

Tires on gravel and the thump-thump of loud music behind closed windows alerted us another car was pulling into the driveway. I planted a kiss on Tanner's mouth, and he held me in place until every possible inch of our bodies that could touch…touched.

"That wasn't what I had in mind," he said.

"Me, either." I lowered my heels to the floor.

Tanner slipped by me and headed down the hall. I stepped out to greet my sons.

"Cool wards, Mom," Thatcher yelled.

Harper and Thatch were standing to either side of the Jeep, extracting whatever goodies they'd picked up from working at the farm and helping out at the market. They each hefted a box, slammed the Jeep's doors shut, and tromped up the stairs, leaving little rectangular clumps of dirt in their wake.

I didn't have to remind them to leave the boots and boxes on the deck and hose down whatever they'd hauled home. They were on it.

"Not the pies!" Thatch laughed. He handed over two familiar white boxes with red lettering. One oozed fruit juice along a bottom seam. "Sallie gave us a broken blueberry pie. And we bought a strawberry rhubarb."

I took care of getting the dessert into the house. Tanner had seated himself on the couch, with his leather bag nearby and his laptop open on the low table.

Thatch paused at the bottom of the stairs. "Sallie's having a rough time, Mom."

"Did she say anything specific to you?"

"Yes. And no. She really wants to move out of her house."

I felt the request coming and shook my head. "No. There's too much going on to invite her to live with us, Thatch. I hope you didn't—"

"I didn't, Mom, but I wanted to." He lifted his arm in my direction. A new bracelet looped his wrist. "See what she made for us? She's trying to see if she can afford to live on her own so she's experimenting with making stuff to sell. Harper has one too."

Crouching down, I held his wrist and thumbed the braid until I'd seen the entire circle once, then twice.

"Did she make this on you, or did you pick it out randomly?" I asked, curious as to how Sallie had hidden the ends of the cording.

"She made one for each of us and tied them on while we waited." He pulled his wrist away and flicked at the braid. "Hm. She really hid the ends, didn't she?"

"Did you and Harper talk to her at all about what's been happening?"

"Nope. Sallie's cool, Mom, but she's not in our circle of trust."
He shrugged. "Got a towel for these veggies?"

I ducked into the closet and handed out a stack of worn dish-
towels. "Did she talk at all about why she wants to move out?"

Thatch shook his head and twisted the new bracelet around
and around his wrist. "Not everybody gets a mom like you. Or a
brother like Harp."

Tuesday night was blessedly calm, and Wednesday was
almost boring. After a full six hours, I left the GIAC's office
early to give myself time to prep for the great unknown of the
coming ritual. I ended up in my garden, watering, weeding, and
enjoying the calm before whatever was coming next.

Rounding the side of my house, I hung up the garden hose
and took off my gardening gloves. An unfamiliar car slowed at
the end of the driveway. When the driver rolled down the
passenger side window and tooted the horn, there was no
mistaking the beaming face behind the oversized sunglasses.

"Rowan!" I yelled, waving my gloves and picking up my pace.

Rowan pulled over and turned on her blinker. "Can I come in
for a visit? I'm kind of curious to see the before-ceremony
Calliope so I can compare her with the after-ceremony
Calliope."

I laughed. "Park your car and come inside. I have to dash, or
I'm going to flood right here."

The first floor of the house was empty, but deep voices
rumbled from one of the boys' rooms as I passed by the stairs on
my way to the bathroom. Given that tonight was such a big night
for me, I kind of expected the guys to be making dinner, if not
seeing to my every need.

I ducked into my room, hoping to find the cluster of necklaces the witches had given me at my first ritual on my bureau.
Or maybe my underwear drawer. I wanted to show them to

Rowan and get her opinion on whether to wear them to my Blood Ceremony. And maybe even get her opinion on Tanner.

Ugh. I hated forgetting where I put things. And this kissing business between me and Tanner wasn't cutting it. We were unattached adults. We also carried so much relationship baggage we could have used one of those wheeled luggage racks to help haul it all around.

I needed to stop thinking about Tanner and sex in the same breath. Maybe that werecougar was still available.

No. No, no, no.

My stomach rumbled. The fruit I had at breakfast was not getting me through this day, which only added to my woes. I found a clean pad, soaped up a washcloth, and forgave myself for being out of sorts.

Rowan must have read my body language as I dragged myself down the hall. She patted my cheeks and pulled a wrapped package out of her bag.

"This is for you," she said, taking me into a quick, hard hug that crushed the paper package between our chests. "It's for your special night." She pulled another package out of the bag and undid its twisty tie. "This is also for you. Hibiscus flowers. For tea."

"You read my mind," I said, grateful one of us was thinking ahead.

"How's your belly?"

"Ugh. Feels like my organs are battling. Remind me why I missed this?"

She shooed me toward the living room. "Go. Take a load off. I'll bring this over when it's ready."

I rearranged the pillows on the couch and plopped myself down. The pink tissue paper wrapping called to be crinkled and pinched. I answered the call and stared at Rowan as she poured water over the hibiscus flowers and stepped back to admire the color of the steeping petals. I toyed with the pink-and-silver bow, considered repurposing it for my hair. One of my fingers poked through the paper, and as sure as night follows day, a torrent of feelings made random stabbing motions at my heart.

I wanted to cry. My love of the color pink had been leeched out of me when I was a little girl. Pink—and orange and turquoise and anything flowery or bright in my clothes and accessories—had slipped away after I lost my mother. My aunt's drab outlook on life extended to the clothes she wore, as well as the ones she bought for me. I never had the drive to challenge her, and I never felt like I had permission to play with the baubles my mother left behind.

"Honey?"

It took me a moment to connect the voice to the request. Neither had anything to do with the color pink or my mother, except that honey and sweetie-pie were endearments I stopped missing a long time ago.

"I'm a mess." I couldn't stop the tears rolling over my cheeks or my sweaty palms from sticking to the beautiful wrapping paper.

Rowan stopped her tea preparations and ran over to the couch, embracing me in the sisterly hug I'd been craving since I first blurted out my sexual escapades from the safety of her office chair. "What's wrong, Calli?"

I lifted up the ruined packaging. "It's the pink. And the honey. And I kissed Tanner, and his old girlfriend's not happy about that, and I cut off Doug's hand..." I burrowed my face into her shoulder and let the tears go where they wanted, which was mostly out.

"Calliope? Who's Doug?"

I started giggling. "My ex-husband."

Rowan patted my back. "He must have really pissed you off."

I giggled more and released Rowan from our very soggy embrace.

"Let me go clean my face," I said, "and I'll tell you all about it."

When I emerged from the bathroom the second time, Rowan had finished setting up the tea tray and brought it into the living room. She waited for me to sit down, and handed me a cup and saucer. "I was going to ask if you were a tear-it-open or a recycle kind of gal when it comes to wrapping paper, but I think I have my answer."

I giggled and tried to not slosh the tea and ruin the paper even more.

"Under normal circumstances, I'm a recycler," I admitted, wiggling my toes and feet.

"Shall we try this again?"

"Yes."

Rowan handed the mangled package to me.

I cooed and oohed and aahed and attacked what was left of the pretty wrapping until my fingertips caressed silk and beading. I drew my brows together and whispered, "This feels expensive."

"Oh, it was!" Rowan laughed and squeezed my calf. "But we all chipped in."

"Who is 'we all'?"

"Me and Rose and the other women who were at your first circle."

I held Rowan's gaze and clutched the silk to my cracking chest. "Thank you."

"Don't stop there. See what it is."

Swinging my legs off the couch, I stood and let the cloth unfold until a dress unlike anything I had ever worn or even let myself covet hung from my upraised hands. Tears threatened to spill over again, more out of joy than hormonal frustration. "This is so beautiful. Where did you ever find it?"

Rowan clapped her hands and danced in place. "I have connections," she trilled. "Come on, come on, put it on!"

The garment was simple in design. Narrow straps led into a bias-cut, ankle-length dress of layered, gauzy silk and cotton. A smattering of glass beads decorated the entire outer layer, like tiny stars in a blood-red sky.

"And don't forget these." She handed me something that had dropped to the floor in my emotional melee.

"Oh my Goddess, Rowan, underwear too?"

She nodded. "I was working with a theme."

Grateful the bit of satin wasn't one of those skimpy thongs, I hooked it over one finger,

"What time do you have to leave?" she asked. "I so wish I could go with you. I haven't been to a Blood Ceremony in a long time."

"Belle's picking me up at nine. And I wish you could be there too." It had occurred to me that somewhere along the way I'd neglected my friendship-building skills. Another thing I could change, beginning right now. "It's probably too late, but I could ask Rose."

Rowan's eyes went wide. "Rose terrifies me."

"Me too! Is she the head witch?" I asked. "The leader of the pack?"

"Mm, I think 'leader of the pack' would refer more to shifters. Rose is the head of all the covens in the Pacific Northwest, which means she's also in charge of organizing and leading the big rituals."

I relaxed back into the support of the lumpy pillows. "I wish I knew what exactly was happening tonight. Do you know?"

"One of the purposes of the blood ritual is to tie you to this place, symbolically and magically. Using your menstrual blood adds more layers of meaning and connection." She shrugged. "One of these days, I'm going to talk to Rose about guiding my initiation. I haven't had one, but I would like one. My life since I was sixteen, seventeen has revolved around caring for women at the physical level. I became a gynecologist so I could practice in the human realm as well as the magical one. But I don't want to do my Blood Ceremony here until I know this is a place I want to stay."

My phone buzzed with a text from Belle, reminding me she'd be at the house at nine. "I'm sweaty again," I admitted. "I'm going to take another shower and then I'll put on the dress."

"Would you mind if I took your picture once you're dressed?"

"I would love that."

In the privacy of the bathroom, I dropped whatever pretense remained and let the weight of what was coming sink further into my body. I was nervous. My hands trembled as I put my new dress and underwear on a hanger. Pulling my hair up and away from my face, I formed a small topknot to keep it out of the shower's stream and pinned the loose tendrils at the sides.

When I'd prepared for the ritual beneath the sacred Sitka trees, I'd been coated with dust and feeling a bit tossed around from the long drive over the logging roads. This evening, I had time to think. Which also meant I had time to stress about all the unknowns. As I stood under the stream of water and soaped up my washcloth, I pictured washing away things I wanted to be rid of and notions of myself that no longer felt right.

Such lofty thoughts for a shower.

Clean water sluiced over and down my limbs and torso. I turned off the faucets and paused to take a deep breath; I couldn't hide in here all night. A thin stream of bright red blood trickled down my inner left thigh. Another wave, sent from the Sea of Transitions, gathered. I tensed my thighs and let the wave curl itself like a cat's tail around my legs and eddy down the drain.

A text from Rose waited for me on my bureau top, instructing me to gather soil from the different quadrants of my property and put it into clay pots. It would have been nice to get that before showering. I threw my summer dress back on, let Rowan know what I was doing, and made the ambit of my yard with trowel and pot in hand. I managed to keep myself relatively dirt-free.

By the time I maneuvered myself into my silky underwear and dress, it was after eight. The five people standing in a half circle at the open end of the downstairs hallway had apparently been patiently awaiting my emergence.

"I clean up rather nicely, don't I?" I asked, giving a slow twirl and dropping into a half-curtsy.

Thatcher grabbed my wrist and pulled me forward. "We have something for you, Mom."

I pressed my hands to my cheeks to cool my face and to keep from crying. Harper was holding something tied together with the repurposed pink and silver ribbon.

"It's my day for presents." I took the gift to the table, removed the ribbon, and gasped. Red leather gauntlets, decorated with an intricate pattern of embossed symbols and all the charms presented to me by the other witches. I was overcome. "Where… who did this?"

"We all did," said Thatcher, gesturing to Harper, Leilani, Tanner, and Kaz.

"Is this what you've been doing upstairs?"

They all nodded, teens and grown men alike. "Bet you thought we were playing video games," said Harper.

I laughed and extended my arms. I couldn't wait to wear my custom-made armor. "The thought did cross my mind," I admitted, "but I never would have guessed you were doing this."

Tanner wrapped one gauntlet around my right forearm and laced it on, while my sons worked together on the left.

"Thank you. All of you." I hugged each of them in turn. "I feel so different." From my sparkly red dress to my new, red gauntlets, I *was* different. I was adorned in a way I'd never been, not even for my wedding, and it was a feeling I would never forget.

"Picture time!" Rowan shooed everyone out of the hallway and into the living room and managed a handful of shots where everyone's eyes were open at the same time. Leilani insisted we get pictures of me and Rowan and another of the three "girls."

A car horn sounded from the road, breaking up the love fest and reminding me I had a long night ahead. "That's Belle, and I bet she can't get in because of the wards."

"I'll see to her," said Kaz. He strode up the driveway, made a line of marks in the packed dirt with a stick, and waved Belle in.

"Halloo, Calliope, are you ready?" The fancily-attired witch enveloped me in a lavender-scented hug before admiring me head to toes and wrists. "Those are *smashing*," she cried, peering closely at my forearms, "and now I want a set too. In yellow."

"The guys made them for me," I said. "I think I have everything."

Belle glanced at the clay pots and nodded. "Good. Glad to see you got your soil. All you need is a sweater to keep the chill away and something on your feet."

"Let me go say goodbye."

"I'll wait in the car with Kazimir."

Grabbing a market basket from the jumble, I added the two pots of soil and left it on the stairs while I went into the house to hug everyone one more time. I slipped my arms into a sweater and my feet into my faithful work boots and declared myself ready.

Tanner picked up the basket and followed me to the car.

"Can you pop the trunk?" he asked Belle, and when he and I were protected from view by the raised hood, he lowered the basket and wedged it in place. With one hand gripping the edge of the hood, Tanner cleared his throat, tugged at the back of his pants, and presented me with a pair of delicate sandals fashioned from long strip of ruby red leather. "This is one occasion where something a little more festive would be appropriate."

Clutching my fancy new footwear in one hand, I threw my arm around Tanner's neck. He slid his free hand to the small of my back.

"Calliope," he whispered. I heard a question in his voice and answered it by planting a kiss on the center of his mouth.

"I have to go." The gossamer-like layers of my dress created a slippery surface between us, clinging to me in places where my skin was sheened with a fine sweat. He slid his hand higher, cupping the back of my ribs. I swayed in place, the little beads along the hem of my dress tickling my ankles and the backs of my calves.

"Calli, time to go-o!" The car jostled side to side as Belle buckled herself in and Kaz departed.

I could have stayed suspended in the moment, in the circle of Tanner's arm, for much, much longer. He kissed my forehead, lowered me until my feet met the ground, and stepped away from the car.

I toed off my boots and handed them to him. "Wish me luck."

CHAPTER 20

Belle was surprisingly quiet the entire ride, only speaking to ask me a general question or to check that her driving wasn't too slow or too fast or too anything. I explored my new gauntlets, pressing the pliable leather against my skin and tracing the lines of the repeated designs.

The sky darkened into ever deeper shades of blue. We turned off the main road connecting the upper and lower sections of the island and drove into an unkempt grove of stone fruit trees, past an abandoned house and barn and other decaying outbuildings. A pond grown over with lily pads and purple marsh flowers offered lambent bits of color.

"I don't think I've ever been here before," I said, half to myself, wondering how that could be and hoping I would have an escort on my way out. When Belle pulled up to a squarish plot where the lines in the grass had been flattened by car tires and parked, I was sure this was my first visit to this property.

I collected my basket from the trunk, admired my prettily laced sandals, and followed Belle to a hidden path that guided us through a narrow section of forest before opening to yet another orchard.

"Where is everyone?" I asked.

"They're finishing setting up," Belle said, "and they're just about ready for you."

A path made by dozens of feet wound its way across the un-mowed field toward a stand of the largest apple trees I had ever seen. As Belle made her way to the one in the center, I could see the area around the trunk of the ancient one had been cared for during the dry season. The grass was green and soft underfoot. Handfuls of wildflowers bloomed in a wide radius to the outer-most drip line of the tree's hooked and twisted branches, with the weight of the ripened fruit drawing the boughs close to the ground. Fallen apples, split and overly ripe, added a heavy sweet-ness to the air.

I waited outside the periphery of the ritual circle, my gaze resting on the rose-colored flesh of the apples. I hungered to taste the fruit, to take its magic into my body and let the sweet-ness feed an unnameable emptiness I had recently begun to resent.

Other women emerged from the gloaming, creating an open circle to my left and right. The occasional bat swooped between bodies and laden branches, chasing insects and weaving a lacy net of dark, delicate threads over the ritual space.

The women to either side of me turned in unison. One kneeled to loosen the lacing on my sandals. The other reached under my dress.

I nodded my understanding, and my permission, and stepped out of my sandals and underwear. I had my period, which was the instigating reason for this ritual, and I was being asked to trust there was a reason for every element of the ceremony and that the women knew what they were doing.

I relaxed as best I could. Women in other places, other times and other cultures had let their blood feed the ground. I could do the same for one night. I'd already fed my heart to the sky during the first ritual.

The familiar witch in charge of smudging approached, her string-wound bundle of sage and sweetgrass glowing at the tip. L'Runa blew a gentle, steady breath across the top of the smudge and began to cleanse the air around me as well as the layers of my ceremonial garb. A gentle nudge indicated when I should lift the innermost layer of the dress, step my feet apart, and accept the sacred smoke across my feet and up my legs.

Crickets' voices faded with the light. Barred owls again added their calls to the aural opening. Hoots filled the air, adding their feathery brown threads to the lace overlay and connecting the taller trees at the far-off periphery with those in the ritual space.

I tried to stay aware of everything happening around me but found it impossible. The original thirteen women with roles at my first ritual had tripled, with the additional women taking up scattered positions in the field. The sensation of being in the middle of a field, at night, amongst mostly strangers was intense. Sacred. Eerie.

Unexpectedly heart-filling.

All this was being done to help *me*.

I remembered the party thrown in our honor when Doug and I shared news of our engagement, followed by a wedding shower, the wedding, and baby showers for each of the boys.

But this ritual…

This felt different. Very different. Rituals were meant to mark special moments along the path of life. This one felt like an entire stage or platform was being built while I stood barefoot in the cooling grass, cleansed by smoke and waiting for the next set of instructions.

The bellow of a conch shell shocked me into the moment. I'd missed the calling in of the cardinal directions and quickly raised my arms to the sky when the sun was invoked and dropped to my knees when it was time to honor and welcome Gaia, Mother Earth.

This honoring I knew. Toes curled under, knees touching cool grass and quiet earth, palms down and fingers spread, I opened a connection to the land through my limbs and waited for the pulse of response.

It came, that slow, liquid beat I'd felt the day I stepped onto the Pearmains' property and touched Clifford and Abigail. Even in the thrall of a powerful spell, their land pulsed through them. And later, when I'd been in the orchard with Tanner and heard the bee-like humming in the ground. The land spoke to me then, and it spoke to me now. I was here to listen, and never again would I shy from my duties to care for the one that gave life and accepted death and had forever been my ally.

Startled, thinking my name had been called, I raised my gaze and looked into the distance, beyond the costumed bodies of a field full of women. I went farther still, picked out a set of eyes glowing gold as they caught the last sparks of the setting sun. The visage of a bear, hunkered in the grass, its fur disguised by tall strands of wheat, shimmered next to a set of wolfish eyes.

"Calli. You can get up now," the woman to my left said.

The bear disappeared; the other animal blinked its eyes and disappeared. Strong, slender hands cupped under my arms and lifted. I brushed my palms together and stood, once again present to the moment. The women at the outermost reaches of the field began to walk toward me, slow and deliberate, their voices vibrating with the repeated phrases of a chant. I could not hear the separate syllables, but I felt them in my bones. One day—soon—I would learn the words.

Once again, I was the only one dressed in red. This time, everyone else wore black, and at a signal from Rose, they donned the masks hanging from their necks, small masks to the front and larger versions facing away from the backs of their heads. A few of the women crouched and stood, emerging with drums of assorted sizes in their hands. They added muffled percussive beats to the chanting, creating a low, thrumming, undercurrent of sound.

Rose stepped closer, took my hand, and led me forward into the start of a dance. The spiral revealed itself after a few turns around the tree in ever-widening circles. Joining my voice and my feet with the rhythm set by the drums, I left my head-centered space and connected further with everything around me. As the spiral turned back in on itself and drew me closer and closer to the massive apple tree at the center of the field, my blood answered the call and wet my inner thighs.

More hands than I could count passed me down the line and guided me to face the great tree and the maw that split its trunk. The opening looked less like a mouth and more like a heart ripped open from the inside.

"You must enter Her, Calliope." Whispered words coming from no one place, no one woman. Maybe the words were in the air or in the ground or dropped from the branches like over-ripe fruit. "Enter the tree."

Bark, loamy and musky on my nose and sharp on my cheek, drew close to my face. A hand on my head reminded me to duck. I gathered the skirt of my dress, pressed my elbows against my sides, and entered. Dropping the layers of silk and cotton, I stood, extended one arm, and the other until my fingertips made contact with the interior surface. The wood was worn smooth. I turned slowly, unable to see anything, and let my eyelids close and my other senses take over.

I smelled honey. My back made contact with heartwood. The wood was surprisingly warm, inviting me to lean in and feel it supporting the entire length of my body, the backs of my shoulders, buttocks, thighs, and calves. Pressing my palms against the inner surface of the tree, I walked my fingers up. At shoulder height, branches split away from the center, offering a set of living wood sleeves. I slipped my arms up and in, dressing myself in the tree, a little girl playing with an ancestor's old gown.

A wider stance was needed for the bottom half of my body to feel balanced, sturdy, and steady. I stepped my feet apart, giving blood space to flow from my womb and onto the ground. Bees buzzed from far up the inner tree and honey dripped onto my head.

The tree began to fit itself to me like a custom-made dress, molding to every curve and bend in my body from wrists to ankles. I had room to breathe—or maybe the tree breathed me—and outside, the drumming and chanting had begun to echo the rhythm of a human heartbeat. The longer the women played, the more I dissolved into the tree until I moved beyond the inner surface, beyond the outer bark, projected into the field and the surrounding forests and coastline until I wasn't one body—I was a million bodies with a million umbilical connections.

And a little too late for me to do a damn thing about it, an ancient presence slipped inside the tree with me and whispered the word, *mine*, *mine*, over and over again until my blood fed the earth, my breath fed the sky, and my brain synapses sparked in time with the twinkling stars.

I giggled and cried until I burst apart.

Sounds of suction breaking drew me back into my tree-bound body. The release of wood wrapping flesh began around my ankles and travelled upward until only my wrists and fingers were encased. I took in a deep breath, felt no restriction in my chest, and took in more breaths. I pressed down with my toes, rocked my weight back onto my heels, revelled in the strength of my legs.

"Ready," I exhaled, and the pressure around my leather-wrapped wrists loosened until my arms were free. I lowered them slowly, patted my face and chest, smoothed the front and sides of my dress. My hands stuck to the fabric in places; I was sticky all over—and under—and the bottom of the red dress glowed rose and yellow with bright morning sun. My toenails winked under streaks of blood and dirt, and I waited.

Silence. I bent my knees enough I could slip out the gap in the tree's trunk and lean against the bark.

The pots of soil I'd carried from my garden were empty and neatly queued at the base of the tree. I dropped to my knees and read a note instructing me to refill the little pots with soil from where I had been standing. I scooped up the damp dirt with the trowel provided and filled each pot to the rim.

Done. What was next?

Squatting, I surveyed what was directly within my field of vision. I couldn't see much past my extended arms and the lowest branches, other than the tops of tents scattered throughout the grassy field.

Crawling forward, gathering the layers of my dress to my waist, I grew ever more aware I was covered in blood and dirt and honey, bits of crushed fruit, sticks and leaves. I stopped. The ground lurched into a spiraling movement, and I fell over, onto my side, and watched a line of black-winged birds circling above the wide reach of the mother tree's branches.

Blood. And honey. I wanted blood, and I wanted honey. I wanted to pierce my skin and lick my self-inflicted wounds, fly in the company of bees and drown in flower cups of fresh nectar. I wanted to eat dirt and tickle beetle bellies and rush up the oak trees like squirrels after branches full of ripened nuts.

My giggles grew into a full-bellied laugh. The birds and branches were joined by a ring of masked faces peering at me. More faces gathered, until the skin tones and hair textures and wildly painted features blended together in one eternally recognizable face, and I passed out again, because if Gaia wanted to claim me for Herself, I was ready to go.

V*oices.* All of them feminine. Hands explored my face, fingers tried to open my eyes, and all I could do was grin, turn my face to the loamy soil, and seek sleep.

A deeper voice, urgent and bossy—definitely bossy—joined in. A strong, thick arm insinuated itself behind my knees, and another arm supported the back of my shoulders, while softer, smaller hands cupped my hips and the back of my head.

Golden. The sun kissed my eyelids. I smiled at the gift. My body met the cool surface of a car's interior, and my heart reached for the door, pressed at it, willing it to stay open so I could escape the machine-made confine and make my way back to the Earth.

The door won. Grass then macadam, unfurled under the tires. I rocked with the rhythm of the road, left my resistance someplace I might never remember, and drifted to sleep again.

W*ater.* Warm water, softened with soap and scented with strawberries.

Support. My shoulders once again cradled by an arm thicker and stronger than my own. I opened my eyes slowly. A pulse on a throat. The curve of an unshaved jaw. Hair, wet at the tips, grazing a muscular neck and shoulders.

My bath. Tanner's gaze on my knees where they broke through the bubbles coating the surface of the bathwater.

"Why are you here?" I asked, my voice scratchy.

His head turned in slow motion, and his eyes sparked bronze, as though the irises were newly forged and piercingly hot. "Rose called me."

"Oh." I closed my eyes, let my knees drop together and my head loll toward Tanner's shoulder. My bones were missing. He was shirtless. I was defenseless. I took a long inhale through my nose and found his musky scent underneath the light-hearted soap. "Did I do okay?"

"I'd say you passed. You more than passed, which is why Rose asked me to come and get you. She thought if I brought you home, you would find yourself faster."

"Was I lost?" I sounded drunk. I *felt* drunk.

"I don't know," he whispered. "I don't know. But you're here now, and that's a good thing." Tanner pressed his lips to my forehead, extracted his arm from behind my shoulders, and placed a folded towel over the edge of the bathtub.

I rested my head against the thick terrycloth and sighed a breathy, "Thank you."

"You okay to wash yourself?"

I had to think about that before I flipped to my side, seal-like, and nodded. I didn't want to let go of his eyes, his beautiful, gem-like eyes, a mother lode of crystal in a lightless cave. "Yeah. But if I'm not out soon, check on me."

"I'll do that." He reached for the tall glass on the counter beside the sink and handed it to me. "Drink. It's water with electrolytes. And if you feel dizzy when you get out, yell. I'll wait for you in your room."

"What time is it?"

"It's almost dinner."

Mmm, did Mama make honeycakes?

I sighed, slid under the surface, one hand gripping the curved edge of the tub so I wouldn't go all the way under and swim down the drain and follow the call to the sea. Eyes closed, I ran my free hand over my skin, felt for my hair. Tanner must have washed away the dirt and blood I vaguely remembered coating me when I crawled out from inside the apple tree.

I emerged from the bath, steadying myself on the rounded sides of the old standalone tub while I bent forward and squeezed the excess water out of my hair. Fresh towels were stacked on the toilet seat. I unfolded the top one and wrapped it around my head. Standing tall in my terrycloth turban, I patted dry. My skin was too tender to rub or scruff. A jar of wild rosehip oil sat near the glass of water. I sniffed the oil's familiar healing notes and poured a generous portion into my cupped palm before drizzling it up and down my limbs and around my breasts.

I followed that with rubbing the oil over my joints and into the folds of my labia.

Pulling my hand away from between my legs, I noticed no blood. And after I toweled my hair and went to detangle sections with my wood-toothed brush, the stroke kept going, two or more inches longer than usual. I separated out a hank of hair and pulled it away to examine the color under the light above the mirror.

Chestnut brown. Thick. Luxurious.

I tugged. Not a wig.

My hair.

I looked down the front of my body. My hands travelled over my skin, found my waist, rounded my hips and my breasts. Maybe no one else would notice, but I did. My skin was smoother, more taut. My waist nipped in, not to its pre-babies circumference, but missing a little of the layer of fat that had arrived on the heels of my fortieth birthday.

I patted my cheeks and breasts again. Still full and maybe sitting a tad higher. I walked naked from one side of the bathroom to the other, chin lifted, hips swaying, feet confident as I landed, heel to toe, heel to toe, on the firm tile surface. Assaying the front of my body again, wanting to make sure this was really *me*, even my pubic hair was more lush.

I hadn't thought to check my appearance in the mirror. The reflection would confirm one of two things: either I was crazy or the ritual in the apple tree had laid some serious consequences on my biological processes. My bathrobe hung from its hook on the back of the door. I slipped my arms through the sleeves, folded the halves across my chest, and tied the belt snugly at the waist.

Curious, I spread the robe open to look at my belly one more time. The remains of the tattoo were completely gone.

Tanner said it was time for dinner. I had the sense I was forgetting something. Something more important than clothes.

Patting the thick fabric so it would soak up the last bit of water from my body, I opened the bathroom door and paused.

Rose said I had to put the dirt back, that I was to blend it with the soil in the most sacred spot of my property. I couldn't very well sprinkle it over the floorboards of the house that provided a safe haven for me and my sons. While my head deliberated where the soil should go, I followed my feet down the hall toward the busy part of the house and out the door, passing Tanner, Harper, and Thatch without them stopping their debate.

The basket with the pots and trowel was parked at the bottom of the porch steps. My clean, pink toes took me there, waited while I picked up the basket, and walked me around the house to the crabapple tree. I crouched. Loosened the soil. Tugged at clumps of dried grass and needled them into giving up their hold. They did, eventually, leaving patches where I could mix in my blood-nourished contribution to the health of the old tree.

Satisfied I'd done a decent job, I whacked the back of the trowel against the trunk. The metal rang out a high, clanging note.

"Mom? What are you doing?" Harper said, Leilani by his side, elbows on the railing of the porch. Lei-li waved to me when I glanced up.

"I had to put the dirt back." Wasn't that obvious?

Harper quirked his head to the side. "Oh. Well, you know there's a party in your honor tonight, right?"

Huh. I snugged the belt tighter, leaving a few muddy smudges on the white cloth. "Guess I better change."

CHAPTER 21

Hallway, bathroom, bedroom. The bureau had been my aunt's, and the mirror had known generations of faces. These everyday objects were familiar—and foreign, like someone had cleaned my house in my absence and replaced everything slightly askew from where it usually resided. I faced the chest of drawers, pressed my belly against the edge, and searched for myself in the mirror.

Calliope Jones. Earth witch. Daughter, mother...I couldn't hold my own gaze.

My gauntlets had been polished and were draped over the corner of the cluttered bureau. I patted the leather, smoothed my fingers over the roughed up spots. The skin on my arms was unblemished, but the gauntlets told a story. I could hope to recall it later, when I was out of this off-kilter, in-between state.

The red dress Rowan gave me was clean and folded and placed on the spindle chair sitting beside the bureau. I wasn't sure I should wear the same dress for the evening's festivities. The red had served its purpose.

"Calli?" Tanner's low voice came to my ears from the end of a long tunnel. His body arrived at my door, followed by an animal-like presence that positioned itself protectively against the solid panels of wood.

"Come in." I could enlist his help picking out something to wear for the party. I wasn't making sense of anything on my own, and I was far more drawn to calling on the beast in my hallway to curl up with me on my bed than making small talk with guests.

Tanner opened the door and paused at the threshold. He wore snug white jeans and a silk shirt the color of antique turquoise. His feet were bared. I slid my gaze between each and every one of his toes, followed the upward arch at the bottoms of his feet to the inward curve of his ankles. The pant fabric cupped his calves and gathered a little around his knees before stretching taut over the sculpted muscles of his thighs and the tumescent bulge of his cock.

My druid was aroused. I lifted the damp hair off the nape of my neck, noted its luxurious weight, and turned, every cell of my skin aware of Tanner's gaze clocking my movements.

He undid the belt to my bathrobe and separated the front halves of the garment. I hissed when the rough terrycloth grazed my nipples.

"You really should be getting dressed," he whispered, cupping my breasts and testing their fullness.

I nestled my head underneath his chin and closed my eyes. This was where I wanted to be. This was the man I wanted to be with. And nothing, not a surprise appearance from my ex—or his —was going to take this moment away.

"Calliope." Sensitive bundles of nerve endings throughout my body throbbed at his voice. I wanted Tanner to finish removing my bathrobe, take me to bed, and spend the rest of the night drawing his magic on my skin.

Voices reverberated from the far end of the hallway. Inhabitants from the world outside expressed the opinion I'd been gone from sight too long and tapped on my door.

"Calliope, are you ready?" asked Leilani.

Tanner tightened his arms around my chest, opened his mouth wide against the side of my neck, and bit gently.

"Almost," I answered.

The druid pressing his length into my buttocks laughed silently. I joined him.

"So much for my sexy goddess routine," I said, ridding myself of my bathrobe and walking naked toward my closet. "I don't suppose you brought me something to wear?"

Getting dressed took longer with Tanner's help than it would have had he left me to fumble in the closet by myself. The gladiator-style sandals he gifted me survived the Blood Ceremony none the worse for wear. Those could go on my feet. And pushed to the far end of the clothes rod was a hippie-chic dress with colorful flowers embroidered across the bodice and straps.

Tanner insisted on lacing my sandals and managed to run a series of kisses and nips up my inner thighs as he crossed and re-crossed the leather around my ankles. He landed more kisses and licks on my belly and up under my breasts in what I took to be approval for my night's attire. More likely he was casting his vote that I forego wearing a bra.

He won, but I insisted on wearing underpants.

Tanner also helped with lip-plumping, deploying his special brand of bites. He denied being part vampire, but suckle marks high up the inside of each thigh presented a counter argument. I was just about to swat him away when another yell from the kitchen signalled my delay had been noted and I should expect an escort if it extended much longer.

"You and I have a date, Calliope Jones." Tanner kissed his invitation across my forehead and along my jaw. "Once the party's over and everyone's gone home, it's our turn."

"Are you asking me or telling me, Agent Marechal?" I asked, running my hands over his ass and giving a proprietary squeeze, when what I really wanted was to shut the closet door and wrap my thighs around his waist.

He held me at arm's length and gave me a slow once-over. "Ms. Jones, I'm telling you I want uninterrupted hours of your time, and I'm asking you to grant them to me at your earliest convenience."

"Ooh, so formal."

He dropped to his knees, grabbed my hips, and planted another kiss right on my prominent mons. His voice husky, his fingers digging into my flesh, he murmured, "I'm on my knees for you, Calliope."

I brushed his hair back from his forehead. "Then you have my unequivocal yes, Tanner."

He slid his body up the front of mine as he stood, fixed his pants, and tucked his hair behind his ears. I preceded him out the door and down the hall, giving an extra sashay to my step. The soft groan behind me had me wishing the party was over and we were heading back to the sanctuary of my room.

My kitchen was in an uproar, and from what I could see through the windows and doors, the activity had spread into the living room, out the front door and all across my property. Harper and Thatch were hovering around the dining table, stabbing at platters of hors d'oeuvres with knives. New knives, from what I could see of the carved handles and the telltale swirls of hand-forged blades.

"Mom," said Harper, folding and pocketing his knife at my entrance, "did you see we hired caterers?"

That explained the three people clad in server aprons bustling figure eights around my kitchen and living room. "I do see some unfamiliar faces and I would love it if you'd make introductions," I said, holding out my hand. "I'd also love to hear about those shiny knives hiding in your back pockets."

"Oh, you mean this?" asked Harper, showing me his blade. "They're gifts from Kaz. He gave them to us the day we carved the runes for the wards." He folded his knife in half, pocketed it again, and tugged on a cord around his neck. "The handle of each knife is made out of the same wood as our amulets."

Thatcher stood closer to his brother and pulled out his knife and the amulet attached to the cord around his neck. "Kaz had us choose which one felt right. It was pretty cool, Mom."

"I'm glad you have these," I said.

A surprise wave of apprehension washed over me. Not one of those cold, heavy waves weighted with dread. More the portent-filled variety that accompanied those moments when I saw my sons as the young men they were becoming, with all the waiting joys and possibilities and challenges.

"How long was I in the bathroom?" I nudged Harper and took a longer look at my oldest son. "And where did you find an iron?" His flat front khaki pants were pressed, with a crisp line down the center of each leg, as was his shirt.

"Mom, we have an iron and an ironing board upstairs. Thatch presses all our shirts. Didn't you know that?"

Huh. "Who's here?"

"Lei-li's parents would like to meet you. Let's start with them."

The entire outdoor area of the property had been utterly transformed while I was soaking, dressing, and being distracted by Tanner's attentions. Garlands of herbs, leaves, and wildflowers looped around the rails fronting the deck and alongside the stairs, and little glass jars with votive candles glowed along the risers and the deck's perimeter.

"Mom, this is Malvyn Brodeur and James Brodeur. Mal and James, my mother, Calliope Jones," Harper said. Leilani unlinked her arms from her fathers' elbows, her eyes twinkling with pride, and stepped behind Malvyn to embrace Harper.

"Malvyn, I'm delighted to meet you," I said. "Especially now that we've figured out we have a few things in common."

Both men greeted me in the European fashion, a kiss on either cheek, and both smelled absolutely divine, a citrusy scent that could have been custom-blended.

"Congratulations on making your Blood Ceremony, Calliope," said Malvyn. "Sorcerers have something similar, but we are tied to an object, not a place." He leaned in and undid one more button of his immaculate shirt, revealing a collar of linked metallic pieces. The collar sat low enough to hide underneath a regular T-shirt. "This never comes off."

"And I studied botany," said James, "bolstering my half-witch status with a great deal of science and an intuitive approach to plants and propagation." He wore a similar collar under his open-necked, caftan-style shirt, only his links were delicately tooled renditions of leaves. His sleeves were folded to above his elbows, and a hammered gold cuff wrapped each wrist.

"May I?" I asked, gesturing to his adornments. "Do these have a specific function?"

"Simply to show my affection for my husband," said Malvyn. "And I might have added a little something to ward off overly inquisitive men."

The husbands shared a quick kiss and a heated private look.

"Your daughter has a very intuitive approach to her baking," I said. "But you knew that already."

"We did know Leilani has a gift for imbuing. The most obvious transference occurs when she's in the kitchen; she can't seem to keep her emotions out of the ingredients as she's mixing them," agreed Malvyn. "We're working on helping her moderate that, and we've also been at somewhat of a loss as to how to educate her further."

"It's a question we knew would need addressing come her eighteenth birthday," added James. "Given she's nearing eighteen-and-a-half and with the recent revelations happening under your roof, we need to begin her magical studies as soon as possible."

While we were chatting, Harper and Leilani wandered over to another section of the yard, and Tanner had made his way over to me.

"You've met Tanner Marechal?" I asked, slipping my arm around his waist.

"We have, and earlier today we were reviewing his material for the mentorship program. I suspect Leilani will be enrolling for this September. We would like to make ourselves available in some capacity as well," said James.

"I would be honored to have both of you as mentors, and as it happens, we're low on male witches," said Tanner.

"Malvyn, I wonder if I might turn our conversation to a different topic?" I asked.

"Certainly." He redid the button that would hide his collar. "Would you mind if we chatted while James and I filled our plates? I came over straight from the ferry, and I'm famished."

"I was told you work in the financial sector," I began. He nodded and distributed plates to the four of us. I kept going. "Would you happen to know anything about the Flechette Realty and Development Group?"

"I know quite a lot about the Flechette Group," he said, filling his plate with savory puff pastries and assorted tapas. "Very little of which I can share with you."

"Then let me ask you this—is there anything you *can* tell me about their current property acquisition plan?"

"I can only share with you that which is already in the public domain, which is the founders, two sisters and a brother who worked their way west from Toronto, were known to have snapped up parcels of land that should not have been for sale in the first place, and they essentially built their empire on a foundation of stolen goods. I will also add—and you may *not* quote me on this—that same ethos appears to be guiding the current Board of Directors."

"Can you tell me what their magic is?"

Malvyn stared at me a good bit longer than was comfortable. "Fae," he answered, "and not the hidden folk-type you'll find in pockets here and there throughout the Gulf Islands. Fae from the

Old Countries, with the ability to hide their true visages and weapons using glamour. As an officer on the Province's Board of Magical Governance—and as a new friend—I would advise you to tread very carefully around any organization bearing the Flechette name."

The bite of spinach and feta pastry heading toward my mouth went back to my plate. "Douglas Flechette is my ex-husband and Harper and Thatcher's father. I'm afraid he's been the cause of some of the challenges we've had this past week."

James spoke up. "Leilani mentioned there was tension between Harper and his dad, but we didn't put all the pieces together. I'm feeling rather guilty at the moment. My research has had me practically sleeping in my greenhouses, and Mal's had to spend a lot of time in Vancouver." His shaking hands underscored his concern. "I don't want to go so far as forbidding our daughter from seeing your son, but…"

"James and I have not had to call on our magic for much of Leilani's life," interjected Malvyn. "But if a storm is gathering in the Magical realm, we would appreciate being brought up to speed."

"For a celebration, this party is starting off on a low note. At least for me." I pulled Tanner aside after we parted ways with Mal and James, who had offered to host a gathering the following night at their house for us and any other druids and witches we saw fit to invite. "Although I'm dying to see what a sorcerer's home looks like."

"Probably much bigger than yours," said Tanner, "with a tower or a widow's walk and at least one room dedicated to his collection of objects and one to his books. They're the crows of the magical world, with an innate pull to acquire shiny things.

"Shiny, magical things," he added.

I scanned the crowd. More people had arrived while I was

speaking with Leilani's fathers, most of them witches I remembered from the full moon ritual and from the Blood Ceremony.

"I'm going in," I informed Tanner, patting at the sides of my dress and straightening my spine.

I stopped at the drinks table, picked up an alcohol-free mojito, and made my way to Rose, hoping to pay homage and dispense with my rising case of performance anxiety-related nerves. Rose was standing with L'Runa, not far from where River was sitting and chatting with Abigail and Cliff.

"Rose, L'Runa," I began, "thank you so much for coming by tonight."

L'Runa ran her hands down my free arm and took my hand in hers. "Calliope, what a powerful ceremony that was last night. For all of us. How are you feeling now?"

"Honestly, I feel different," I said, laughing lightly, "which I'm sure everyone says, but also like I'm slightly...off center."

She kissed my forehead and tightened her grip on my hand. "Entering the Mother Tree and taking the journey with Her is a profound experience of being out of body and out of time. Give yourself at least another twenty-four hours for your missing pieces to find their way home." L'Runa's smile was genuine and kind.

And I was still in awe of her palpable essence, some of which was circling its way around my left arm and over my shoulder, a snaking sleeve of invisible protection.

Rose nodded at her friend, tucked her hands behind her back, and lowered her voice. "Calliope, your Blood Ceremony did not follow the sequence most others do. You had uninvited..." She paused mid-sentence as L'Runa elbowed her gently and spoke into her ear. "Let me rephrase that," she said. "You had *unannounced* guests, and while we always expect there might be visitors from other realms, one of yours was..." She searched the darkening woods surrounding my house and rubbed her upper arms. "One of your visitors lingered at the periphery of the ceremonial area in a way that whispered of a threat. And two other visitors came in their animal forms, as though to protect you from that threat."

"When moments like that occur during a Blood Ceremony or even during one of the lesser ceremonies, Calliope, our policy is to let it unfurl without interference," said L'Runa, lifting a lightweight shawl out of her capacious bag and handing it to Rose. "Much as one would, say, when watching an outdoor theater production or musical performance. One cannot always control the weather or the actions of the local inhabitants while the show is going on."

"But," Rose interjected, "we had to ask Tanner for help once the sun rose and you emerged from the tree."

"I remember some of that," I said. "Thank you for taking care of me."

"We're glad to see you alive and well on this side of your ceremony, Calliope. It's the best of all possible outcomes."

My conversation with the two witches left me pondering what the not-so-best of all possible outcomes might have looked like. I shook off the thought, found an empty chair in a cluster of round tables, and let myself be surrounded by well-wishing family and new friends.

S tifling a yawn from the lack of sleep, I took stock of the party. Harper, Leilani, Thatcher, and Sallie had spread a blanket at the far end of the property and were on their backs, pointing up at stars, and seemingly deep in conversation. Nearer to the house, other clusters of partiers had me calculating how much longer I should stay before it was acceptable to gracefully usher myself off to bed.

Where I would gracefully await the dark-haired druid standing with his back to me, in lively conversation with his trio of druidic cohorts. Watching Tanner could easily become a favorite pastime, and a rush up my spine confirmed my crush was real.

Enough mooning. I was chilly. Rubbing my full belly, the feeling of fullness extending into my heart, I excused myself and went into the house to find a sweater.

The moment I planted my foot on the strip of lawn between the house and the driveway, I knew something was different. The ground was askew in a way that was simply wrong. Though the surface of the lawn looked smooth, my feet couldn't find purchase, and my gut clenched in reaction to a presence I could not see. Lack of hysteria in the remaining partygoers pointed away from the possibility of a mild earthquake.

I whirled to my right then left. Underneath where I stood, an undulating presence extended its long-fingered reach, and each of those fingers created fissures in the thick underlayer of fine, intertwined roots.

Did no one else feel what was happening? The teens were still on their blanket. Rowan was head-to-head with Wes, the reds of their hair a coppery glow in the light cast from a nearby torch.

Nearer to the house, River and Rose were with Clifford and Abigail, gathering sweaters, jackets, and purses while continuing their conversation. At another table, Mal, James, Kaz, and Belle were laughing. Tanner was walking toward them, a bowl of cookies from the dessert table balanced in his hand.

I pinched the fabric of my flowy dress so I wouldn't flash anyone and scooted back up the stairs, darted through the house to my bedroom, and went to grab my wand.

Which was now becoming one with its twelve-inch replacement. Tiny branchlets clutched the old stick to the new. I picked up the conjoined pieces, thinking I could separate them like bamboo chopsticks, but the branchlets and leaf buds were having none of it.

"Okay, okay, I get it," I whispered.

I peeled off my dress, rolled myself into a sports bra, and wedged the conjoined wands between my breasts.

Wands. Gauntlets.

What I wouldn't give for an instruction manual.

I slipped the gold hoops out of my earlobes, pulled on a pair of clean jeans and a T-shirt, and affixed the bear and the apple to the top of my T-shirt and called myself ready.

No one looked at me when I skidded to a stop at the top of the porch stairs, locked and loaded for the cosplay part of the evening. But when Tanner and the other druids turned as one and faced the road as the wards ringing the house snapped to life, most everyone else came to their feet on high alert.

"Calliope," Tanner barked, waving me toward him.

"Something's coming," I said, shoving my arms with the unlaced gauntlets at him. "Is it the Apple Witch? If it is, there's something very different about her approach. And she hasn't said anything."

He closed his eyes as he laced me up and shook his head as he answered. "If she's here, she's being very restrained." He pointed toward the road and the trees and bushes to either side of the entrance to the driveway. "Company's coming from that direction, if the wards are any indication."

Tree limbs and leaves glimmered with the now familiar flecks of emerald green lights, stronger to the North and East. With a bit of squinting, I could see dimmer lights flickering throughout the woods.

I took a couple of deliberate steps away from the house, thinking I had time to get a read of the underground, when a posse of silvery gray SUVs with tinted windows and extra antennas roared to a stop and blocked the entrance of my driveway. The tires skidded on gravel, and six high-beam headlights went dark at the same moment.

The driver's side doors faced the road. As each one opened and the driver exited, more drama was added to the entire performance in the extra beats it took to reveal who, exactly, had arrived.

Oh, for fuck's sake. Meribah Flechette—Doug's mother and my ex-mother-in-law and self-appointed judge and jury. She was joined by the woman in the passenger's side of her car and Doug and Roger, who exited the lead vehicle.

"Calliope," Meribah started, "we heard you were having a party, and we hoped we might join you and share in whatever it is you're celebrating."

CHAPTER 22

I wanted to laugh at Meribah. Someone must have suggested the Merry Widow and her band of sycophants watch all three *Men in Black* movies and take notes: black pants and two-button jackets for the men; tight black skirts and form-fitting jackets for the women; pressed white blouses and shirts for all. Their faces feigned a stoic attitude and absolutely none of the movie's underlying humor.

"I can't imagine why you're really here," I said, palming my wand and securing the thicker end into one gauntlet.

And now that I knew she was Fae, everything that had always been flawless about her exterior, everything I had compared myself against and come up wanting, took on new meaning. My ex-mother-in-law had been hiding her true self from me the entire time I was a member of the Flechette clan. I should have paid more attention to the discrepancy behind her perfect mien and the venom in her words and actions.

"I'm here for my grandsons," Meribah said. "Douglas informed me their magic has begun to rise, and they are Flechettes first and foremost and should receive their training under my aegis."

"Will you be providing the same level of training you gave your sons?" I was ready to spar with Meribah—on my own turf, bolstered by the strength of my bonds to the soil under my feet and the reinforced wards around the property line.

As long as she and her crew stayed outside the wards and I stayed inside.

She cackled. "You're the idiot who never suspected a tattoo had anything to do with your diminished abilities."

Ouch. "He's the idiot who lost his hand."

"Douglas, show Calliope your hands."

He stepped forward, pushed up his jacket and shirt sleeves, and turned the undersides of his forearms to face forward. The bones in his hands glowed dark blue, and one by one his fingernails elongated into pointed claws. He seemed mesmerized by his shiny new weaponry. "You did me a favor by allowing me to justify the expense of an upgrade."

"Dad?"

Doug peeled his gaze off his hands and glanced past my shoulder to Thatcher. Spreading his arms and fingers wide, Doug asked, "Pretty cool, hey, son?"

"Put those away, Douglas. You're scaring your children," his mother commanded.

The speed with which he obeyed his mother was embarrassing. So much of our marriage was beginning to make sense.

"Meribah," I said, my wand inching its way into my right hand, "you have no claim to my sons. They come and go between this house and their father's, and if you want to see them, you should reconsider doing anything that would cause me to place restrictions on those visits." I could sense people moving closer to my back. A quick check to either side showed both sons had stepped up beside me. "That said, I will also honor their wishes. Last we spoke, Harper and Thatcher wished to continue living with me and attending school on this island."

The forward doors to the middle vehicle opened. A woman

emerged from around the front, and a man stuck one leg out the passenger side while turning to face the back seat.

Meribah smirked. "You might change your mind when you see the special guests we've brought."

The wards crackled and grew brighter. Man in Black Number Three opened the back door of the SUV, reached in with both arms, and tugged. When he stepped away, two males of shorter than average height, with bindings around their wrists and bags over their heads stood next to the vehicle.

"Bring them closer, Josiah," Meribah said.

Josiah Flechette. Meribah's brother. As soon as he'd taken two steps closer to where the wards held strong, I recognised the man's face in the ambient light. And when the woman driver closed the car doors and took her place to the other side of the bound figures, her name registered in my brain—Garnet Flechette. These were Sallie's parents.

"I will allow these two guests to remain on the island and continue the work they came here to do," Meribah said, "if you release one of your sons into my custody. Mine, not Douglas's."

"Absolutely not. I have no idea who or what you've got under those bags, but my sons are not up for sale, barter, or trade."

Meribah shrugged and lifted her right arm as though waving off a pestering bug. A blue glow, similar to the glow in the bones of Doug's hands, only more concentrated, shot down her index finger and continued, revealing a long, thin blade with a pointed tip. She raised her arm above her head, touched the edge of the ward with the tip of the blade, and sliced a hole through the magic-charged air.

The woman accompanying her, who had yet to speak, grabbed one edge of the slit and held it to the side, allowing Meribah to step through and place one booted foot and then the other onto my land.

I sucked in my breath, expecting all hell to break loose, just like it would in the movies, with explosions and lasers and sound effects.

Silence.

"There are old wards here, wards that know my blood." Meribah gave me her cold, brutal smile and a one-shouldered shrug. "They don't like me, but they know me." Reaching behind her, she held hands with the woman I didn't recognize and pulled her through the opening.

With that, the wards shattered, falling like brittle glass curtains ringing a massive stage.

Josiah and Garnet each placed one hand at the back of the necks of their captives and pushed them forward. Garnet took the rope attached to the wrist bindings and handed it to Doug's mother.

I sucked in a breath, certain I was about to drown. Saltwater filled my lungs, and overwhelming panic blacked out my ability to see a way around the bizarre situation unfolding in front of me.

Until cracks and snaps rose out of the wooded area on the other side of the driveway. *Ivy bind?*

Yes, I breathed. *Ivy wind, ivy bind.*

My vision cleared. Before I could send a more specific instruction to my loyal invasives, Garnet grabbed the hoods covering the men's heads and ripped them back. Both men choked and dropped to their knees.

"Peasgood! Hyslop! What are you doing with my boys?" Abigail's low wail rose from the guests gathered behind me.

I whipped my head side to side, searching to see who was positioned where.

"Abigail, no!" Clifford ambled across the grass, trying to keep Abigail with him, but she slapped his hands away and continued, spindly arms outstretched.

Josiah and Garnet stepped away from the two shackled men,

giving tacit permission for them to stumble forward and be met by their grandparents.

I spun in place. Behind me, Tanner, Rose, River, L'Runa, Wes, and Kaz had spread out, forming an arc with their bodies. Belle and Rowan were hustling Leilani and Sallie into the darker part of the yard, with James protecting the rear. I didn't see Malvyn anywhere.

The four Pearmains huddled in a tight bundle of hugs and tears on the grass between me and the invading Flechettes.

"What the hell are you trying to accomplish here, Meribah?" I demanded.

"Land, Calliope," she said, as smug as I had ever seen her. "I want more land. And I will do anything I have to do to acquire it."

"Including murder?"

She shrugged, and the drop of her shoulders signalled the start of a transformation. Her glamour faded, as did Doug's and Roger's and those of the other three. Ears elongated into points, and bodies morphed into taut, battle-ready silhouettes. Weapons strapped to their torsos and hidden behind their cultivated facades appeared, crackling with magical charge.

"Ivy wind; ivy bind. Ivy wind; ivy bind," I murmured, sweeping my wand across the array of altered Fae standing in front of me. I urged the vines to start with my ex and his twin brother.

Bursting from the ground as tendrils, the vines thickened, growing thorns and oily leaves as they threaded over and around one another in a rush to follow my command.

Doug and Roger reacted by unleashing their claw-enhanced fingers. They dodged the Pearmains and headed for my sons, who had the presence of mind to run in opposite directions. Wes and River followed the Flechette brothers then stopped, dropped, and shifted into their river otter forms. I had no time to gawk at the beauty of the transformation, only a second to wish them sharp claws, sharp teeth, and all the viciously protective instincts they could muster.

I whipped my attention back to Abigail and Clifford, terrified her frail body wouldn't withstand the violence of the erupting chaos. Having my attention diverted away from my sons ripped at me, but I had to trust my vines and the druids.

The wards reactivated, flaring brighter and taller than before and further lighting the scene in front of me.

From the side of the road, an explosion rocked the cars.

I could see the upper half of Malvyn's body on the other side of the lead SUV. His arms were raised to shoulder height. A spinning wheel of red hovered in front of each palm.

Garnet and Josiah's arms flailed out as the backsides of their bodies slammed against the side of one of the SUVS, held there by Mal's spell. Arms up, elbows locked, he skirted the vehicle and slapped his hands against Josiah's wrists then Garnet's and again at their ankles, leaving the husband and wife manacled to the metal doors.

Two of the six Fae were contained, and two more were close to going down, leaving Meribah and the mystery woman to me.

Adelaide. It was Adelaide Dunfay, the realtor who'd left her card with the Pearmains week after week, trying to get them to sell.

Anger rose along my limbs. I wanted that woman disarmed. I wanted to know why she'd chosen the Pearmains, and if she had anything to do with the deaths of the hidden-folk. But I knew charging at her, my untested wand raised to the sky and a battle cry on my lips, was a laughable tactic.

In the next breath, the animal presence I sensed outside my bedroom door approached my left side. A light gray snout nudged my fingers, and the silver-white fur of a ghost wolf pushed its weight against my hip. And then it was gone, folded into the shadows.

As if all this wasn't enough, *she* arrived. The Apple Witch.

I felt her longing, her confusion, even as Meribah and Adelaide joined hands, swung their blades out to the sides, and move in Abigail's direction.

The Apple Witch would have to wait.

I had given my blood to the soil on this island. I would protect the next generation of hidden folk, the ones who would shepherd the trees safely into the future. I mustered my energy to try a naming spell like the one I'd inadvertently used on Tanner. *"Meribah Gratiana Flechette, Adelaide Flechette Dunfay —stop."*

Meribah and Adelaide jerked to a stop. I had a handful of heartbeats to savor the shocked looks on their faces before their mouths morphed into twisted grins, only to change again into cries of shock as they were knocked to the ground from behind.

The ghost wolf planted his paws on Adelaide's backside, bit at her jacket, and threw his head side to side, tugging the jacket down her arms until they were trapped behind her. The beast took her wrist in its mouth, shook its head, and dislodged her weapon. It yelped when it tried to bite the blade.

Meribah was rolling away faster than I could get to her. She sprang to her feet, slicing at the air around her until she fell a second time, onto her back, kicking as the wolf went after her ankles.

I tore forward, landed my knees onto Adelaide's back, and tried the naming spell again. This time, I put more into my delivery and added a caveat. *"Adelaide Dunfay Proctor, do not move."*

Her body stiffened, and a growl of frustration rumbled in her throat.

Meribah and the ghost wolf were circling each other; another blade, as thin and deadly-looking as the first, extended out of her other hand.

The wolf tensed to leap—I could read it in the way his joints bent, loading his tendons for power and height. Meribah must have read it too. She burst into a spiral, going from stillness to a blur of movement from one moment to the next, building force and momentum from her feet to the ends of her swords.

I had no counter-spell for that.

The wolf rolled to the edge of the grass, and by the time it reached the trio of massive fir trees, Tanner emerged naked, crouched and eyes fixed on Meribah the untouchable.

"Rocks, Calliope," he yelled. "Get me rocks."

I ran to the bottom of the porch steps, gathered two handfuls of gravel, and swerved toward Tanner.

"Throw them at her." He had a larger rock in each hand and held them the way Malvyn held the spinning red wheels.

Ball-tossing was never my forte. I sent out an abbreviated plea for accuracy and threw one handful and then the other.

Tanner slammed his rocks together once, and again, setting up a rhythm. Each time his rocks met, the gravel flew at Meribah and away, toward and away, until she lost her momentum, absorbed her weapons, and ran for the nearest SUV.

"Adelaide, Douglas, Roger, come!" she called.

Footsteps thundered from around the backside of my house. Adelaide's prone form shot across grass and slammed against the rear wheel of Meribah's SUV.

Adelaide stood, shakily, the front of her shirt shredded and bloodied. I opened my mouth to use her name against her one more time and froze at the look of malice on her face. She pivoted, hopped into the front passenger seat, and slammed her door shut as her SUV and the one carrying Doug and Roger peeled away and sped down the road.

Whatever Malvyn used on Josiah and Garnet continued to hold. He'd added a collar around their necks, keeping the two mercifully silent even as their mouths moved and they fought against the restraints.

The house lights were blazing. Tanner, naked, disappeared through the front door. Below the deck, figures moved. I had to assume everyone I hadn't kept track of during the fight was okay. Or would be.

I turned and ran to Abigail. She lay on her side, a bunched up man's jacket tucked under the side of her head. Clifford was on his hands and knees beside her, weeping. Peasgood and his brother hadn't been able to do much beyond use their bodies as a buffer between their grandparents and the irate Fae. I dropped onto my hands and knees on the other side of Abigail and gripped the grass with my fingertips and toes until the spaces in between my digits were jammed with soil.

These two elder folk had dedicated their lives to preserving the descendants of Idunn's apples and so I called to the Apple Witch to show herself, to show me she could be something other than a greedy ex-lover. I called to her to drop whatever she had against me, look beyond whatever selfish needs motivated her pursuit of Tanner, and use her formidable strength to protect the very people who served as stewards of Idunn's treasures.

Below me, the Apple Witch's presence lit up the earth, running through the fissures and lighting them with liquid phosphorescence.

I sent one more pulse, one more request, into the ground, praying she would heed my call to protect Abigail and do no more than what I asked. I placed one hand on Abi's shoulder and one on Cliff's.

"It's going to be okay," I said. "Help is coming."

CHAPTER 23

Abi was so still. She didn't respond to my voice, but she had Cliff and their grandsons and I needed to see that my sons were safe.

I found them on the far side of my garden. My brilliant vines had taken a different tack than I'd envisioned. Instead of attacking Doug and Roger, they'd attached themselves to Thatch and Harper, weaving a protective cage that pinned the two to the ground. I grabbed fistfuls of vines, felt the adrenaline rush leave my body, making room for tears, shaking muscles, and a torrent of what ifs, and all I wanted was to make sure my boys were okay, that the vines hadn't cut off their ability to breathe or—

"Mom, we're okay, we're okay. Where are Leilani and Sallie?" Harper asked.

Ivy, unbind; ivy unwind. Ivy, unbind; ivy unwind. And thank you.

The vines writhed in my clenched hands. I let go. They unwove themselves and whipped away, leaves waggling like round, green fingers, to the areas we designated as theirs. I grabbed Harper's face and kissed his cheeks, and Thatch let me do the same.

"I think they're with James and a couple of the other witches,"

I said, as they came to their feet and shook dirt out of their hair. "Belle and Rowan set up a triage area in the living room. I'd appreciate it if you two would check in with them."

They tried to protest.

I tried to wield the wand of parental authority, realized they'd been through enough, and waved them off. "Go," I said. "Do what you need."

Their hugs squished the air out of my lungs. They tore off, passing Wes as he trotted up from the back yard.

"I'm sorry they got away, Calliope," Wes chuffed, coming to stand beside me. "But now we know who killed the wee trolls."

"Do we know?" I asked. Because I had the sinking feeling Doug and Roger were in this mess more deeply than I wanted to imagine.

"Sallie, lass, come here." Wes waved her over from where she'd been waiting under the deck and wrapped an arm around the distressed teen's upper back. "Tell your cousins' mum what you told me."

"I'm so sorry." Tears poured down Sallie's cheeks, mingling with the bloody streaks on her face, throat, and the front of her dress. "I'm so sorry I didn't figure it out earlier so I could warn you."

"Warn me about what?" I asked, bringing her into a hug to soothe her tremors.

"My parents. It was them. They've been going after the hidden folk, threatening them, trying to get them to leave the land so Aunt Meribah could buy up the properties."

Wes looked at me and nodded. "There's more."

Sallie let out a long, shuddering breath. "They've been away from the house so much. I got lonely, which was why I started my pie business, and one day, when they'd actually been home for longer than five minutes, I asked about getting apples and other ingredients wholesale. They told me to be patient, that pretty soon I would have access to as many apples as I wanted. I just wanted to have something of my own, Aunt Calliope, something of my own I could be good at."

I hugged her tight. There was nothing I could say, no more questions I could ask. "Wes, can you take Sallie to Belle and Rowan, please? And Sallie? You can stay here, with me and Harper and Thatch. You don't have to go back to your parents."

I hoped I could stick to that promise. With the teenagers accounted for, I went to check on Abigail.

She and Clifford were gone.

I ran into the house, asked Rowan and Belle if they'd seen or treated either of the elder Pearmains or if they'd left with anyone. They hadn't.

Standing on the front deck, I scanned the yard. Sections of turf had been disturbed in the melee. I took the stairs in one jump and ran to where chunks of sod been had been sutured together, their edges rolled and tucked under. I tried to wedge my fingers into the grass and rip the sections apart, but the ground was not giving up what had been taken.

Tanner had followed me out of the house.

"She took them, Tanner. She took them," I said, scrubbing at the ground with my flattened palms.

"We'll find them," he assured me.

Hyslop and Peasgood were on their backs some distance away and likely going into shock. I had to let go of my grief and help them. Or get them to someone who could. Tanner picked up one of the men, jogged him over to the care of our witch healers, and returned for the other. When he returned the third time, he grabbed a scarf off one of the chairs and wrapped it around my shoulders before lifting me to stand.

He crushed me in his embrace.

"I think I know where she's taken them," he said, smoothing my hair, his breath running ragged on its way in and out. "I have to go."

Tanner released me and gripped the braided cord of his necklace, the very one I had never seen him take off. He pulled the cord over his head and from around his waist and placed both loops around my neck. "Calliope, do not take this off for anyone but me. Can you promise me that?"

He tucked the burnished pouch under my blood- and dirt-stained shirt and pressed his hand against the center of my chest.

"I promise," I said. "Please, be careful."

Tanner nodded once, turned, and ran toward his truck.

"And please come back." I wasn't sure he heard me.

The emptiness threatening to submerge me in that moment was an emptiness I had known a few times before. When I crossed the threshold into the A-frame house after my mother had died and understood her laughter would never again entice me into her room for a tea party. Again, when Doug walked out of our house after telling me he wanted a divorce—more than a divorce, to wash his hands of me.

And now.

We were so lucky that only two people had been lost in the fray, but those two people were dear to me. They were gone, taken by an entity I did not understand, with motivations that were still unclear, to a place I might not ever find.

"Calliope."

I didn't recognize the voice calling me. I scanned the over-turned tables and chairs, the matte black silhouette of the Old One, the house lights blazing over the front and back porches.

"Calliope."

The voice was coming from high in the treetops or the roof of the house.

I looked up. "Who's there?" I asked. "And what do you want?"

A figure rose to standing at the peak of the roof. The outer garment they wore stiffened and opened out to the sides, and what I thought was clearly a tall man in a billowing overcoat became a tall man with wings. With a repeated, sharp-edged *whoosh, whoosh,* he swooped down the long expanse of the A-frame's roofline and landed a few feet from me.

The night had painted his cloak a charcoal black when he was on the roof. Up close, the cloak—his wings—were mostly white with pale gray speckles. His silvery white hair was longish, sweeping across his forehead and covering his ears, and he was old. Not nearly as old as Clifford, but his face was lined and the stubble along his jawline and under his throat shone white in what little light was coming off the torches.

I had never seen this man before. I had never seen a bird-man before. I wasn't sure he was even real.

He took two steps toward me, tapped the pins attached to my T-shirt, and enveloped me in his arms and wings.

"Granddaughter, I have so much to tell you."

CHAPTER 24

Tanner was gone. River, Rose, and Belle had bundled Peasgood and Hyslop into Rose's sedan and driven off soon after they heard Tanner was going after the Apple Witch. Rose wanted to take the young men to the Pearmains' farmhouse and continue the search for Cliff and Abi from there. River gave me a knowing look and expressed the hope he might be able to catch up with Tanner.

The bird-man followed me across the lawn and into my house, the tips of his feathers brushing the grass. I stared toward the road; Josiah and Garnet's limbs were shackled to the exterior of their SUV, and their lips were clamped together through magical means. Inside, Malvyn was at the head of the dining table, ringed to either side by James and Leilani, Rowan and Wes, and Sallie, Kaz, and my sons.

"I am on the Province's Board of Magical Self-Governance," Mal said, leaning his weight onto his fingertips as he surveyed the group of gathered Magicals. "Josiah and Garnet Flechette will be remanded into custody pending our investigation into their involvement into the murders on this island and others."

Sallie's face paled, and she dropped to her knees, her elbows against the edge of the table and quiet sobs wracking her body. Rowan wrapped her arms around Sallie while Wes bent to lift her into his arms. They walked the young woman to the couch.

I turned my attention back to Mal. "You can take them now?"

He nodded, his face a mask of impassive gravity. "I have not had to invoke my authority in this manner very often. Taking custody of those two means I will be off-island for at least three to four days."

James drew Leilani snugly against his side. "We'll be okay, Mal. We have the safe room."

A quiet hand on my shoulder reminded me my grandfather was in the house. Harper tore his gaze from Leilani and scratched at his upper back. "Mom," he said, drawing out the sound, "who's behind you?"

"That's the bird man I told you about the other night, Harper," said Kaz. "You picked a hell of a night to show up, Christoph."

"My granddaughter was in trouble. I'm sorry I didn't get here in time for all the excitement." Christoph walked around the table to Harper and Thatcher and studied my sons.

"Are those real?" asked Thatcher, pointing to the wings Christoph had pinned tight against his back.

"Yes."

"Did you just call our mother your granddaughter?" asked Harper.

"Yes, I did."

Kaz cleared his throat and stepped closer to me. "Calliope, I had no idea you were related to Christoph. I should have seen the connection the night Harper first feathered."

I pressed my palms to my face and scrubbed, letting my fingers massage my hairline. A headache of epic proportions was brewing behind my forehead. "It's okay, Kaz."

"Granddaughter, do you have an extra bedroom I could use?"

I rolled my eyes behind my hands.

"Can you prove you're related to our mom?" Harper shouldered his younger brother to the side and planted himself in front of Christoph.

My grandfather—the bird-man—stood taller and appraised Harper slowly, from the top of his head to his feet. "For this moment, you will have to take my word, Harper. You have the gift of flight. Would you like to learn how to use the wings that are waiting to break free?"

Harper's gaze wobbled side to side. He unbuttoned his dress shirt, slid the shirt off his shoulders to his elbows, and turned. "Are you telling me these will turn into wings?"

Christoph took one step closer to Harper, hesitated, then placed his palms and fingers against the reddened area near Harper's upper spine and the backs of his shoulders. Harp's chin dropped, tension eased out of his body, and my grandfather closed his eyes and chanted until the follicles disappeared.

"They will turn into wings when you are ready, great-grand-son. The choice is yours to make." He lifted his hands from Harper's skin and repositioned the shirt over his shoulders. "You should know you are in possession of a rare gift."

Harper turned and focused on buttoning his shirt. "I'll take that into consideration," he said. "Right now, I just…" He pressed his fingertips against his eyes, unable to stop the tears. He shook me off when I reached for his arm and fled to the stairs and the sanctuary of his room.

"Great-grandpa?" Thatch glanced at the ceiling and back to Christoph. "Please don't leave. You can have my room. Harp'll be okay. He's just really kind of fucked up about our Dad right now. And the feathers." Thatcher wrapped his arms around Christoph's chest in a quick, tight embrace and ran up the stairs.

"Dad? Papa? I need to talk to Harper before we leave," said Leilani.

James and Mal nodded.

"James will help me get Josiah and Garnet in their car. We'll drive them to our house." Mal turned to me. "Calliope, your house might be the safest place for our daughter tonight. Might Leilani stay here too? James can pick her up in the morning, once I've left for Vancouver."

"Of course," I said.

"You need a healer here, Calli. I can stay and help," Rowan said.

I'd forgotten about Rowan. Her warmth and expertise—and friendship—would be a welcome addition.

"Kaz and I can take the night shift," said Wes. "We'll repair and strengthen the new wards. But if the old ones truly were made with Meribah's blood, they'll continue to recognize her. We'll have to make removing any vestige of her presence a priority."

I moved my gaze across everyone circling the table and those in the living room and upstairs. Four teenagers just coming into their magic. Two druids, two and a half witches—one of whom was also a healer—a sorcerer, and Christoph, whose magical category was as yet unknown.

My ragtag collection of Magicals. I had sheets and towels enough for everyone and food to last through the next day at the least.

We would get through this.

River and Rose would find Abi and Cliff, Tanner would find the Apple Witch, and somehow, somehow, I would figure out how to keep my sons safe without dimming their potential.

"I'll put on a pot of coffee," I said. "Let's get to work."

ACKNOWLEDGMENTS

Jeni Chappelle, Editor. THANK YOU for guiding me into a new genre with a steady hand; for believing in these characters (especially Calliope); and pushing this conflict-averse writer into finally blowing stuff up. Let's do that *again*!

Elizabeth Mackey, Cover Design. Thank you for bringing an important aspect of Calliope's story to life and for always finding the right balance.

The Beta Belles ~ Leslie Mart, Diane Castro, Kimberley Kennard: Thank you for answering the call with thoughtful comments and suggestions, and for your enthusiastic support. (The next book should be ready soon, so…?)

Raquel Erbach, Graphic Design. Thank you for answering that eleventh hour DM for a simple silhouette of a tree. Besos!

The divas of Romance Chat: Thank you for being endlessly entertaining and supportive, at all hours of the day and night, and for always being willing to hit that 'Retweet' button.

ABOUT THE AUTHOR

Coralie Moss loves everyday heroines and complicated witches, layered magic and earthly moments, and will always believe in the power of love. Whether she's writing Urban Fantasy or Contemporary Romance, her characters get her up in the morning and Assam tea keeps her going. She lives on Salt Spring Island, British Columbia with her HEA, their son, and two globe-trotting rescue cats.

Reviews left at Goodreads and/or your point of purchase are always appreciated.

facebook.com/CoralieMossWrites

twitter.com/moss_coralie

instagram.com/authorcoraliemoss

bookbub.com/profile/coralie-moss

goodreads.com

JOIN CORALIE'S NEWSLETTER

Want to get news updates and alerts about Coralie Moss and her new books, including the next Calliope Jones novel, MAGIC RECLAIMED?

Sign up for her newsletter to get information on upcoming releases, giveaways, and more.

Summer Rules, a novelette (Contemporary Romance)

READ the eBOOK for FREE!

As far as Elaine is concerned, when summer's tourist season arrives on Salt Spring Island, it's the off-season for romance. Her mini-empire of gourmet food trucks needs her undivided attention, and from the end of June through Labor Day, her ironclad Summer Rules are in effect. Sex is off the menu.

Richie's on hiatus from relationships period until he meets the renowned entrepreneur, Elaine Atkins. She needs his lumberjack skills to take down the tree threatening to land on her most popular food truck. And when her assistant calls in sick, Richie can't say no to Elaine's plea for a temporary sous chef.

The saucy rapport and spicy heat inside her popular taco truck aren't all coming from what's cooking on the stove. Elaine's a vital woman in her mid-forties, and though Richie is twelve years younger, he deftly handles everything she tosses at him, starting with her resistance. By the end of the lunch rush, he's ready to ask her for a date. And that's when Elaine finds out just how hard it is to stick to her Summer Rules.

Invisible Anna (Contemporary Romance)

Anna Granger wants a second chance at love. But she hasn't been on a date in five years and has no idea where to begin. Her best friend wants Anna to make herself more visible. But that means leaving her comfort zone and giving the unknown a chance. When a college flame resurfaces and a captivating furniture designer rents the cottage next door, Anna is thrust into a series of personal and professional dilemmas. Will it prove smarter—and safer—to stick with what she knows? Or can she drop her guard—and her resistance—and meet love and passion head on?

∼

Opening Nights (Contemporary Romance)

Opening Nights *is a sizzling intrigue between a talented costume designer and an upper-crust Bostonian with a bad-boy reputation.*

Chase Witherell's preferred milieu is any place but his family's Beacon Hill mansion. Overseeing global projects keeps him where he wants to be —in the air and on the road. Touching down in Boston, he attends a fundraising gala where he's smitten with the show's lead costume designer. Could this stunning and talented single be the one who prompts him to unpack his bags?

For workaholic Luna O'Rourke, life revolves around the theater, where she's just one production away from her dream job. That is, until the conniving actress, Fiona Marchess goes into overdrive to sabotage Luna's promotion—and love life.

When the costumer's meticulously scripted life falls apart, she must figure out whom to trust. Can Luna—who's always worked from behind the curtains—step out and embrace the limelight with her leading man?

∼

TANNER

Tanner drove his truck to the place where he first met the remarkable Calliope Jones. He maneuvered onto the Pearmains' drive, made a three-point turn in front of the gate, and parked the back end deep within a tangle of thorny bushes. The paint on both sides of the truck was already so scratched, he'd never notice the addition of more.

He was careful to leave his knife in the glove compartment, lock the cab's doors, and pocket his keys. He passed through the gate stripped of trinkets and strode around the perimeter of the empty house, following the path's right fork into the orchard. Past the newer trees, to the older ones. He slowed his pace.

Ripening apples swayed on short sections of branches. Leaves waved in the dark, whispering temporary sound prints that dissipated as he passed.

He continued on, deeper into the orchard, until the presence of the oldest trees slowed his stride. Hobbled by age and disease, somewhere amongst these ancient beings was another force he hadn't met face to face in so many years he'd lost count.

Tanner's night vision kicked in, calling forward a piece of himself he kept at bay. Every knotted tree was worth his attention, but he sought only one and found it, found the great trunk blatantly split and spread like the opening to a giantess's womb.

He planted himself near the tree, undressing with slow deliberation, exactly as he'd imagined undressing in front of Calliope. If he lived through this, her house, her touch, and the healing waters in her deep bathtub would be his next stop.

And if he was lucky, she would care for him as he had cared for her after her Blood Ceremony.

Clothes folded and stacked with meticulous care, he faced the tree, stepping close enough to shudder when rough bark met the sensitive skin of his penis. He tried to step away, but the ground shifted underneath his feet. He stumbled and turned as tentacle-like roots swept up the backs of his heels and calves and circled his legs, followed by ones at his waist, shoulders, and wrists.

Slammed against the tree, he expanded his ribcage, tried to keep his chest open and wide against the creeping tightening of whatever was attaching him to the tree.

Tanner Marechal. Bonsoir, my wolf in the night. My apple. My seed.

Bark formed like a warrior's armor along his forearms and upper arms and capped his shoulders. More formed on the fronts and backs of his calves and up the fronts of both thighs. The outer layer of his skin and covering hairs rose to meld with the bark. The process was both painful and charged with an earthy eroticism he'd longed for his entire adult life.

The area over his heart was left free, as was most of his buttocks, his genital area, and the ladder line of dark hairs rising from the base of his penis to his sternum.

He could move, barely. The bark had formed a plate-like exoskeleton up the front and back of his torso and limbs and created a freeform helmet as it cupped the sides of his neck, the area around his ears, and the back of his skull to the hairline.

The Apple Witch showed herself once he was fully ensnared. She rose from the ground, a nubile sapling speeding through its growth until it hit peak strength. She shed her outer layer of darkened bark, slid her smooth surface against his inner legs and thighs, and positioned herself over his groin. Delicate growths of spring-green branches tipped with delicate leaves reached for him, stroking, calling, arousing.

And then she entered him as she enfolded him, and he was lost to sensations. He was stroked, probed, licked, milked, heated, fed, and sucked dry. He was there purely for her pleasure, and it seemed to pleasure her to no end to discover the empty vessel within him and fill it, empty it, and fill it again until he reached his peak.

Tanner spilled his seed as the tree consumed him. His chest rose, his ribs spread, and he shed his bark-like armor. Little roots and supple vines fell away, leaving him breathless, leaning against the tree, freed.

95542550R00170

Made in the USA
Middletown, DE
26 October 2018